To Hale and Back

By

Marie James

Hale Series Book Four

Copyright

To Hale and Back

Chapter 1
Josie

I lean back on my heels on the bathroom floor. Whoever said morning sickness only happens in the morning was a liar. I knew it was a possibility because I read it in several of the pregnancy books I've been scouring. Up until this point, I haven't felt any different. My body has been extremely sore and I've been incredibly tired, but I just chalked that up to being tied up in a closet for over two weeks.

"Oh, Josie," I hear Kaleb say softly just as I feel his hand rub small circles on my back. I turn my face to look at him, not able to control the huge grin on my face. "You're smiling? You just got sick."

I nod at him and my smile grows at the look of utter confusion on his face. "The books say that morning sickness means the hormones are high, which is usually a sign of a growing baby."

I pray that it's true. I was shocked to find out we were expecting. I mean who wouldn't be. I've been on birth control for years to help moderate my cycle and it's quite possible that we conceived the very first time we made love. I can't imagine having a baby with anyone else, even though it's super early in our relationship. What concerns me the most in the whole situation is that the doctors found trace amounts of methamphetamines in my bloodstream. That, coupled with the fact that I'd practically been starved and left to die in my own bodily filth, has the doctors keeping a very close eye on me. My hCG hormones have been doubling like they are supposed to and that is promising. I've known for less than a week about this baby and I'm already invested more than I ever could have imagined.

"You okay now?" His voice is full of love and concern. I know in any other situation his actions since we've been back home would be considered hovering, but I like that he's been so attentive. I know it won't last forever and eventually it will begin to annoy me, but, for now, it's just what I need; a loving touch and gentle voice to let me know we are in this together.

I nod my head and let him help me from the floor. A shiver reminds me that I had to run out of the shower when the nausea hit and I'm still sopping wet with shampoo in my hair. I make a quick detour to rinse my mouth and brush my teeth before stepping back into the shower with Kaleb.

I tilt my head back and let him rinse the suds from my hair. The feel of his hands working conditioner into my hair feels wonderful. A low hum escapes my lips.

"Feel good?" He whispers against my neck.

I hum again. I'm exhausted and I'm certain the sex we had moments before getting into the shower canceled out the nap we took after getting back from the doctor this morning. I do however have enough energy to soap up the shower sponge and run it over every inch of Kaleb's golden skin.

We spent the next half hour in the shower kissing, petting, and caressing each other. Not one word was spoken as we showed each other with our hands and mouths how we felt for each other. It was absolute heaven.

The second I walk out of the shower Kaleb is wrapping an incredibly fluffy towel around my shoulders and he guides me to the edge of the tub and uses another equally soft towel to dry my hair.

"You're pampering me," I tease.

"For the rest of your life, Mariposa," he vows just before planting a soft kiss on my temple.

How in the world did I get so lucky? Not taking into account the horror of the past couple of weeks I can't help but wonder what I did to land not just an incredibly sexy, skilled lover, but a man that seems to want nothing but the chance to please and worship me. I let fear settle in my gut, not able to keep the thought that the other shoe will drop and something tragic will happen. The perfect guy and the promise of a family? No one gets as lucky as I have.

"What's wrong?" He must have noticed my mood shift. I'm not very good at hiding my emotions.

I don't want to give a voice to my fears; doing so will give it even more power. "I'm just tired." I stand from the edge of the tub, making sure that my towel is wrapped snuggly around me as I unwind the cord from the blow-dryer.

I begin to dry my hair and watch in the mirror as Kaleb dries his body. Although he's so economical about it, for some reason it's incredibly sexy. I lick my lips and bite my tongue; my body going from tired to needy with a mere glance at his sculpted form.

He looks up just as he swings the towel around his back to dry his shoulders. Noticing the look in my eyes his movements falter and his lip twitches in a partial grin. The sight of his sudden yet still growing erection makes my breath hitch. I shake my head and smile; he's well aware of how he affects me.

"What?" He asks as he drops the towel and stalks toward me.

I turn the blow-dryer off and place it on the counter just as his muscled chest hits my back. I suddenly regret the towel that is still currently wrapped around me, my body craving the skin to skin of his touch.

"I…," I swallow roughly. "I just can't believe you're real." I lean my head to the side as he rests his head on my bare shoulder, watching our reflections in the mirror. "And mine," I whisper seductively.

"Yours," he responds reverently lowering his hot, sinful mouth to the delicate spot just below my ear. "Perfect." His fingers are gliding over the exposed skin of my arm leaving goose pimples in its wake.

I huff absently. "You won't think that when I'm as big as a car!"

He nips at my neck and slowly raises his head as his hands tug my towel open; I keep my eyes locked on his as it falls to the floor.

"Even then," he whispers in my ear as his hands find my suddenly heavy breasts. "Even then, Josie. You will be perfect."

I close my eyes as his warm breath coats my skin and his thumbs sweep across my pert nipples.

I open my eyes as I feel his right hand begin to make its way down my body; I want to see the second his fingertips skate over my center. His hand stops below my belly button and his fingers flex. "You and this baby are my world, Mariposa. And my world is perfect."

"I love you, Kaleb." I do, with every atom of my being. Our relationship is nontraditional and traveling at the speed of light, but somehow it feels like it's ideal for us. I turn my head so I can look in his eyes rather than being separated by a reflection.

"Te Amo," he whispers against my lips before slanting his lips over mine and licking into my mouth.

I moan when his hand slides lower and he slips two fingers into my quivering heat.

***

I bolt awake just as the nightmare is trying to grab hold of me. We were incredibly distracted when Kaleb carried me out of the bathroom earlier and we didn't manage to turn off the light. I'm grateful for it since the extra light aids me in orienting myself quickly.

I snuggle deeper into Kaleb, making sure every possible inch of my naked body is touching some part of his equally naked body. I hear a rumble of approval in his chest causing me to look up. He's wide awake and looking down at me with those intense green eyes.

"Hey, baby," I whisper as I caress his chest with my cheek.

"Sleep well?" He asks softly as he reaches for my hand.

"I always sleep well in your arms." He caresses my left hand and I tilt my mouth to him, offering it.

He kisses my lips gently. "Then you should stay in them."

"Forever," I say momentarily breaking our kiss.

"Promise?" He pleas. I nod my head. "Forever?"

I smile up at him. "Forever," I vow.

He brings my hand to his lips. The ever present light from the bathroom glints off of a brilliant diamond solitaire that is now adorning the ring finger on my left hand. I gasp and my eyes dart back and forth from my hand to his face.

"Kaleb!" I'm speechless. He proposed in an off the cuff fashion in the hospital and has been at my side practically every second since. "It's beautiful! How did you...?"

He clears his throat. "It was my mothers." I know my eyes are wide with shock. He continues, "the ring my father proposed to her with." He shifts his weight and positions me so I'm straddling him and cups my face in his very large hands. "Will you be my wife, Josie? Will you allow me the chance to love you, cherish you, and worship you for the rest of our lives?"

"Yes," I pant against his mouth just before I slide my tongue across his.

His hands leave my face and I feel the grip of his fingers on my hips. He shifts my weight forward and then back. I moan when he slips inside of me.

Chapter 2
Kaleb

Damn I'm one lucky bastard I think as Josie collapses on my chest, panting, her tiny body covered in a light layer of sweat. I've barely softened and can still feel the periodic pulses from our synchronized climaxes.

"Will it always be like this?" she asks into my chest.

"I sure as fuck hope so." I wrap my arms around her as she settles her weight to my left side. We're a sweaty, sticky mess and I wouldn't have it any other way.

I watch as she holds up her hand and admires the small diamond ring again. I'm nervous about what she thinks of it. Lorali is marrying a billionaire and has a rock the size of Texas on her hand. Alexa and Garrett may never get married, but I couldn't imagine hers would be any smaller.

"You like it?"

"I love it," she says and turns her eyes to me. "I love you."

I kiss her forehead. "I love you, too."

We both settle into the embrace. I wish I could resist her more. She seems overly tired and even though I take into consideration what she's been through in addition to being in her first trimester, I'm still concerned about her lack of energy. It's in total contradiction to how she was before she was kidnapped. I'm concerned that she may be fighting depression and not just dealing with fatigue from her pregnancy.

I hear her stomach growl and feel her smile against my chest.

I shift to move out from underneath her, but she clings to me tighter. "Let's get you something to eat."

"Will you tell me about this?" I look down and notice that she's gently rubbing a finger over the circular scar just under my right pectoral.

I never wanted to have to talk to her about this. Not because I wanted to keep it from her, but because I wanted to protect her from that terrible day in my life. Maybe to protect me from reliving it as well.

"I was shot," I say simply.

She whimpers and squeezes me tight but remains quiet, giving me the opportunity to continue.

I clear my throat and pray for strength to get through this story.

"I was a rookie." I tell her as my mind wanders back to that horrible day. "I had only been out of the academy for six months. Barely enough time to even wrap my head around being a cop, much less the skills and mindset needed for that fucked up day."

The rubbing motion of her hand on my chest settles me. "I was with my dad that day. We were serving a warrant on a known dope house. My dad wasn't very concerned about the situation. He had what he considered a reliable informant that told him the people in the house were stoned all the time and he'd never seen a weapon there. It was Friday and we were in a hurry to get home. We had backup en route but he didn't want to wait and I trusted his instincts even though every cell in my body was telling me it wasn't a good idea, but what did I know? He'd been a cop as long as I had been alive. Fuck," I mutter. "He didn't even wear a vest anymore. They were optional back then and it was hot as hell that day, so I didn't have one on either."

"Oh, god," she mutters against my chest. She of all people, since her father is a cop, knows how dangerous it is to let your guard down even for a minute.

I hold her a little tighter and rub her back when I feel the slight tremble of her body.

"My dad and I were standing side by side, not using an ounce of the tactical training that had been drilled into my head in the academy and into my father the twenty-five years he was on the job. He reached up, knocked on the door, and announced us as law enforcement. Before he could even pull his arm back, the door exploded with two shotgun blasts." I squeeze my eyes shut when I feel the burn of tears behind them.

I can feel Josie sobbing into my chest and I want to comfort her, but I have to tell the whole story now because I don't know when or if I'll ever have the strength to revisit the subject.

"One of the pellets hit me in the chest. My dad," I clear my throat against all of the emotion that wants to come bubbling out. "My dad took the rest. I blacked out almost immediately. I was told my dad was gone before he even hit the ground."

"I never understood why my mom was always a nervous wreck when my dad put on his uniform and left the house. I knew it was dangerous, but I thought she was overreacting a bit. Now I know. Now I know my heart will break every time you leave the house." She's full on crying at this point, sobbing uncontrollably into my chest.

"Shhh, Josie," I rock her gently and kiss the top of her head. "I never want to leave you, Mariposa and I will do everything in my power to come home to you every single day. There's nothing like losing your dad and almost dying yourself to make you very diligent about safety. I'm very cautious at work. I have been since that day."

"Have you talked to anyone about it?" she sniffles against my chest.

"I did the mandatory six months with the house shrink. I struggled the most with what the shrink identified as survivor's guilt. I blamed myself for not speaking up when I had a bad feeling about the situation. I'm much more verbal at work now. If my gut tells me something's not right, I make sure to say something about it."

"How is your mom doing?" I love that she cares enough about me to ask me about the one other person who's life was devastated that day.

"She seems ok. I mean as ok as someone can be when they've lost as much as she has. She goes to church a lot." I laugh.

She pulls her head back to look at me. "What's funny?"

I smile at her and kiss the tip of her nose. "She has a guy friend at the church. She says friend, but they spend a lot of time together. They seem to get along well."

"How do you feel about your mom dating?" My smile falters slightly.

I shrug my shoulders. "You know." I can't tell her that the idea of her loving someone other than my dad makes my skin crawl. "I don't want her to be lonely."

"Baby?" She must sense my issue I have with my mom's situation.

I flip her over on her back, quickly sucking one of her nipples into my hot, eager mouth, hoping she doesn't get too upset with my diversionary tactics. I begin nipping my way down her flat belly when her stomach growls again, louder this time than it did earlier.

Food! That's a great way to deflect her attention. "Come on," I say backing away from her and offering her a hand. "Baby's hungry for food!"

She grumbles at me. "Yes, but mommy is hungry for daddy." Her voice is seductive and the way she's biting her lower lip almost convinces me, but when her stomach growls again, I can't be swayed.

I laugh as I tug her off the bed and hand her the robe that's hanging inside the closet door. "You remember the last time we had pizza delivered?"

Her eyes light up at the mentioned hint of the multiple orgasms I gave her while we waited for our food to be delivered. "Yes," she pants breathily.

"I think we should order Chinese." I wink at her. "They tend to take slightly longer to get here."

Chapter 3
Alexa

"Fuck!" I snarl as I once again crash into the oversized table that is taking up way too much space in the entryway. "I wish he'd leave a fucking light on," I mutter under my breath.

I'm going to have another bruise on my knee I think as I slam my keys down too hard on the table and limp into the living room. Plopping down on the couch I reach down and tug my shoes off. These twelve hour days are for the birds, but it's my cross to bear since I'm playing catch-up from all of the time I missed after being shot and while Josie was gone. I should count my lucky stars I still have a job.

I smile because I know that after today everything is caught up. I also know I got caught up so fast because of the effort I put in prior to the shit hitting the proverbial fan the last two and a half months. Everything should settle now that I've been released to full duty and Josie is home.

She's knocked up and engaged now, but home safe. Knocked up! *Hell no!* I think I'd die, either from shock or Garrett killing me! I make a mental note to talk to my gynecologist about getting a tubal or something. There's no chance I want kids and I'm certain Garrett feels the same way, but I'm sure the doctor won't take drastic measures since I'm so young and childless. Just the thought that someone has the ability to make decisions about my body pisses me off.

I attempt to curl my leg under me on the sofa and wince at the pain in my knee. Old Alexa would guzzle a bottle of white wine to ease the pain; current Alexa is too tired to even get off the couch to get some Advil. I palm my phone and decide to text Lorali.

Alexa: We still getting together tomorrow night?

I open my social media app, wasting time until she responds back. After several minutes of perusing pictures of acquaintances' partying, her text response rolls across the top of the screen.

Lorali: That's the plan. I've texted Josie twice today and she's not responded. I know she's probably fine, but it's got me a little worried.

Alexa: I'm going to call her real fast. Hang tight.

I swipe over to my contacts list and select Josie from my favorites. I hold it to my ear and listen to it ring. Just as I'm pulling my phone from my ear to hang up, I hear it connect. Rather than hearing Josie say hello I'm tortured with a feminine giggle and the rustle of bedding.

"Who was it?" I hear Kaleb's accented voice ask.

The "Ah!" from Josie followed by a sexy whimper explains exactly why she's not responded to Lorali's texts. I battle with myself, struggling between listening and hanging up. Kaleb's gruff "Fuck, you taste so good." Has me clicking off. As hot as the situation is, Josie is like my sister and yeah….no.

Garrett and I have been like ships passing in the night this last week and I'm definitely feeling deprived, even more so after that little phone faux pas. I shake my head and attempt to clear dirty thoughts from it.

I can't *not* tell Lorali about this so I opt to call instead of text. She, unlike her sister, picks up after two rings.

"Hey," Lorali says into the phone. "What did she say?"

"Well," I can't even hold in the laugh. "She said 'AH!' and then he said 'Fuck you taste so good!' So then I hung up."

By the time I get all of that out I'm full on laughing which sets off a smaller giggle from Lorali. "Jesus!" Lorali snorts.

"Pretty much." I hold my stomach which is now hurting from laughing so hard. "I'm pretty sure she meant to hit ignore rather than answer."

"I'd hope so! She's not our little Josie anymore is she?" Lorali says somberly.

"Nope. All grown up, engaged, and having a baby." I sit back further on the couch. "So, needless to say, she's a little busy right now. I'm sure she'll get back with you when her and Kaleb wrap-up their…meal."

Lorali snorts again. "I bet she will."

"Okay, so we're on for tomorrow evening. I need to get off the phone so I can let Garrett know what his dinner plans are for the evening." I let out a mischievous giggle.

"Funny thing." And I can tell she's smirking. "Probably close to the same thing Ian's going to have!"

As soon as I hang up the phone I text Garrett.

Alexa: Little Red is home all alone and waiting for her big bad wolf

I know he's incredibly busy so I don't expect to hear from him anytime soon. He usually gets home between eleven and midnight and there's no way I'm waiting up for him. Too tired to even worry about dinner I strip as I make my way to the shower, leaving a trail of clothes in my wake.

I manage the fastest shower in the history of showers before hand-drying my hair with a towel and falling into bed, exhausted. So grateful that tomorrow is Sunday and I can finally sleep in.

***

I'm startled awake by a sharp bite of pain to my nipple only to realize that my arms are tied over my head and something that smells surprisingly like my perfume is tied around my head, preventing me from seeing anything. I'm in total darkness.

My heart is thundering in my chest and a light sheen of sweat is suddenly covering my entire body.

"G…Garrett?" I whisper timidly. Because seriously, who else could it be?

"Nope," he pants in my ear, startling me because I didn't realize he was so close. "The big bad wolf," his mildly menacing laugh sends another chill over my body and an echo of need to my core.

"Why did you tie me up? Blindfold me?" *Please tell me it's because we're going to play.* Oh, how I've missed the Garrett from when we first started hooking up. I'd been released from the doctor weeks ago, but with Josie's kidnapping and our work schedules, we've barely had time for shower quickies these days.

"You are all trussed up in your clothes because they were left strewn all over the floor." I moan loudly as he twists my other nipple. "I'm hoping after tonight, you'll remember to put them in the laundry where they belong."

I huff. "If leaving my clothes lying around makes you tie me up, you should expect my entire wardrobe on the floor tomorrow."

His hand suddenly slaps my clit and I realize just how close to euphoria I already am.

"You like that, Angel?" I nod my head because I know he's paying very close attention to me, monitoring every nuance of my body and its reaction to him. "Such a pretty mouth you have." I feel his finger skate over my bottom lip as he gets back into the big bad wolf persona.

I feel his body shift and his finger touches my lips again. I sweep my tongue out to lick it, an attempt to elicit some type of reaction from him. Rather than a finger, my tongue makes contact with the drop of precome that was no doubt clinging to the tip of his erection.

Knowing he is so close I raise my head up from the bed and wrap my lips around his engorged shaft.

"Fuck," he hisses as his hips jolt forward, propelling his cock deeper in my mouth. I hum my approval around him.

I'm struggling to get a rhythm seeing as I'm tied up and flat on my back. Sensing my predicament he generously holds my head in place and begins to slowly fuck my mouth. *I love it.* I'm in paradise when his velvet covered steel length glides over my wet tongue. He's trying to remain stoic, but the flex of his fingers against my scalp tells me I'm affecting him more than he wants to let on.

He swells further in my mouth and just when I think he's going to release he wrenches away.

"Goddamn," he mutters under his breath. I grin, a slight feeling of triumph on my face.

I shouldn't be surprised he didn't climax in my mouth. He always wants to be inside of me when he goes. One of these days I want him to be so out of it with bliss that he forgets and just let's go, but tonight is not that night. Tonight, somehow, he's able to maintain his control.

I feel his warm breath against my neck and can tell he's settled on the bed beside me. His hand trails down my body just as he begins nipping the skin where my neck and shoulder meet. A rough bite to the muscle at the top of my shoulder, combined with a hard twist of my nipple makes me cry out. Fuck, this man plays my body like a concert pianist. He knows when to stroke gently and when I need a little more.

His hand glides down my stomach, making the muscles bunch and flex and I hiss when his middle finger makes initial contact with my clit, which of course is swollen and ready for whatever he plans to give me.

"I see you found your dinner," I pant as he makes slow, lazy circles against my overly sensitive bundle.

"Is that right?" he asks just before sucking a nipple into his mouth.

"MmmHmm." The extreme suction on my pebbled nipple is bordering on too much pain which means it feels just right.

He releases it with a loud pop. I love being blindfolded, it heightens every other sense; the anticipation of not knowing what he's going to do next keeps my entire body on that fine razor's edge of bliss.

"Funny thing," he mumbles against my belly button. "It's exactly what I was hoping was on the menu."

"Shit!" I scream as his mouth closes over my sex and his teeth clamp down on my clit. I continue to whimper as he rocks his teeth back and forth, my tender bud still between his teeth. Even though I'm almost certain he's going to draw blood, I can't help but mewl and beg for more.

Finally, he releases me and laps at me as the blood flow returns to the delicate area. I'm overwhelmed by the sensation of the throb he's created in my body. I struggle against my restraint and angle my hips harder against his mouth.

"Please," I beg.

"Tell me what you need, Angel," he demands as he slowly licks my quivering entrance.

He's teasing my body with only the most delicate touches, refusing to give me what I want, what I need until I'm begging for it. Well, it's been too long and there is not one ounce of sexual pride left in my body.

"More," I pant, frustrated. "More of everything."

His lips cover and suction to almost my entire core and his tongue begins flicking in earnest against me. Up and down and circling around with absolutely no pattern; his mouth is chaos on me. The best type of assault.

Just as one hand is sneaking up my body to cup my breast, I feel his thumb lightly caress the tight pucker below his mouth. The strategic pinch of my nipple and the soft plunge of the tip of his thumb past the sensitive ring of muscles catapult me into oblivion.

I'm still clenching uncontrollably when he stuffs two very large fingers into me and begins to stroke my front wall, which prolongs or sets off another orgasm; which I'm unable to decipher.

"Best meal ever," he praises as he pulls his fingers from me. "Here, taste," he whispers as his wet fingers touch my lips.

I suck his fingers into my mouth the same time that he slams into me. I nearly clamp down on his fingers as I'm stuffed full of him. *God, I love the first thrust.*

Unbidden, the thought of a pregnant Josie slams into my head. "Garrett, no!" I try to turn my body away from him, an impossible task since I'm tied up.

The thrusting stops immediately. As far as he's taken me, as many things as I've let him do to my body, I've never told him no. He understands the gravity of the word from my lips even though it's not my safe word.

"What's wrong, Alexa? Did I hurt you?" His breath is coming out in shallow bursts and I can feel the slight tremble of his muscles, no doubt from trying to control his body that is surely loaded with adrenalin right now.

"We need to use a condom," I explain.

"But you have the implant," he offers and slowly starts to roll his hips. "I need to feel you, Angel. No barriers."

"But Josie," I explain. He quickly shifts his hips back and pushes into me, his incredibly ample cock finding the end of me. "Oh, God!"

I feel his weight settle over me. "We'll find another way," he promises against my neck as he begins very purposeful thrusts, the tempo ever changing so I can't settle in and predict what's coming next.

The grip of his hand on my hip, the angle he holds me at, and deep reach of his thick cock sends my body into orbit, shattering apart and clutching at him, begging for more.

"Fuck, Alexa," he grounds out. "Too soon!" I sigh as the pulsing of his orgasm joins the erratic beat of my own.

"I needed that," I finally admit after several long minutes.

"I had planned on more," he protests and kisses my lips softly.

"You didn't have to come," I chide him.

"Yeah, tell that to my cock that was being strangled by your pussy." He nips my bottom lip as his thumb strokes over my still hard nipple.

"Sorry," I gloat. "I can't seem to control her around you."

"Apparently," he agrees as he reaches up and frees what I realize now is my shirt from my eyes. I blink up at him, my eyes focusing on the magnificent man that I'm privileged enough to lie next to every night.

"Well," I say coyly. "If you're that upset about it, you can always spank me and teach me a lesson."

His eyes light up like it's the best idea he's ever heard and suddenly I'm flipped over on my stomach. He growls just before his heavy hand slaps my ass.

Chapter 4
Garrett

Nothing worse than an incredibly hot night filled with sex and moans loud enough to wake the neighbors, then waking up alone in a cold bed. Alexa has been leaving me since the first time we made arrangements for a one-night stand months ago.

Maybe if you get the riding crop back out, she will remember to wake you with the lithe movements of her body against you rather than an empty spot.

I'm mulling over these thoughts as I struggle to cage my morning wood into a pair of sweats, of which I pulled from a dresser: where they belong, as opposed to the floor where her clothes were thrown once again last night.

I can't help but smile to myself. Alexa and I are opposites in almost every aspect of our lives except where we line up perfectly in the bedroom. I'm punctual; I don't think she owns a clock. I'm neat and like things ordered; she could live out of a suitcase or off of the floor. The most disconcerting difference is the one I try not to think about the most, and just happens to be the one I can't seem to shove out of my mind.

Never did I ever think I'd have the ability to love someone with every piece of my heart after the shit my ex-wife pulled, but I find myself caring for and loving Alexa more than I ever did Jamie. Before Alexa I would've rather eaten glass than try to picture a future that included one woman. I mean, who would want that? My guess is any man who's never been inside of Alexa Warner.

Now? Now, I have all sorts of crazy shit plowing through my head, thoughts I can't seem to control, and images of what my future, *our future*, can look like. So what's the problem?

Alexa.

She's the problem. Despite my declaration of love after she got home from the hospital, she still seems aloof, just out of my grasp. I mean don't get me wrong. We get along great damn near every second and we are beyond combustible in the bedroom, but she seems just out of my reach. No matter how much I try to prove to her every chance I get that she's it for me, I can't help but feel like she tries to stay one step ahead in an attempt to protect her heart, no doubt a result of my reaction to the first time she told me she loved me. Apparently yelling 'FUCK' and storming out of the room wasn't the right thing to do.

Daily I'm riddled with the guilt of being a lesser man and not telling her how I felt; the realization, however, came a few minutes too late. The consequences were of epic proportions. Alexa left my penthouse that night, got shot, and nearly died, but that's only part of it. The shooting and very quick arrest of Blake Evans set into motion tragic events that ended with Josie getting kidnapped and held captive and starved for over two weeks. Every single horrible thing that happened after Alexa left my house that night rests heavily on my shoulders. I've vowed to make sure that she knows how much I truly love her every second of the day.

I scrub my face with my hands, once again trying to abate the tendrils of guilt that try to consume my every waking minute that she's not in my arms.

Rounding the end of the counter heading into the kitchen, the sight in front of me stops me in my tracks. Alexa is bent over in front of the refrigerator, my white button down sneaking up the back of her thighs, only hinting at the secrets beneath.

I groan as my previously flagging morning wood is resurrected and throbbing behind the suddenly abrasive texture of my sweats. I position myself behind her and slowly begin to lift the white cotton of her shirt out of the way.

"Oh God," I slur as my head begins to swim. Her ass and half way down her thighs are splattered with red angry welts. I run my fingertips over the damage, disgusted with myself and somehow incredibly aroused at the same time. This isn't the first time I've left such marks on a woman, but somehow seeing them on Alexa's skin troubles me.

She hums at my touch, stands, and turns to face me. The lustful look on her face dissipates when she sees what I can only imagine is the horror at her injuries and confusion about my pulsing cock.

"No," she says suddenly angry. "You don't get to turn something incredible from last night into something you regret this morning."

"But I've hurt you," I challenge.

"I loved every minute of it." She rubs her hands down my arms and steps closer to me, the very tips of her cloth-covered breasts hitting my chest first.

"I didn't mean to leave marks. It looks like it hurts." I plead forgiveness with my eyes.

She clasps my hands in hers, directing one to her bottom and one to the center of her thighs. "Every time something touches it," she forces my fingers to grip her ass. "It makes me wet," she pants against my lips as she guides two of my fingers into her.

Suddenly my guilt begins to fade and is completely absent when she comes on my fingers while standing in the middle of the kitchen with the refrigerator door still wide open.

***

Alexa managed to convince me that I needed to be punished for her injuries if I felt so bad about marking her skin. She decided that edging me for two hours and coming in her mouth was enough of a punishment for me. Now she has a ridiculously sexy grin on her face which is a good change from the sultry smirk she had on the drive over to Ian and Lorali's house. I don't think I could handle another minute of her whimpering and thigh clenching as she squirmed needlessly in her seat.

I'm distracted by the over exaggerated sway of her slender hips as we walk to the front door. I pull her up short. Leaning down towards her ear. "Keep that shit up, Angel and you'll find yourself getting fucked in one of the empty rooms before we leave."

She turns her face and clamps her teeth down on my earlobe causing a searing hiss to rush past my lips. She places a soft peck on my lips. "I know you're trying to use that as a deterrent to control my behavior, but honestly I just see it as a challenge."

She leaves me speechless as she saunters up the grand steps to the front door and walks in without even knocking leaving the door wide open for my entrance. *Yep, definitely getting fucked before we leave.*

I follow the clicking of her heels and laughter to the back patio. The pool is sparkling and incredibly inviting and it's good to see this area open. Before Lorali, Ian hardly ever came out here, his self-imposed heavy schedule preventing it. I'm beginning to think I should follow his example. My lead bartender Johnny has been all but shoving me out of the door every night anyways and *Ampere* has run like clockwork even with all the time I missed the last few months.

I smile and shake both Ian and Kaleb's hands as I watch the girls squeal at each other like they've been separated for years; then I cringe at the knowledge of the actual separation they are still recovering from.

Somehow we've ended up segregated by gender, us guys are on one side of the patio and all three girls are huddled together opposite of us. I'd feel like a pussy at the loss of Alexa's touch if Ian and Kaleb didn't look as equally distraught.

"So," Alexa says loudly and clears her throat for effect. "Josie, I called you yesterday." I watch as Josie's eyes grow big like she's anticipating what Alexa is about to say. "Seems I interrupted Kaleb's little snack."

Josie gasps, drops her head to her hands hiding her face, and I see Kaleb shift in his chair.

"Dios mio," he grumbles.

"I…I thought it went to voicemail," Josie stammers. Then her head snaps back to Alexa. "How long did you listen?"

"I didn't *listen*," she emphasizes. "I made a phone call and was forced to hear just how much Kaleb liked the meal you presented him with!" I love it when she's indignant.

What the hell is she talking about?

Then Alexa's words and the memory of the dinner she gifted me with last night hit me. *Sly little fox.* Seems she had some inspiration. All three women are grinning now and I cut my eyes to Ian, who has a look of understanding on his face as well. Just how much do these girls talk about our sex lives with one another?

I play ignorant. "I'm confused. Josie, why are you embarrassed that Alexa called while you guys were eating dinner."

Her face flushes and reddens immediately. I hear Kaleb snicker beside me, obviously enjoying her mild discomfort.

Lorali, the ever-protective sister, jumps in to save her. "Well, Garrett," she says drawing my attention away from Josie and back to her. "Kaleb was the only one umm....eating," she chokes the last word out.

I tilt my head, maintaining a look of confusion and almost failing to keep the laugh that is beginning to bubble in my throat at bay. Lorali in her attempt to save Josie has ended up just as embarrassed. Seems they can speak to each other about our sex lives but struggle in mixed company.

"Yes, Garrett," Alexa says with a smirk. "Kaleb had the same thing you had for dinner last night."

"Pussy," I answer.

I watch as Ian sprays beer out of both his nose and mouth and smile in Lorali's direction. "Seems Ian had the same thing, if I'm not mistaken."

"Best damn thing I'd eaten all day," Ian confirms with an ear to ear grin.

"Here, here," Kaleb says holding up his beer in salute.

I wink at Alexa and watch as she grinds her ass harder on the chair, knowing she's doing it so she can feel the sting of the marks on her ass.

"Wait," I glare at Alexa. "So that's why."

Now it's her turn to tilt her head in confusion, only I can tell she really has no line on my train of thought.

I look over at Kaleb and then back to Alexa. "You may have wanted to *feed me* after that little phone call, but you also demanded I use a rubber."

"Fuck that," I hear Ian mutter.

I'm an asshole and it's blatantly clear when Josie shrinks down a little bit in her chair. Kaleb leans forward and places his beer on the table, ready to get up and comfort her.

"No offense, Josie," Alexa says as she glares at me. "I just don't want children." *Never?* "And you know you were on the shot. And I was just a little freaked out."

"And," Lorali cuts in. "Ian's rude *fuck that*, was about using condoms not about having children." She smiles at her fiancée. "He'd actually prefer a baby over ever having to use one again."

"Yeah," Alexa says her head shifting between the other girls. "Not me. I'm actually thinking about contacting my gyno to see if I can get a tubal, so I won't ever have to worry about it."

"No." My voice booms before my head realizes the word came from me.

Her face snaps towards me and she narrows her eyes, the look on her face telling me we'll talk about it later. I smirk back at her, hoping she can read the *don't make me take you over my knee*, look I have. If the squirm in her seat is any indication she read it loud and clear.

Chapter 5
Ian

Seems Garrett and I had more in common than both eating pussy last night. Lorali tried to pull that *wear a condom* shit with me last night as well. When I told her she couldn't get pregnant if I came in her ass, she relented. I'm glad she saw things my way and I'm only a little upset she hasn't consented to anal. I'm wearing her down and eventually she'll give in.

"So," Lorali says to Josie once everyone has calmed down from sharing their dinner plans from last night. "Have you guys set a date?"

It isn't until Lorali mentions them getting married and I watch Josie lovingly cradle her left hand in her lap that I notice the engagement ring on her finger. *How did I miss that?*

"Oh, Josie it's beautiful," I hear Alexa say, which is surprising since Alexa has always been very anti-marriage and I wonder if she's doing it for Josie's benefit. I immediately throw the thought out because Alexa is anything if not one hundred percent genuine.

"It's the ring his father proposed to his mother with," I hear her tell the girls, and suddenly I feel like a dick for buying the biggest fucking rock I could find and even more so for asking Lorali to marry me in a fucking club, rather than somewhere that is more meaningful.

I have to keep telling myself that Lorali isn't Josie and different things make them happy. Lorali tells me all the time that she could do without my money and from the way she's acted since we've been together, I know this for the truth, but fuck me if her eyes don't shine with pride when I catch her looking at her ring. At this moment, I realize she loves it because she loves me, just as Josie loves hers because it's what Kaleb gave her.

"We haven't really had the chance to talk about a wedding yet," Josie says as she smiles in Kaleb's direction. "I want something small, but we haven't discussed anything."

"Well," Kaleb says and leans forward resting his elbows on his knees.

"Hold that thought for a minute, man," I say as I stand and make my way over to Lorali. I pick her up easily and settle into her chair and place her on my lap. "I just needed to get a little more comfortable," I explain.

"Thank fuck," Garrett says and angles his head towards Alexa, who pops up and goes to him.

Kaleb, not missing an opportunity to be near Josie moves over to her. My world has been set to rights.

"Sorry for the interruption, Kaleb. Please continue." I angle my beer towards him before taking a sip.

"I was just going to tell Josie that I think a small wedding would be perfect." He kisses her neck and she seems to just melt into every crevice of his body.

I hear Alexa hiss and cut my head in time to see Garrett whisper something in her ear and pull his hand from the apex of her thighs.

"Okayyyy," I say and shuffle Lorali to her feet. We need to do something else before this turns into an orgy of some kind. "How about we all get changed and jump in the pool?

Everyone nods, murmurs their ascent, and stands to make their way to different locations in the house to change into swimwear.

From the growl I just heard from Garrett and giggle from Josie I think it may be a bit before either pair makes their way back out to the pool, which is fine by me because I have plans for the next half hour or so.

"Take your time!" I yell at everyone's retreating back.

They each have what Lorali and I consider their own rooms here, carry-over from when Josie was abducted and I've made sure to let them know that they're welcome here anytime.

"You seem distracted," Lorali says as I close the door to our suite.

"I want you practically every second of every day," I tell her. "But do you find it weird that I stay rock hard every time we get together in a group like this?"

"Really?" she asks and her face lights up. She sighs loudly. "I'm glad I'm not the only one."

"I have no idea why. It kind of freaks me out a little bit." I explain.

"I think it's because there is so much love and attraction around it just electrifies the air or something," I nod in agreement as I push her beautiful honey colored hair off of her shoulder so I can kiss her there.

"Mmmm," is her response as her hands make their way under my t-shirt and her nails lightly score my back.

I unzip her jeans and slide them, along with her underwear, off of her luscious ass, dropping to my knees to push them to her ankles. My face is near her cleft and I'm unable to keep myself from inhaling her intoxicating scent. I toss her jeans to the side once she's stepped out of them and run my hands back up her legs to the inside of her thighs.

I kiss her just below her belly button and pull my head back as I reach in with my thumbs and spread her swollen lips apart; she's all but dripping on the carpet. I lean in to taste her and she stops me with her hands on my head.

"I thought the rule was you're not supposed to eat anything before swimming?" I look up at her evil little smirk.

"I'll stick to the shallow end then," I growl at her before burying my face between her legs and slinking an arm around her, already predicting her reaction to my bombardment. I'm a fast learner and it only took us once of her falling for me to make sure I'm holding her tight when my tongue hits her clit.

"Jesus," she pants and tugs on my hair. It's just long enough for her to wrap her fingers in and I live for the moments when she lets herself go enough to try to force me into action. I'm certain she doesn't even know she's doing it.

We've been together for months now and I'm just as excited to get my mouth on her, my cock inside her as I was the first time I ran into her, possibly even more so now after all of the tragedy that has hit our small group. Nothing like a couple of near deaths to make you appreciate what you have.

I groan against her hot body as she comes so much that her juices are dribbling down my chin. I love that I've never had to use a drop of lube on this beautiful woman.

She's trembling as I wipe my mouth on the inside of her thigh and stand up. "You're worried about me drowning in the pool so you decided to try and drown me in here instead?" I tease as I wipe more of her off my face with the t-shirt I just tugged over my head.

She giggles and I toss it to the floor and work my pants off, freeing my rock hard cock. I kiss her lips and sweep my tongue in repeatedly as I reach around her back and lift her against me. I grunt the second the hot flesh of her pussy makes contact with my throbbing cock. I'm not even in her yet and already I'm thinking of the next time.

I pull my mouth only a hairsbreadth away from hers. "You know I never want to rush with you, but we have guests today." I nip her bottom lip. "So I'm going to fuck you hard and fast and you're going to love every second of it." I tilt her head and bite her ear lobe. "I'll make it up to you once our guests leave."

Her hooded eyes watch me with expectancy. I walk her toward the bed, lay her on her back with her feet against my chest, and slam into her without further warning.

"Shit," I hiss. I told her hard and fast but me blowing my load in two seconds is not what I meant. I lean over to kiss her, practically folding her in half, *thank you yoga*, to give myself a second to prevent this turning into a very embarrassing situation.

"Relax, baby," I beg against her lips. "If you stay clamped down on me like that things are going to end faster than I intended."

She attempts to take a calming breath and I rock my hips back and forth turning it into a moan instead.

The tingling in my spine has subsided a fraction so I grab her feet from my chest and spread her legs as wide as my arms can reach. "You ready?"

She nods energetically and bites her bottom lip. I slam into her shoving her across the mattress a few inches. "Hold on to the edge of the bed down by your ass, baby. I don't want you scooting away from me."

She obeys and I begin to pound into her relentlessly. She's magnificent with her hair spread across the duvet and her amazing tits bouncing to the rhythm of my pulverizing hips.

"Goddamn it, Lorali. You need to come soon." My voice is pleading because there is no way to stop the train that is coming. "Play with your clit, baby." I'm practically growling at her.

She whimpers at the first contact of her fingers. "Oh God!" she says loud enough so the whole house should know she's about to peak.

"Come, Lorali. Now." I say through gritted teeth.

She does, ridiculously so. The first hard clench of her tight pussy is my dick's permission to let go, my orgasm releasing in hot bursts inside of her. I slowly flex my hips, dragging my still hard cock in and out of her, relishing in the oversensitive sensations until she whimpers and tries to wiggle away. I bury myself to the hilt, place her smooth legs around my hips, and rest some of my weight on her chest.

Her eyes are closed, no doubt exhausted from the past half an hour, and she looks amazing. Her cheeks are flushed the most incredible shade of pink and her lips are slightly parted to allow for her erratic breaths.

I stroke her cheek. "Lorali," I grin at her when her heavy eyelids flutter open. "I love you, baby. I'd love nothing more than to stay in this room making you moan all day, but we have to grab a quick shower and head back out to the pool."

She grumbles at me. "You have to get out of me so I can get up."

In an attempt to torture her I roll my hips and thrust in and out of her a few times which ends up tormenting me as well, but I finally relent and vacate her. I sweep her off the bed and walk us into the walk-through shower.

Chapter 6
Lorali

As always I get my way. I convinced Ian that it is 'Tit for Tat Sunday' in the shower and since he made me come twice, once with his mouth, I insisted I return the favor. I love the taste of him and go after it every chance I get.

What annoyed me was rushing his blow job to get back out to the pool and discover that the other two couples haven't made it out yet. I grab the plate of deli made sub sandwiches and set them on the table on the patio and begin making trips to and from the fridge and the patio.

Ian insisted that we order the deli food, stating that there is no need in wasting time on making food when he can pay someone to do it. Each time he gets this way, I argue that it's wasteful, but he just shrugs me off. We've had the argument more than once but this last time when I told him to do whatever he wanted with his money he corrected me and said it was *our* money. He wasn't very happy when I told him to stop spending *my* money so frivolously. I told him he needed to invest it and stop throwing it away, which then led me to being placed in front of a computer while he pulled up his very substantial portfolio. So in my attempt to get him to stop wasting a hundred dollars on food he shut me up with knowledge of the millions he has at his fingertips.

I know the food will be well received as I'm sure everyone has worked up an appetite from changing into their swimsuits. I know Ian and I did.

I decided on a subdued navy and red, chevron print bikini for today since we're in mixed company. I've only been in the pool a few times since it warmed up enough but that was with Ian and there was no clothing involved, so this is the very first time I've been in a bathing suit around Ian. He strokes or pats some part of my body each time we pass carrying food out to the patio. He can't seem to keep his hands, eyes, and mouth off of me. I know he's building the anticipation for tonight and hell if it isn't working.

I'm standing facing the pool and Ian is at my back with his arms wrapped around me, whispering all of the things he plans to do to me later when I hear the back patio door open. I turn my head and see Alexa strut out in a fire-engine red, barely there bikini with Garrett close on her heels, a scowl on his face. He apparently is not impressed with her choice of attire in front of others.

I'm used to Alexa being wild and showing the world everything the good Lord blessed her with, this is until now. Now my insecurities come to a head when I see my gorgeous, red-headed best friend step out in tiny scraps of fabric in front of my fiancé.

I turn in Ian's arms to try to gauge his reaction to them when they walk towards us. He grins and when I follow his line of sight I can tell he's smiling more at Garrett's reaction than the sight of Alexa.

"She's beautiful. Isn't she?" I whisper in his ear.

He nods his head noncommittally. "You're beautiful," he responds and pecks my lips. "And Garrett has his damn hands full."

I can't help but laugh as I watch Alexa make her way around the table of food, deciding what she wants to eat as Garrett trails behind her with a towel obviously trying to get her to cover up.

"He's tamed her," I advise him.

He huffs. "She's far from tame," Ian disagrees. "I'd spank your ass if you tried to go out in public in that suit."

My jaw drops when Alexa makes her way around the table and her back is to us. Red streaks and lines are halfway down the back of her thighs. I can tell they're not from today because the swelling is minimal. My eyes dart to Garrett and I'm shocked to see a twinge of guilt on his face as he breaks eye contact with me, steps behind her, and wraps a towel around her waist.

"What the fuck?" I whisper to myself.

Ian laughs, then clears his throat when I glare at him. He shrugs his shoulders, "Garrett's known to spank an ass every so often."

"She's covered in marks, Ian," I say in an angry whisper.

"Look at her," he tells me with mirth. "Does she look like she's bothered by it?"

I glance over at Alexa and watch her as she kisses Garrett's mouth and look away when I see her hand glide down his stomach and cup his cock.

"I'm thinking," Ian says. "Alexa may enjoy what Garrett does to her."

"They do look happy," I conceded as he lowers his mouth to mine.

Ian swatted my ass once when we were in Paris a few months ago but hasn't since. Honestly, I loved the way my ass stung from the swat of his big hand, but those marks don't look fun to me at all. *To each their own I guess.* I make a mental note to talk to Alexa about it later.

I hear a feminine throat clear and pull my mouth away from Ian's. Peering around his shoulder, I see a flushed Josie and a very sated looking Kaleb step out on the patio. Josie, true to form, is in a

Tankini with boy shorts, no way she'd be caught dead in something like Alexa is wearing.

"You guys hungry?" I ask the final couple joining us on the patio. "We have loads of food."

Josie and Kaleb both grab a plate and begin adding food. I notice Josie only gets some fruit and a couple cubed pieces of cheese. "You don't want a sandwich, Josie?"

She looks a little embarrassed, which leaves me confused.

"The books say deli meat is unsafe in pregnancy," Kaleb informs me. I had no clue.

"Oh, okay." I shrug my shoulders. "Would you like me to grab you something else?"

Josie shakes her head no and beams at Kaleb. "You've been reading the books?"

I almost swoon at the sight of his loving smile as he nods at Josie, kisses her cheek, and places a gentle hand on her lower belly. He's going to be an incredible dad and husband. I turn my head and look at Ian, who is watching me with adoration and suddenly I'm sad that my own womb is empty.

I smile at him when he quirks his eyebrow up and beams a huge smile at me; just like with everything else he can read me like an open book. I know where our discussion is going to go later.

I turn away from him to attempt to abate my longing to take him back to our bedroom and begin the baby making right now. I grab a plate and grab a few random food items and join the others back at the patio furniture.

The conversation naturally flows right back to the weddings which I know Kaleb and Ian are looking forward to, the planning? Not so much.

"Why don't we all get together next Saturday and go shopping?" Alexa recommends. "That gives you and Kaleb a week to discuss what you guys want." She directs the last part to Josie.

"I'd love to!" I exclaim. "I'm way behind from…" I let my voice trail off. How completely insensitive was that? Did I really just almost blame my sister's kidnapping on my suspended wedding plans?

I look over at Josie, ready to apologize, but she's not even paying attention to me. Instead, she's watching Kaleb's hand rub her flat stomach. The smile on her face tells me she either didn't hear me or she wasn't bothered by my rude words.

I look over at Alexa, who is glaring at me, obviously mad at my slip. My eyes start to water and a blanket of guilt covers me. Just as my eyes start to water, Alexa shakes her head slightly, an apology for making me feel worse than I already did.

"What do you think, Josie?" Alexa asks breaking into my remorse. "Want to go shopping next Saturday?"

Josie looks to Kaleb for assurance and suddenly I realize she's terrified to be away from him. I cut my eyes to Ian, begging for him to step in.

"That's a great idea ladies," he leans forward conspiratorially. "I'll have the limo available to you." He cuts his eyes to Kaleb and continues. "Ramon will be there to help with the bags."

Kaleb nods at him. Ramon is not only Ian's limo drive but also his bodyguard. Both Kaleb and Josie are well aware of whom he is and it sets them both at ease. I squeeze Ian's hand as a thank you and he draws it to his mouth and kisses the inside of my wrist.

"Any idea which boutique you want to go to?" Josie asks me.

I hear Alexa huff playfully and I turn my head to her. "What?"

"We'll have a limo and Ramon is carrying the bags? We'll go to all of them!" We all laugh.

I pop the last grape from my plate into my mouth just as Ian bends his head to whisper in my ear, "you ready to get in the pool?"

I nod my head, unfold myself from his lap, and stand. The others follow suit. "Let's get wet," I say to no one in particular. Josie nearly chokes on the water she's drinking.

I can't help but grin, engaged, pregnant, and still flustered by an unintentional sexual innuendo.

"You seem to be less stressed," Garrett says in observation of Ian's laid back demeanor in the pool. Garrett's right. Ian is normally wound very tight.

We're all coupled up hanging onto the side of the heated pool.

"I've hired a few more people at work to help weed through the minutia before it makes it to my desk." He explains and grips my hip, positioning me in front of him against the wall, his arms still on the wall and my legs wrapped around his hips.

He emits a low groan when I tilt my pelvis fractionally, rubbing my slit against his thickening cock. He bends his head down and nips at my earlobe. "I will fuck you right here in front of everyone if you don't stop."

My body's response to his delicious threat is surprising. I know it's an empty threat; Ian is not the type to perform in front of others and I honestly have no desire to either, but his words have caused me to grow slick and my breasts heavy with need.

"Yes, sir," I respond on a mild whimper in his ear.

He turns his attention back to Garrett. "I just need to find one more person to fill the Philanthropy Director position and I'll be able to clear my plate a little more."

"Any interviews lined up?" Alexa asks joining into the conversation.

"I have a few people lined up, but I'm being very selective. They need to have the right feel for the job and I've been less than impressed with the people who I've spoken to thus far." Ian explains.

Alexa smiles. "You know who would be great? Mallory King." I nod in agreement. "I know she's been looking for something a little more structured to focus on.

"Your friend that visited you in the hospital?" Ian asks in recollection.

"Yep. I'll email you her information." Alexa offers.

Ian nods in appreciation. I know how much of a relief it will be when he finds someone he trusts to take over that workload.

Chapter 7
Kaleb

It's late by the time we make it home from Ian and Lorali's. After hours just hanging out in the pool talking, we played a few hands of poker. It's the first time I'd played poker with Ian in months. It, of course, had a totally different feel with the girls around than a poker night with just the guys.

Josie decided it was time to go once Alexa, after a few glasses of wine, suggested the next hand include strip poker. I agreed with her quickly and Ian and Lorali started yawning, suddenly too tired to play anymore. Garrett sure as hell has his hands full with that hellcat, but he and Alexa seem like they were made for each other.

"Mariposa?" I whisper in Josie's ear after tugging the truck door open in the garage. She doesn't even stir.

She's fallen asleep on the drive home so I reach in and sweep her up in my arms to carry her to bed. I run my nose along the curve of her jaw. She's practically weightless and incredibly tiny in my arms, and I can't wait to be able to carry our child exactly the same way.

I lay her softly on our bed and slowly begin to undress her as gently as I can. I know she's tired just being pregnant but coupled with a full day in the sun she has to be exhausted. I slip her shirt off and unhook her bra. I run my fingers down her arms taking the lace lingerie with them; my need to touch her is palpable. A trail of gooseflesh follows my fingers down her arms. Unsnapping her jeans I tug them down her hips, leaving her green silk panties on. I kiss the top of each of her feet as I free them from the legs of her skinny jeans.

I see her shiver and I'm hit with a pang of shame. I'm standing here undressing her slowly, torturing myself; all the while she's cold and uncomfortable. *Way to be a dick, Perez.*

I tug the blankets over her legs and pull it up to her chin. She immediately snuggles into their warmth. I turn to leave the room and hear her voice.

"Baby?" The sound of it is soft and comforting.

I turn back to her and stroke a blond wave of hair from her cheek so I can look into her sleepy eyes. *Love.* Her amazing blue eyes shine with love for me.

I gently kiss her lips. "I'll be right back. I have to feed Mia and let her out to use the restroom."

She nods her head gently in understanding. "Love you," she whispers as her eyes drift closed once more.

"Te Amo, Mariposa," I declare, my lips brushing her forehead.

***

"I need you," I hear as Josie's breath ghosts across my cheek and her tight, silky core wraps around and sinks down on my engorged cock.

I go from deep sleep to wide awake in the span of less than a second. I was having what I thought was a dream of her stroking my length. I never saw her face in my dream, but her touch is something that has been ingrained and seared on my brain since day one.

I open my eyes to find her on her knees, bouncing up and down my erection vigorously. I reach up and grip her hips to slow her movements. I was so close to orgasm in my dream it's about to come to fruition embarrassingly fast.

"Fuck, Josie," I pant out. "Slow down."

She whimpers when I hold her hips static, preventing her from moving. I reach my hand between her legs and sweep my thumb over her engorged clit. She responds by clamping her hands over her full breasts. Her hips begin to buck as she gyrates her hips against my thumb.

She throws her head back and moans loudly and I feel her insides grasp at my length repeatedly. *Thank God!*

I lift her hips up and slam her down twice and then I'm releasing into her. She gives me a sleepy grin and collapses on my chest. I think we're both back asleep before our heart rates return to normal.

***

My vacation ends Monday at four in the morning with a phone call from the county jail forcing me to unwrap Josie's delectable body from mine. I love being a cop but I wish criminals would take a damn day off once in a while.

I grin as she grumbles when I try to maneuver myself out from under her. I lift her arm from my chest as she squeezes me harder and growls.

"Did you just growl at me?" I lean in to kiss her and she just grumbles into the mattress. I sweep her wild, sleep tussled mane of gorgeous blond hair out of her face. "I couldn't hear you, Mariposa."

She turns her head only slightly, "I asked if you wanted me to make you lunch," she mumbles from the corner of her mouth.

"I have a better idea. Why don't I come home and have you for lunch?" Her offer to get out of bed and take care of me, even when I know it's probably one of the last things on Earth she wants to do right now has me rock hard.

She moans softly and I can feel her weight shift under the covers, no doubt she's rubbing her thighs together.

"Keep it warm for me," I plead before kissing her head one last time and hitting the shower.

The drive to the county jail was quick since no one in their right mind is up and about this early in the day. Once I arrived, I checked in at the front desk and met up with the patrol sergeant who's doing me a solid by letting me come in and talk with a guy I've been looking for.

Felipe Espinoza is a middle-level man with the Cortez Cartel. He has a misdemeanor warrant out of Denver PD for a domestic assault on a girlfriend last year. He was booked, released, and blew town all on the same day when the girlfriend signed an affidavit of non-prosecution. He's a smart player and knows exactly how to play the game. I don't expect him to say a thing, but I'm also not going to turn down the chance to speak with him.

I step into the interrogation room just as Marco Hernandez is cuffing him to the table. I recognize Marco as the jail sergeant that was in charge the day Blake Evans was murdered in the jail bathroom. Blake Evans is the bastard that not only almost killed Alexa when he shot her but set into motion a series of events that ended with Josie being kidnapped and starved for nearly three weeks; which consequently also ended with the death of three people during the shootout during Josie's rescue.

Without making eye contact, Marco slithers out of the room without so much as a nod of his head acknowledging my presence. I have the utmost respect for all people in law enforcement, but that guy rubs me the wrong way. He seems like the type of guy who cuts corners and doesn't give a shit about his job, and that mindset gets people killed.

Felipe Espinoza is a weather-worn man, with a paunchy gut, tattoos on his neck, and a front gold tooth. He seems dirty with greasy hair and a sneer which would make almost any man think twice about crossing him. Not the type of man I'd want to meet in a dark alley, but I have a job to do.

I lean against the wall from him with my legs crossed at the ankles and my hands resting in my pockets. I'm going for nonchalant, but I get the feeling that Felipe has seen the inside of an interrogation room many more times than I have.

"What's the Cortez Cartel doing in Denver?" I ask finally breaking the silence.

Felipe doesn't respond and he actually seems to be looking through me rather than at me. I know he'll never answer my questions which piss me off, even more, considering I had to leave Josie alone in our warm ass bed for this bullshit, for that alone I want to slam his head on the table.

"Only two people above you in the cartel and your ass gets stopped for running a red light because you can't pay attention enough when getting road head?" I bark out a laugh. "Cartel's really scraping the bottom of the barrel these days I see."

He sneers at me, his menacing gaze holding mine. *Hello, Felipe glad you could join me.*

"I'm here on a misdemeanor warrant, Detective." He spits my title out like it's a hunk of rotten meat in his mouth. "I'll be out of here in less than forty-eight."

I laugh again and see the flash of confusion on his face when I don't take the bait.

"You're right about that, Mr. Espinoza." I agree with him quickly. "Less than forty-eight actually. Transport is already being set up for later this afternoon." He narrows his eyes at me and I continue. "Denver only has you on a misdemeanor, but SoCal has more than a dozen federal charges waiting for you. "You'll be eating breakfast at MCC San Diego tomorrow." I unfold myself from against the wall and smile. "I'm sure the Denver charges will be left pending indefinitely."

I hear him mutter "Puñeta" as I turn and walk out of the room. *Fuck is right Mr. Espinoza.*

I close the door behind me and grab the first uniformed deputy that I see. "Let Hernandez know Espinoza is ready to go back to his cell."

"Marco just left," He informs me. "Said he had food poisoning or some shit." I glare at him. He was literally just in the interrogation room and seemed fine with me.

"I'll let them know to get someone down to get him." I nod at him. *Better.*

Chapter 8
Josie

The suggestion of wedding shopping last week was terrifying until Ian offered the help of Ramon, his bodyguard. I've had a hard enough time alone in the house while Kaleb has been at work this week. I've practically barricaded myself in our bedroom, as far from the front door as possible. I even lock the bedroom door and Kaleb has to knock when he comes home for lunch. I haven't left the house except with Kaleb and I'm a little more than mildly apprehensive about him not being with us today.

When I agreed to go wedding shopping with Lorali and Alexa, I didn't even consider that Kaleb would be home and I would be gone. He has been my lifeline lately and I'd much rather be wrapped around him napping in our bed than doing any sort of shopping. I know I need to get out and get back to some form of normal life but my hands start sweating and my body trembles when I just think about it.

"I can't wait to marry you in a few weeks," Kaleb says as he kisses my shoulder.

I'm in front of the bathroom mirror in nothing but my bra and panties pulling my long hair into a messy bun.

"You sure you're okay with a small wedding?" He's agreed to every suggestion that I've had about our nuptials, but I wonder if he would have a difference of opinion if he didn't think I was so fragile.

He grins at our reflections as he wraps his arms around my waist. "I don't want you to take this the wrong way." My body stiffens at his warning. "I'm less concerned about decorations and location and more looking forward to our first kiss as husband and wife."

"Really?" I whisper my body relaxing.

"I mean don't get me wrong, I can't wait to see you walking down the aisle to me, but I'm most excited about getting my ring on your finger." He runs his nose along the column of my chin, his hot breath sweeps across my shoulder eliciting a wave of goosebumps down my body. "I need to know you're mine."

I hum my approval. "I'm yours now, baby," I assure him as I swivel my hips against his towel covered erection.

"Are you nervous about today?" He asks as his hand drifts over my lace covered center. I nod slightly because honestly I am. "Let me see if I can relax you then?"

He turns me in his arms and gently glides me backward until my thighs are touching the sink and then he pulls my panties to the side and sinks two fingers in deep. "I wouldn't want you leaving here nervous," he pants in my ear as I moan from his touch.

"So wet for me already," he murmurs against my neck. "So greedy. You're clenching around my fingers already."

My eyes roll in my head as he begins to stroke that delicious spot he always gravitates to. My legs begin to tremble and I'm near collapse as Kaleb runs his other arm around my back and lifts me to sit on the edge of the sink counter.

"Still nervous?" His eyes are dark green and his mouth is slightly open to allow for harsh intakes of breath and I love that he's just as affected by me as I am by him.

I nod my head and bite my lip; toying with him.

He grins salaciously and drops down to a crouch between my legs. "Let's see what we can do about that."

My head hits the mirror at my back when my body arches into his mouth. I pull my legs up and place them on his shoulders; his ears and the scruff on his cheeks deliciously abrading the delicate skin on my inner thighs. I pick up my hands from down by my hips to grip his head, the action causing me to lay further back. I hiss at the shock of the cold of the mirror against the heated skin of my back.

Kaleb continues to flick and tease my outer bundle of nerves with his tongue while his fingers probe and torture my core. I'm breathless and teetering on the edge of no return when he pulls his mouth away.

"Kaleb," I beg as he also pulls his fingers from me and rubs my slickness on my swollen tissues.

"I crave you, Josie," he admits with a gentle kiss against my body giving my sensitive clit one final lick before moving his face further up. "I love you, baby," he whispers against my lower tummy, a declaration to our unborn child.

When he fully stands the towel around his waist falls to the floor and my eyes gravitate to the thick, proud erection jutting toward my center. My tongue sweeps my lower lip just before he leans his mouth down to mine. Slowly he feeds himself into me and I wrap my arms and legs around him.

"Like this," he says as he untwines my legs and places my feet on the counter, my legs spread wide. I move my hands back down by my hips for balance. His cock at my core is the only point of exquisite contact between our bodies.

We both bend our heads down and watch as he glides inside of me. I moan as he slowly finds the end of me and withdraws. His hips begin a slow, torturous rhythm and the fire he'd been stoking rages to life once more.

"Harder," I beg.

He grunts as he cups my ass in his huge hands and lifts me off the counter, my legs instinctively wrapping around him. Within seconds I'm bouncing up and down his length, my arms gripping his shoulders.

"Yes," I praise him as my core prepares for release. Less than a handful of thrusts later and I'm shoved over the edge of reason. "Kaleb!" I shout as the throbs turn to a full blown explosion.

He's patient with me and gently thrusts in and out of me, draining each aftershock from my body.

"My turn," he says as he places me on my feet, turns me around, and folds me over face down on the counter. I'm wound tight again the second he slams into me from behind.

Both of his hands grip my hips as he pistons in and out of my body. When his orgasm finally hits, he's holding me up and my toes are not even touching the floor. The throbbing spasm of his length inside of me sets off another explosion in my core and I'm a whimpering mess by the time he pulls out and carries me back to the shower.

***

"I'm glad we're doing this," I say to Alexa and Lorali through the curtain as I slip a dress with an empire waist over my head. I really like this one and the price is better than the others I've tried on today.

Kaleb gave me his credit card as I was leaving the house and told me to have fun with it, but I feel awkward about it. I know we're getting married, but I feel selfish spending his money on clothes and a wedding when we have a baby coming. We haven't spent time talking about finances or the specific logistics of being a family.

I shake my head as I step out of the dressing room, trying to clear the self-doubt and shame that hits me when I think about how everything in my life has happened all at once.

"Yes!" Alexa encourages me and Lorali gasps and brings her hand to her throat.

"It's perfect Josie," my sister says with a huge smile.

I do a little spin. "I think so too," I agree with her.

"What about shoes?" Alexa asks. "I have a perfect pair of Manolos!"

I clear my throat to begin explaining about our wedding. "I'm planning to wear flats because we're getting married at the house."

Lorali beams. "Kaleb's back yard is perfect. His view is amazing, an excellent backdrop for a wedding."

Alexa nods in agreement. "Guestlist?"

"Family and a few close friends," I tell them as I swish the dress around my hips in front of the mirror. "Super small. Maybe thirty people tops."

"Is that what you want?" Leave it to Alexa to not beat around the bush. I love and hate that about her.

I meet her eyes in the mirror and smile. No sense in being dishonest. "It is now." I shrug my shoulders.

"What does that even mean, Josie?" Lorali crosses her arms over her chest.

I sigh and flop down on the couch in the small dressing room. "It means that I never pictured myself being pregnant when I got married." I fiddle with the hem of my dress. "I never saw myself getting abducted either."

"Oh, Josie," Lorali says as she sits beside me and takes my hands in hers.

I smile at her. "What I pictured was finding the perfect man who treats me like a princess and loves me unconditionally, and I found him. I always thought I'd be courted and wooed and then I would get married and plan a family. I never thought I'd fall in love in less than a week and get pregnant practically the first time we made love." I raise my head and in this exact moment let go of every ounce of shame I have about my situation.

"This may not seem like a fairy tale to others, but this is *my* fairy tale. I just didn't have to wait months and months like others do to find my true love and happily ever after." I grin at both of them.

"I totally get it," Lorali agrees. "It was pretty much that way with Ian and I…well except for the baby part."

"Same here with Garrett," Alexa concedes and I know she's talking about the love aspect of it and not marriage or children.

I slap my legs and stand up, ready to continue on with my day. I pull the tag from under my arm and wince slightly. It's less expensive than some of the other ones, but I've never spent five hundred dollars on a dress before.

"What was that noise for?" Alexa asks.

"It's expensive and I feel weird spending Kaleb's money," I explain.

Lorali nods her head in agreement. "I get it. I hate it when Ian demands I spend his money."

Alexa laughs. "You are both crazy as shit! Your man wants to spend money on you; spend his fucking money!"

Lorali shakes her head and laughs. "Ian has too much money. He just throws it around; even wasteful with it."

Alexa huffs. "Has he asked you to sign a prenup?"

"I wish he would," Lorali mumbles. "I don't want him to ever think that I'm with him because of his money."

"Do you plan to talk to him about it?" I ask Lorali. I may need to mention it to Kaleb as well. I have no clue about his finances but it is apparently something we need to talk about.

"Hell no!" Lorali exclaims. "He keeps telling me to quit my job because I make so little he doesn't see the benefit of it. He wanted me to take over the charitable donations sector of his company."

"Why don't you," Alexa asks.

I watch her shrug her shoulders. "I don't like rich people. Ian's not like most wealthy people. I don't want to do that every day."

Alexa laughs. "Lorali, you already work around very rich people with your job."

"Good point," Lorali says.

"Lor?" I begin. "I was hoping I could ask you a favor."

"Anything," she offers.

"Think you can host Mom and Dad and possibly a brunch the Saturday after the wedding? Kaleb's house is only big enough for his mother and cousin that are coming into town for the ceremony." I smile big and bat my lashes.

"That won't be a problem at all. If you have any others you need to house they're welcome as well," She offers.

"Thank you," I tell her as I slide back into the dressing room to change back into my street clothes.

I buy the dress and find a lovely pair of shimmery flats at the next boutique. I also find a gorgeous hair clip to wear that has beautiful pearls and tiny green butterfly. Perfect for my wedding day; perfect for Kaleb.

"What do you guys want to do now?" Alexa asks as she hands several bags to Ramon for him to place in the trunk.

"Lunch!" I bark out. I smile at the speed in which I answer her.

"Getting your appetite back I see," Lorali says as she opens the back door for us all to slide in.

"Seems like it. At this stage in the game, it is either eat or sleep. I'm tired all the time." I explain.

Less than twenty minutes later we are being seated in a fancy Italian restaurant. If I'm not tired, now I will be after I'm loaded down with pasta!

My cell phone dings and I smile when I see it is a heart from Kaleb. I love spending time with Lorali and Alexa, but I can't wait to get back home to him.

"So what are you guys doing for your honeymoon?" Lorali asks as she grabs a seasoned breadstick from the basket in the center of the table.

"Kaleb has one week of vacation left before the end of the year. He said something about maybe Reno." I smirk. "I don't care where we go as long as the bed is comfortable."

Alexa full on laughs. "That's my girl!"

I giggle. "That's not exactly what I meant. I'm so tired all the time. The books say it's normal, but I literally take naps all day long."

"That bad huh?" Alexa asks.

"Yes. I think today is the longest I've stayed awake since before I was…taken." Crap I didn't want to think about that right now.

"I bet you're bored. Staying home all day while Kaleb is at work with nothing to do. I'd take naps too." Alexa offers.

"You guys could always take this summer off and come hang out with me all day." Lorali laughs like it's the craziest suggestion in the world.

"I'm actually thinking about opening my own spa." Lorali and I both tell her how wonderful of an idea it is.

She shrugs her shoulders. "Garrett has an incredible business mind and he thinks I'd be happier if I made the executive decisions."

"Are you having trouble at work?" Lorali sits back in her chair as I sneak another bread stick.

"Not really. *Elite* is just a little stagnant right now and the owners aren't very progressive. It's hurting the company, but they aren't ready to make changes." She explains. Alexa manages the spa at a very high-end resort and she's very good at her job, but you can only do so much when your hands are tied by the owners.

We both nod. I don't even want to think about my job right now. Just the idea of going back to that school makes me nauseous.

Chapter 9
Lorali

"You've been acting weird all day," Ian says as he unzips the back of my evening gown. "Want to just tell me about it? Or do I need to fuck it out of you?"

The discussion about the prenup with the girls last weekend has been running on a constant ticker in my head. Having a prenup is not stressing me out; knowing when I bring the idea up that Ian is going to shoot it down is what bothers me. I hold my finger to my chin in contemplation with a grin on my face. He will be slightly more agreeable once his sexual appetite is sated.

"So be it," he growls as he pulls the lace of my bra down and his lips suction to the tip of my breast.

Sequin covered lace and silk pool around my feet as Ian sucks my painfully hard nipple into his mouth. Before I even register that his hands are around me, my strapless bra snaps open and joins the ridiculously expensive dress at my feet.

Suddenly he grips my hips and I hear my panties rip; then feel the chill as the cool air licks at my blazing core. He's so aggressive and needy tonight and I love it. I bite the top of his shoulder, spurring him on and reach for the buttons of his tuxedo pants.

He pulls his mouth from my breast and my nipple hardens further from the loss of the warmth. I quiver as he watches with hooded eyes as my hands work feverishly to undress him. He looks magnificent tonight in his tailored to perfection Armani tux, but now he needs to get out of it.

"Help," I plead as my fingers start working the tiny buttons at the bottom of his shirt.

He begins working the bow tie loose from his neck and then starts on the buttons at the top meeting me in the middle. Next we each take a sleeve and set to work on the cufflinks at his wrists. He, of course, finishes first and as his hands sweep to the wrist I was working on; I let him take over as I work his pants and briefs down his hips.

Hitting my knees in front of him, my hot mouth wraps around his tip as soon as it is clear of the fabric. His hiss makes me smile around his rock hard length and entices me to take him to the back of my throat.

"Fuck, baby. That feels good," he praises as his fingers work my mane of golden hair from the pins holding it in a messy chignon, allowing it to fall over my shoulders and down my back. He forcefully takes a handful and begins to dictate the speed my mouth runs over his cock. My hands on his thighs register the tremble in his muscles.

"Enough," he grunts as he rips my mouth off of him.

I rise up and step free of the fabric at our feet. Suddenly I'm air born in his arms and then tossed on the bed. Before I can catch my breath, I'm flipped on my stomach and he's pulling my hips up.

With his hand wrapped once again in my hair he tugs my head back at the same time, he slams inside of me. My core begins to tremble immediately, the tiny inner muscles rippling along him and begging for more.

He's relentless as he pounds in and out of me. I know he's acting this way because I smiled and spoke with a gentleman at the gala tonight while waiting for our drink order to be filled. There was nothing remotely inappropriate with our interaction, but from the feel of it Ian feels the need to remind me that I'm his.

"Mine," he spits out just as his hand lands in a stinging slap on the apple of my right ass cheek.

It sends me over the edge, causing wave after wave of clenching spasms to devastate my body.

Just as I begin to sag lower on the bed, exhausted from the orgasm he just gave me he grabs my hips and forces me back up. Folding over my back, "there's more," he promises in my ear.

Each thrust of his is met with a soft moan or whimper from me. Our sweat slickened bodies move against each other as he slides in and out of me easily. I can feel the remnants of my orgasm as it flows down my thighs. His fingers make contact suddenly with my clit and I gasp as my body responds to him immediately.

For the second time in less than ten minutes, my body is convulsing and gripping his cock. He roars as he is engulfed into his own release and I collapse on the bed, pulling him down with me.

"Jesus, Ian," I finally manage with a laugh. "I should talk to other handsome men more often." My giggle stops suddenly when he pinches my nipple.

"You did it on purpose?" He asks incredulously.

I turn in his arms so we're chest to chest. "No, but I may from now on if that's how you react."

He's slipping from the frame of mind I need him in for the conversation we need to have. I position my chest over him and kiss his lips. "I only have eyes for you, Ian." I kiss him again but settle once more against his chest, exhausted from the two very incredible orgasms he just blessed me with.

I close my eyes and smile against his chest as his fingers trace up and down my back with a whisper like calmness, the gentle touch welcome after such an aggressive session.

I open my eyes slowly so I can watch my finger trace around the magnificent tattoo on his left pectoral muscle.

"I wanted to talk to you about something," I begin and wait for him to respond. A low murmur is all I get so I continue. "When I was out with the girls last weekend, Alexa brought something up."

"Well this sounds like trouble," he responds playfully.

I swat at his chest softly. "She," I pause, mild trepidation running over my body. "She asked me if you had given me a prenup to sign."

"We don't need one," he says softly, his demeanor unchanging.

"I think we do," I whisper. He doesn't respond and that combined with the lackadaisical way he continues to lightly stroke my back is becoming maddening. I expected a fight from him. I geared myself up for one and instead he is just throwing the idea out of the window and seems like he won't even consider it.

I pull my head back from his chest so I can look into his eyes. His hand calms on my back but his eyes are closed.

"Ian?" I ask softly in an attempt to get him to look at me.

"Hmm?" He offers without opening his eyes.

"Can we talk about this?" I pull further away from him and sit up by his side, forcing his hand to settle on my thigh.

I watch as he slowly opens his eyes and realizes how serious I am.

His hand gently begins to caress up and down my leg. "What's there to talk about?" He grins salaciously at me; his eyes pinned to my breasts.

"We need a prenup, Ian," I repeat myself, growing more annoyed. This garners his attention and he brings his line of vision to my face.

He pushes himself into a sitting position so we are both sitting on the bed facing each other.

"Why?" He asks simply.

"I don't want people to think I'm after your money," I answer and drop my eyes to my hands that are now clasped together in my lap. "I don't want *you* to think I'm after your money."

He laughs deeply and the sound makes me snap my eyes back to him; the look on my face stopping it immediately.

He clears his throat, apparently still entertained by this conversation. "Baby," he says and lifts my chin up with a finger when I begin to lower my eyes again. "I know you're not after my money." His smile takes over his entire face, his incredible hazel eyes sparkle at me. "You complain anytime I spend money frivolously."

I frown at him. "Other people," I begin.

"I don't give a fuck about what other people think, Lorali," he interrupts me. "And," he says before I can respond. "Even if we do have a prenup, how would they even know?"

I shrug my shoulders noncommittally.

"Are you afraid I'll cheat on you?" He questions softly.

"What? No!" I shake my head. "Why would you even ask that?"

"Most prenups are for the protection of assets and the protected party loses more if they have cheated on the unprotected spouse."

"I don't think that way at all, Ian." I tell him and hope he can see the level of trust I have for him in my eyes and my expression. I've never had trust issues, aside from the asshole boyfriend from high school. Alexa is the one who struggles with trust since she's been betrayed so horribly.

"Then why do you insist on one?" He reaches out and clasps my hands in his; both of his thumbs stroking the delicate skin of my wrist as he speaks.

I shrug because I've already told him, but he does not want to listen. "I have no other way to prove that I'm with you for you, and not your money."

"Will you quit your job?" He asks softly.

"Seriously?" My face and the tone of my voice changing slightly to include the irritation he's just caused me. Where is this coming from?

"Yes. Will you quit your job and stay at home?" He repeats.

"No of course not." I shake my head so he sees my response twice.

"You don't make very much money working there." His thumbs continue their stroke of the inside of my wrist.

"That's not the point, Ian!" I huff and want to do nothing more than jump off the bed and take a shower, alone. "I have that job because working for the paper is what I've always wanted. The money was never a consideration so long as it was enough to support me."

I watch as he raises his eyebrows at me. "Exactly," he says.

I tilt my head at him slightly in confusion.

"If you wanted me for my money, you wouldn't work. You would quit your job, take my black AmEx, and spend your days shopping." He explains.

I glare at him. He is so nonchalant with this whole conversation. He has an incredible point, but still.

I gently tug my hands away from him and stand. "I guess I'll call everyone tomorrow then."

"Everyone? Why would you call anyone?" He asks as he stands from the bed and reaches out for me.

"To let them know the wedding is canceled." I turn my back to him and walk toward the bathroom. With my hand on the door, I turn back to look at him, registering the pure shock that is on his face. "I won't marry you without one." I close the door gently and lock it.

Chapter 10
Garrett

The phone call I got from my accountant has put me in the foulest mood. In my absence over the past couple of months, things are not lining up the way they should. He hasn't figured out exactly what is going on, but something in the books isn't right.

He began by wanting to question me as to whether or not I'm extorting money from my own damn bar and I shut that shit down real quick. No fucking way I'm stealing from myself. *To what end? Pay fewer taxes? Give me a fucking break.*

There has to be a simple explanation for it, but even knowing that irks the shit out of me. I blaze through *Ampere* without even talking to anyone as I head back to my office. The only interaction anyone gets is the slight head nod to Johnny, who is, as diligently as ever, checking to make sure the bar is fully stocked and ready for tonight. Saturdays are always incredibly busy and Johnny has handled practically every one on his own the last two months. I have full faith in him.

Closing the door behind me, I settle in at my desk and turn my computer on. I have absolutely no chance of finding whatever mistake is being red-flagged at my CPA's office. I'm not an accountant, that's why I hired one, so I don't have the ability to determine what's wrong.

I lean back in my chair and roughly run my hands over my face. I love this club, but this is the very last place I want to be today. It's begun to get harder and harder to leave Alexa in the bed on the weekends. My peak work hours are when she's off. The peak times at her spa are the hours before mine, the men and women getting their treatments and pampering before they head over to places like *Ampere*. We're like two ships passing in the night, with her having to stay up late until I get home or being late in the morning since she has to be to work so much earlier. It's wearing us down.

A knock at the door brings me out of my self-imposed pity party.

"Come in," I grunt at the noise.

Johnny sticks his head in. I can tell he's apprehensive and that's my doing. I'm sure he felt the difference in my attitude when I came through the front door. Normally I would stop by and say hi, or in the least verbally acknowledge the people as I pass by.

"Got a minute?" he asks, still in the doorway.

"Sure, man. Have a seat." I hold my hand out and point to one of the chairs in front of my desk.

The sound of the knock on the door and the interruption almost pissed me off, but Johnny is the least annoying person that could have been on the other side.

"Bar ready to go?" I ask so we can move this impromptu meeting along. I was in the middle of feeling sorry for myself and I'd like to get back to it so I can get over it and never have to be bothered with it again.

"Of course," he answers with a smirk. "You alright?"

"Yeah, you know? Same 'ol, same 'ol." I begin shuffling papers on my desk to avoid eye contact. The last thing I need is a heart to heart this afternoon.

"You seem," he says cautiously, "distracted."

I sit back in my chair and sigh. Johnny is practically my manager; this is something I should be able to speak with him about.

"There are some discrepancies that my accountant found in the paperwork."

He tilts his head in contemplation. "Like someone mistyped some numbers? Or left a zero off or something."

"Fuck. I hope that's the case." *Is it too early for scotch?*

"That was an issue I had at my bar. The accountant figured it out. I'm shit at math." I watch as he crosses his left leg over his other knee at the ankle.

"Hold up. You had a bar? I thought you'd just worked at another bar." I lean up further in my chair, waiting for him to respond.

If he had his own bar, that's why he has been so efficient here. But why would he no longer have one? Poor management? Overspending?

"Yeah," he says as he drops his head, his gaze focusing on his clasped hands in his lap.

"You just decided you didn't want to fuck with owning a bar anymore?" I push. "I think I pay you pretty well, but it's nothing like owning your own bar."

He chuckles and the sound is empty and painful rather than light and carefree, the way a laugh is supposed to sound.

"You hear about the bar a few years ago where a pissed off guy came back after being booted and killed a patron outside?" He raises his eyes and I can see the pain in them.

I sigh loudly. "Yeah, I heard about it."

"My bar," he says and points his thumb at his chest.

"Shit," I mutter. I couldn't even imagine the fallout from something like that. The decrease in patronage if people were too afraid to go because of fear of harm. Nothing like a death on the concrete in front of your establishment that screams 'it's not safe here.' It would be detrimental to a business.

He clears his throat, in an attempt to block the anguish that has just taken charge of his entire face. "My girl," he whispers and I'm not sure I heard him right. It isn't until I watch him wipe a lone tear from his cheek that I understand.

Not only had he possibly lost his business due to a violent act in front of his bar, but he lost his girl.

"Fuck." I say and lean back in my chair again. That one word. That's all I have. No idea what else I can say.

I give him a minute because it's apparent he's struggling with his composure. I don't know exactly how he feels and what he's been through but it takes me back to the minute I heard Ian over the phone tell me that Alexa had been shot and they didn't know if she was going to make it.

It's my turn to clear my throat as the memories of first seeing her in the hospital bed, covered in wires and tubes flash before my eyes.

"I'm so fucking sorry, man." I finally manage to say to him. The words sound empty even though they are anything but.

He straightens in his chair and slaps his legs with his large hands, effectively shutting down the emotions.

"Hard thing to get over," I tell him.

"Damn near impossible, actually." He swallows roughly.

"Your girlfriend?" I ask softly.

He shakes his head slightly. "Wife," he says softly. "My pregnant wife."

I'm speechless. This man has suffered the most horrific pain imaginable. I wouldn't step foot back in this club if it was linked to something as tragic as losing my Alexa and our child. *She'd have to be willing to marry you and have a baby for that to even be a problem.* I think almost bitterly.

"Impossible," I say, confirming his earlier statement.

"Deep shit, right?" He says, attempting to shake off the darkness that is now sitting heavy in the air.

"Deepest," I answer him. "Definitely explains why you never go after the hundreds of girls I've seen try to get you to go home with them."

He chuckles again, sounding bitter. "Last thing I need is a bar whore."

I nod my head in understanding. Most of the girls who come to the club and just throw it at a guy are not the type you want tainting the memory of your deceased wife. I don't know if I'd ever be able to move on if I were in his situation. I'd probably just curl up and die.

"I have just started to see someone, though." I watch as his top lip curls into a small smile. "Her name is Jessica. We met at the coffee shop. Sweet girl. We'll see where it goes."

I grin back at him, encouraged at his change in mood. I feel like a total dick in here throwing a pity party for myself over some accounting issues and this guy is dealing with losing his wife and child; makes me a douche and an unappreciative bastard.

"Well let me know if you need a Saturday off to take her out. I know you're here during 'dating hours.'" I tell him with air quotes.

"Will do, man." I watch as he stands and shake his hand when he offers it. "Back to the grindstone," he says just before walking out and closing the door behind him.

I should take Ian's direction and hire more people. I'd wanted to be completely hands on with this club, but my situation isn't the same as it was months ago when we opened. Now all I can think about is going home to my girl who told me she had no plans today.

I push myself away from my desk and stand. Shutting down my computer that I never even used today, I glance at my watch. It's still early afternoon and that leaves me with hours and hours to ravage my girl and even take her out this evening if that's what she'd like to do.

***

Without fail the ever present shudder is there when I drive past the former liquor store that Alexa was at when she got shot. The feeling of unease seems more pronounced today after hearing Johnny's story.

The building is unrecognizable now. Ian bought the place after he realized it was going into foreclosure and gifted it to Ben Williams' wife. He paid for remodeling and she has turned it into a very lucrative Denver gift shop. I wonder if she has a sinking feeling in her gut every time she crosses the threshold into the building. I know I'll never be able to step in there.

I shake my head clear of those thoughts as I pull into and park in the subterranean garage. I all but jump out of the SUV and sprint to the elevator bank, in a mad rush to get to my penthouse. I'm chastising myself for not grabbing a bottle of wine or a late lunch for us as I unlock the door to the large apartment.

I empty my pockets into the basket on the front entry table. I smile to myself because I know Alexa hates the damn thing. I may actually move it this weekend. Anything to make her happy. I frown as I step further into the apartment and see that the living room and kitchen are empty. I should've called her first before just assuming she wouldn't find something to do, knowing I'd be at work again until late.

I kick off my shoes and scoop them up as I make my way to the bedroom. The door is shut which is odd, but I don't falter in my steps until I hear a man's voice, "Fuck, just like that! Suck it deep."

My hand hesitates on the doorknob because I know when I swing it open my life is going to change. I teeter on the edge of indecision; my broken heart throbbing painfully in my chest. "I'm close, bitch." I hear the masculine voice say.

Two things happen at the moment. I'm suddenly angry that Alexa is doing this to me when she thinks I'm at work, but alternately I'm pissed at this man for talking to my woman like that.

Hatred over the cheating wins out and I swing the door wide. My shoes tumble from my hands just as "What the fuck, Alexa," boils out of my mouth.

She squeaks loudly and tries to pull the sheets over her, but it's too late. She's already been caught.

Chapter 11
Alexa

There are a million things going on at once. I'm shrieking like a crazy woman and trying to pull the damn covers over myself all the while Garrett is yelling at me. My cheeks, I'm certain are a hundred shades of red and the incessant moaning and rough commands from the TV aren't helping my situation one bit.

Busted.

Garrett Hale just caught me flicking my bean. Most embarrassing moment of my life, ever.

I finally manage to get the covers pulled over me and look at him. I see a wash of relief come over his face before his mouth turns up with a salacious grin. *Relief?* What the hell is that about?

"Angel?" He says mockingly as he saunters towards the side of the bed. I watch, wordless, as he picks up the remote and powers off the TV just as the first squirt of the money shot flashes. I'm grateful the grunts and groans have been silenced. I was just as close to release as the guy on the screen, but now my body is flushed with embarrassment and shame.

I hang my head as he sits beside my overheated body on the bed. He tilts my head up and forces me to look him in the eye. He's told me more than once in the months that we've been together every one of my orgasms are his, so there is no telling how this is going to play out.

"I loved the sight of you when I opened the door and found you with your fingers deep in your pussy," he whispers as an unnamed emotion sweeps over his face.

"Y…you're not mad at me?" I stammer. I can't tell if we are about to play or if this is a real conversation we are going to have. He likes keeping me on edge and if I'm being honest, I love it too.

"Am I mad that I found you in here, *alone*, playing with yourself?" I flinch at the emphasis he places on the word alone but let it go when I see the smile in his eyes. "No, Angel. I'm not mad." He sweeps a loose tendril of hair out of my face and moves it over my shoulder. "I'm more concerned."

"Concerned?"

"Yes, Alexa. Seeing you in here pleasuring yourself makes me wonder if I've neglected you." He pulls the sheets down from where I have them clutched at my breasts, exposing them. "Are you feeling deprived?"

I whimper when he gently tugs one of my nipples between his thumb and forefinger. "Bored," I manage to pant out. "I was bored."

He hums in understanding. "I thought you were going to try out one of the books Lorali recommended."

I close my eyes, enjoying the feel of his large rough hands on my delicate flesh. "That's the problem. I was reading *Owned* and it got me all hot and bothered. M. Never really knows how to write a sex scene!"

"Is that so?" He asks as he licks inside of my mouth with that wicked tongue of his.

I'm unable to answer with words seeing as how only moans and whimpers are coming from my mouth. He pulls away and watches my face with half-mast eyes.

"I didn't come." I feel the need to tell him that like it will make a difference. He's very gentle. The second he threw open the door I was sure I'd be tied up and spanked within minutes; punished for not listening to his orders about not masturbating. This is not what I was expecting.

"You didn't?" he asks gruffly as he tugs the sheets completely free of my body.

I'm sitting Indian style so my sex is exposed to him and I grin as I notice the hungry look in his eyes.

"We need to remedy that. Don't you think?"

I moan as he lowers his head; my eager body already anticipating the hot touch of his mouth. The amazing swipe of his tongue on my already puckered nipple is overwhelming and just that fast he has reignited my need to come and brought me to the edge I was about to teeter over when he caught me.

"I figured you'd punish me," I say on a gasping breath as he nibbles my hardened bud.

He pulls his head away with a pop. "Believe me. I was going to do way more than punish you when I heard what was going on in this room before I opened the door." That's the look I was expecting. Anger. Just as fast as it makes itself known it is gone, replaced with a wicked grin. *Oh boy.*

I'm entirely vulnerable to him. I'm sort of a free spirit so I'd rather be wearing as little clothing as possible when it is allowed. So he has found me in our bed stark naked, wearing only finger and toenail polish. I have nothing to protect me against him. I have nothing slowing him down. No clothes to remove to give me more time to think of something. And honestly? I couldn't be happier.

I don't want to have to wait for him to undress me although he would either do it tantalizingly slow or he would rip the fabric from my skin. Now that I think about it, I don't know if he's ever let me undress for him unless he is controlling my movements with his commands.

My eyes flutter uncontrollably as he trails his fingers along the groove near the apex of my thighs, touching me everywhere but the exact dime-sized spot that I need him the most. This is his game. This is what he does to torture me further; his way of keeping all the power and controlling the situation. *Garrett Hale, always in control.*

"Please, Garrett," I beg as he sweeps past my clit, purposefully avoiding it.

"Please?" He taunts seductively. "Angel, you are in no place to beg."

He kisses my stomach, right at the exit wound from my shooting, his lips pausing longer than usual. His actions are in contradiction to his voice. He seems off somehow like something isn't quite right with him. Surely he's not still concerned with the issues at the club. When he left earlier, he was frustrated because there was a problem, but he seems different now that he's here.

"Haven't I told you not to touch yourself when I'm gone?" He asks bringing me out of my thoughts of concern.

My body is thrumming and he's toying with me. I love and despise him for it at the same time. I nod acknowledging that I'm well aware I've been told not to come unless he tells me I can. His thick thumb applies pressure an inch above my clit and he moves his hand higher on my stomach when I tilt my pelvis up, hoping to get contact. I groan my displeasure.

"How should I punish you?" He's twisting both of my nipples with his hands and I can't even think straight much less form sentences.

I feel him step away from me and I snap my eyes open. He's two feet away from the bed, his arms are crossed at his chest, and he's gazing down at me waiting for an answer. This is another one of his games. He knows how much I want his touch; need his touch. So periodically he denies it.

"Huh...what?" I have no idea what's going on at this point. My body is screaming for release and my brain has focused its attention there rather than my mouth where I need it to be.

"How should I punish you for touching yourself?" He repeats each word slowly. He does it sarcastically but I'm actually grateful he slowed it down enough for my brain to grab hold of it.

"Make me come until I can't walk?" I say with a sly smirk on my face.

"Or...not let you come at all," he counters.

I gasp; one of my least favorite games of all. Surely he wouldn't.

"You don't like the sound of that it seems." I'd like nothing more than wipe the smirk off of his face. I love being dominated by him but there are some days when I'd love nothing more than to control him, if only for an evening. It will never happen. He'd never give up his control in our bedroom.

I do the only thing I can think. I slide seductively off the bed and walk towards him with a deep swish to my hips. He notices and I grin internally. *Not completely immune I see.* I cut my eyes to the front of his slacks and see the beginning of the bulge straining there.

I stop just as I reach him. I can feel the whisper of his clothing against my bare skin. Seems I like torturing myself as well. I place my hands on his hard chest, loving the heat that is coming off of his body.

Suddenly he reaches behind me and grabs a handful of hair. I hiss not because of the small dart of pain but from the wetness that has suddenly slickened my thighs.

"What were you watching that was worth breaking my rules, Angel?" He demands in my ear.

"A blow job," I answer truthfully.

"Just a blowjob? I'd like to think I know you pretty well, Alexa and that doesn't seem like enough to cause you to have three fingers plunged inside of you." He's always right. "What about it had you so turned on? Had your cheeks and breasts flushed and pink?"

My eyes had been closed briefly as he spoke in my ear, but they open as I feel him pull his head away from me so he can see my face.

"He was fucking her face," I inform him breathily shifting my body closer to him so I can feel his now rigid erection against my stomach. "He was so rough. She was gagging on it." He closes his eyes on a long blink and I know he's picturing me doing that to him. I move my head so I'm speaking in his ear. "It made me so fucking wet." He groans. "I was almost ready for four fingers." My body tingles when he growls at me.

"Down," he hisses out as he uses his hand tangled in my hair to push me to my knees. "Show me." He bites out.

My pleasure.

I reach for the fly of his pants and waste no time unbuckling his belt, unzipping him, and pushing his slacks off his hips to pool at his feet. His thick, long cock nearly hits me in the face as it's set free of the offending fabric. I have my mouth wrapped around the head before I can take a breath.

He only allows me a minute of licking and teasing his length before he's stepping out of his slacks and spinning me around to the bed. *Yes! Finally, he's going to fuck me.*

The clink of the buckle of his belt causes more juices to appear. I moan and wait patiently for him to slide inside of me.

"Hands, Angel." It's not a question; it's a demand.

I pull my hands up and put them behind my back. In a flash my arms are restrained and I'm back on my knees with his cock in my mouth. I say in my mouth which really means he's halfway down my throat and I love it. I'm gagging and there is enough slobber dripping from my chin to lube an orgy. He grunts every time he slides in and hits the back of my throat. I give in to him one hundred percent because I trust him emphatically and I know he won't give me more than I can handle.

"Perfect," he praises without slowing his deep thrusts. "I'm close, Angel."

I choke even more when I try to grin at his words. They mimic the porn star from the video I was streaming only nurturing in a way and not derogatory like his use of *bitch*.

He thickens in my throat and just when I think he's about to blow he pulls out, his harsh breaths coming in gusts as he tries to calm himself enough to keep the orgasm at bay. Just when I think he's going to let me suck him off.

I'm gasping for air myself. My nerves are on end and my clit is throbbing. This is when he would normally pick me up, throw me on the bed, and slam into me. That's not how it goes today. He doesn't seem to have the patience. Instead, he stalks behind me, pushes my face into the carpet, and slams into me.

"Ah!" I scream at his glorious intrusion. My internal muscles are quivering and gripping him, begging for more.

One more thrust and I'm thrown over the edge.

"Goddamn it!" He yells and slaps my ass harder than I think he ever has. I feel the immediate throb of his cock, telling me he just exploded inside of me. He, apparently, didn't calm enough from the blowjob. We sure do make a pair; him pulsing and me clenching him in bursts.

"Perfect," I mutter as I slide from my bent position and stretch out on the floor. I watch with my head turned as he falls without an ounce of grace beside me on the rug.

"I have no control with you," he says absently.

I huff. That's all he has is control around me. I have no clue what situation he's talking about. It's moments like this that I love so much; when his domination over me slips just a bit and he allows himself to let go.

I wiggle myself closer to him so I can rest my head on his chest. He only has to see my struggle for a few seconds before he sits up and releases my hands from their bindings, allowing me to shift my weight more comfortably.

I nuzzle into his chest and tickle his happy trail as he slides his arm around my back, cradling me against his chest.

"I love you, Garrett," I say sleepily.

I feel him squeeze me closer. "I love *you*, Angel," he says and kisses the top of my head. His voice is husky and filled with emotion.

"Care to tell me what's going on?" I prompt him.

"What do you mean," he asks absently.

I steady my hand on his stomach. "You seem off today."

I wait long minutes before he responds. "I thought…" He clears his throat. "I thought you were cheating on me."

I pull my head back from his chest and glare at him. Of all the things he could have said at this moment, this was one that never would have come to mind.

"What?" *the fuck.*

He cups my cheek and I don't miss the look of gratefulness on his face.

"I came home unannounced and I get to the closed bedroom door and all I hear is moaning and some motherfucker telling you to suck his cock." He closes his eyes and I feel his entire body shudder. "I was prepared to walk in here and kill someone."

He seems almost broken at the idea of me being with another man. I should feel elated knowing he cares enough that he would be shattered and borderline homicidal at the idea but I'm not. I don't like having that much power over him. It doesn't feel right.

I turn his head so I can stare into his amber colored eyes. "You're everything I need, Garrett. I don't need anyone else."

He gently kisses my lips.

"Do I…" I begin. "Do I give you everything you need?"

He grins at me. "For now," he says with a smirk.

"For now?" I smack his chest playfully at his choice of words, but it hurts my feelings that he's being so nonchalant about our relationship. I look down expecting to see the same playfulness on his face; instead I'm met with a determined stare.

"Promise me," he begs.

"Promise what?" Surely he knows I'd never cheat on him.

"Promise me you won't have any type of procedure done to prevent you from having babies."

What the fuck! Where is this coming from? Way out in left field as far as I can tell.

Noticing my confusion he responds. "You are everything I need, for now, Angel but in a few years we may want kids. I don't want you to do something permanent now because you're afraid you'll get pregnant on accident."

"I don't think I want kids, Garrett." I'm shaking my head like even allowing the idea in there will cause problems.

"*Think* is the operative word you used, Alexa. You may not want them now, but that may change." He sighs and it's clear that I'm frustrating him. "We don't have to discuss children now, but you're it for me. If I do ever have kids, it will be with you."

I give him a soft smile more for him admitting I'm it for him and less about the children. "I promise I won't do anything drastic for the time being," I say placating him, but he knows if I promise him something I won't go back on it.

"Thank you," he whispers softly against the top of my head as I settle my head back on his chest.

I grin against him. "You know how you can say thank you? By making me come again." I rotate my hips, grinding against his hip.

Before I know it, I'm on my back and he's settling between my hips. "For the rest of your life, Angel," he promises and he gently glides inside of me.

Chapter 12

Ian

The rest of my weekend was miserable after Lorali locked me out of the bathroom Saturday night. The only way she'd agree to let me touch her in any fashion was after I agreed to talk to my attorney about drawing up a damn prenup. And by touch I mean hold her hand on the couch and spoon her in our bed at night.

She thwarted every attempt I made to get inside of her so it seems that won't be happening anytime soon. I asked her how long I had to wait and she said she be more willing after she had one in her hand. I hope my attorney doesn't mind working overtime because I need it before I leave for the day.

"Can you get Anthony Jones on the phone for me?" I ask my office manager as I walk past.

I settle in at my desk and wait for the beep that tells me my call is waiting. I busy myself with logging into my email and working on that. I'm unable to give it my full attention and I'm certain it has everything to with my situation at home with Lorali, more so her being upset with me than the lack of ejaculating in the last thirty-six hours and that says something!

I pick up the phone the second I hear the chime.

"Anthony," I wait for his acknowledgment. "I need you draw up a prenup."

I hear him sigh. "Thank God. I was wondering if you would ever come to your senses."

If I could strangle someone through a phone, I'd do it.

"I need it done fairly quickly," I tell him.

"How quickly?" I can hear the trepidation in his voice.

"I need a rough copy in my hand before I leave the office at five," I inform him.

"Today!?" He says with a loud squeak at the end.

"Think you can handle that?" I know Lorali feels like I waste my money, but I make sure to pay top dollar for top performers. My personal attorney is no different. I'm his only client and my expectations are set very high for him. He's well aware of this.

"Do I have a choice," he feigns inconvenience.

"Not this time I'm afraid," I tell him.

"Standard stuff?" He asks and I can hear paper shuffling like he's getting ready to take notes.

"Not exactly," I say.

"Of course not," he replies and I can't help but smile because he knows me so well.

***

My conversation with Anthony has left me in a perpetual state of ease. We've worked out a way where Lorali gets her prenup, which means my sudden dry spell will be over soon.

"Mr. Hale?" The small speaker on my phone interrupts my reverie. "Your ten o'clock is here."

My mind is drawing a blank on what I have scheduled today, my focus clearly not where it should be while I'm at the office.

"Remind me again please, Susan." I prompt her.

"Mallory King. Interview for the Director of Non-Profit." I grin. Hopefully, this one interview will clear my plate even further.

"Ah, yes. Please send her in." I stand behind my desk just as the office door opens and Susan escorts Ms. King in.

Her stride is confident and she's dressed impeccably. She has an air of sophistication around her as well as assuredness, all things required to demand respect from the people she will be practically hounding for donations.

She reaches her hand out to me as she approaches. "Mr. Hale." We shake hands. I notice her grip is firm, not dainty like I was expecting.

"Ian, please," I tell her as I sweep my hand toward the chair in front of my desk, indicating for her to take a seat.

"Ian," she says as she begins to lower herself in the chair. As she sits, she brings a small briefcase to her lap and snaps it open.

She pulls free a few crisp pages and hands them to me. "I know my assistant has already emailed my resume," she begins.

I tilt my head. "Assistant?"

Her smile grows. "Yes. Assistant."

I glance down at the resume in my hand and try to recall her name. I've seen her with the girls several times, but I'm unable to focus on anyone else when Lorali is around so I haven't paid her much notice.

"King," I say reaching as far into my memory as I can. "You're the daughter of Raymond King?"

She smiles and nods. "In the flesh."

"He's quite wealthy. Surely you have a trust fund." Why in the world is she seeking a job with my organization?

Her spine straightens and I can tell she's mildly annoyed. "I also have an MBA from Stanford that I didn't earn to just sit at home and live off of Daddy's money."

Fiery, I like that.

She clears her throat when she notices my raised eyebrow. "I spend my time already with various volunteer and non-profit pursuits. I've researched your company and we seem to be champions of many of the same organizations. By working for your company, I'll be able to reach and aid many more people than I could ever endeavor to reach on my own."

She shrugs her shoulders like it just makes perfect sense to use my money and name to help those she's already been trying to help on her own.

"Of course," I say in agreement. I steeple my fingers at my chin and just watch her. Even under my scrutiny, she doesn't falter, proof she's very comfortable in her skin and more than capable of handling the tasks required for this job.

"It's a full-time position," I remind her in case she'd only planned on dedicating a few hours a week to it.

"As it should be," she confirms.

"When can you start?" I ask my mind already made up.

"My schedule opens up the beginning of next week." She beams at me and her enthusiasm thrills me almost as much as the knowledge that the part of my organization I care the most about is going to be well taken care of.

I stand behind my desk and reach out my hand to her as she mimics my actions. "Welcome to the team." We shake hands. "Please stop by Susan's desk and she can give you the intro packet."

I watch her as she walks to the door. "Ms. King," she stops and turns towards me. "Make sure you leave Susan a list of the organizations you champion that Hale Inc. doesn't so we can promptly get them added to our list."

I watch as her eyes glisten at the generosity. She's perfect for the organization if the idea that a few more people will be helped elicits that strong of an emotion from her.

***

The rough draft of the prenup is waiting for me at Susan's desk when I leave the office for the day. Lorali is off on Mondays and I'm usually welcomed home to the sight of her in the kitchen preparing dinner. We don't usually have much time for meals at home, but Monday evenings and a home cooked meal have sort of become our thing.

I frown at the idea that today may be different since our weekend wasn't filled with the normal events, mainly her not being filled with me.

I quietly make my way to the kitchen where the sounds of pop music and the tantalizing smell of Italian food are coming from. I lean against the door frame and watch as Lorali, dressed only in one of my oversized t-shirts, sways her hips in front of the stove as she stirs something in a saucepan. My cock throbs at the sight.

I gently place the legal papers on the counter, step in behind her, and place my hand on her stomach. Pressing gently I persuade her to take a step back against me, my now bulging cock resting against her lower back. She hums at the contact and leans her head back so I can kiss the delicate column of her neck.

"I've missed you so much, baby," I say against her skin and I hope she knows I mean more than just today. We rarely ever fight and even when we do it has never stopped us from joining together in the bedroom. This time has been different. I'm nervous about the way I've arranged the prenup, even slightly scared that it will not be received the way I've intended.

"Turn the stove off," I tell her, but keep my hands on her hips as she leans forward, clicks off the stove, and removes the bubbling sauce from the burner.

She backs into me again, only this time, she raises her arm and places it behind my head; my favorite position to have her in. My hand instinctively reaches up and sweeps a thumb over the hardened bud of her nipple that's jutting out.

She moans and swivels her hips fractionally. I use my free hand to reach blindly behind me until it reaches the documents I placed on the counter. I lower the hand caressing her breast back to her waist and she whimpers. I know she's just as frustrated as I am.

I hold the paperwork in front of our clasped bodies until she opens her eyes and notices them.

"What's this?" She asks reaching for it.

"Your prenuptial agreement, baby." She gasps and turns in my arms, her eyes darting back and forth from mine to the legal sized documents in my hand.

"That was quick," she says as she reaches for it.

I huff. "I had some incentive to get it done quickly," I smirk at her.

I follow her to the dining room and sit beside her as she turns back the cover page and begins to read.

She doesn't say a word as she reads the agreement line by line, but I do watch as her smile fades and her eyes begin to narrow. She's not happy, but she has to understand this is what she gets. Once she has finished, she straightens the papers, closes her eyes, and takes what I presume is a calming breath.

Placing a hand flat over the prenup, she says, "All this paperwork says it that all of your money is my money."

I nod my head yes because basically that's right.

She bites her lip in frustration. "It doesn't protect your assets."

"You Lorali are the only asset I care about," I tell her honestly.

She swallows roughly and just stares at me. I give her my most winning smile, hoping the dimples she loves so much are on full display.

"This isn't what I meant when I said you needed a prenup."

"I know," I say. "But this is what you'll get." I'm not giving into this. I'm not having a document drawn up that limits what she'll get if we split. If she leaves, she might as well have it all because I'll be just as useless as the money if I don't have her.

"And if I refuse to marry you without one?" She says and the blank look on her face makes my smile falter marginally.

"Well," I say pulling her from her chair and onto my lap. "Then we'll just live in sin for the rest of our lives and I'll make you the beneficiary to all my money anyways."

She grumbles into my neck.

She pulls her head back and looks into my eyes. The love I see in hers is all but tangible. "You missed something in it," she says referencing the documents I'd all but forgotten on the table. I incline my eyebrow. "It doesn't say anything about our children."

I smile. "You still want to have babies with me?" I ask playfully and stroke her bottom lip with my thumb, already imagining her mouth wrapped around me.

"Soon," she whispers, her focus on my mouth.

"How soon?" I ask my lips a fraction of an inch from hers.

"Immediately," she answers and I jerk my head back to look in her eyes thinking I heard her wrong.

She beams at me. "Really?" I ask softly afraid she'll change her answer.

She cups my face in both of her hands. "I thought I could skip next month's shot and the birth control should be completely out of my system in time for our honeymoon."

I grip her ass in my hands and stand up, heading toward the bedroom. "I know our children will be perfect, but we should practice a lot just in case," I say against her mouth as I walk down the hall.

"I was thinking the same thing," she murmurs against my lips.

Chapter 13
Kaleb

I can't turn my brain off as I make the drive to work. Josie has been home from the hospital for over a month now and she's just as timid about leaving the house alone as she was the first week I got her back. She has repeatedly assured me she's fine and she continues to see the same psychologist she was set up with in the hospital. The big picture is what has me worried. She will not leave the house by herself. Hell, she won't even sit on the back porch when she's alone.

I know she thinks she's hiding it from me and everyone else, but I notice the tremble in her hands and the quiver of her lips when I suggest she do something as simple as run to the store for something we need while I take a quick shower. She puts on a brave face and leaves the house with me and she's gone out a few times with the girls but only if Ramon's escorting them.

I'd hoped the trauma would begin to settle and she'd settle back into something that resembled her normal. I hate to even admit to myself now that I fed her fear in the beginning. I, too, had been terrified and didn't want her out of my sight. Now she's become dependent on everyone else, exactly the person she'd told me more than once that she didn't want to be. She emphatically repeated she wasn't weak and she hated when people saw her that way. Her captivity changed her, manipulated and mutilated her into the person she didn't want to be. The worst part? She doesn't even realize who she's become. This *is* her new normal.

Movement catches my eye as I exit my car in the parking lot of Precinct Four. Turning my head, I see Detective Jessica Riley standing very close to a man I recognize as Marco Hernandez, the sergeant from the county jail. He doesn't notice me as I grab my gear from the trunk of the car. He's watching her like the sun rises and falls on everything she's saying to him as if his sole happiness in life is dependent on her. I smile when I notice a look of contentment on her face as well.

She turns her head, finally noticing me as I close the trunk of the car and begin to make my way to the side entrance of the building. She startles at first when her eyes land on me but then I watch as a sly grin hits her face. She pulls Marco closer to her and kisses him almost violently. I can't help but chuckle. That's not exactly the Jessica I'd hooked up with a handful of times at the beginning of the year. But hey, who am I to judge?

My grin is from ear to ear as I punch in the code to gain access to the building and it doesn't drop a hair as I settle in at my desk. Josie and I will be saying our vows in five days, and then we will be heading to a quiet, peaceful resort in Montana for our honeymoon. I'd wanted to do something a little more extravagant, but Josie said she felt more comfortable not wasting a bunch of money since we have the baby to worry about now. She'd said it would be irresponsible. I want her happy so I didn't argue; as long as we're together the location doesn't concern me all that much.

And the baby? My face should hurt from all the smiling I've been doing. I stare at the computer screen full of emails as I remembered our trip to the doctor last week.

I hear Josie gasp and feel her hand grip mine tighter. I inwardly register that her strength is coming back.

"That's...?" Josie says affectionately.

"Yes. That's the heartbeat," the doctor says as he moves the jellied wand around Josie's lower stomach that is still as flat as the day I first laid her out and kissed her on my couch two months ago.

I hear her whimper and look down just in time to see a tear run down her cheek. I catch it on my fingertip and kiss her cheek. I close my eyes and let the sound of my child's heart fill my soul.

"Everything looks great," the doctor says as he points and clicks the mouse on the screen, periodically stopping to type information. My fears about the possible consequences from her abduction will never leave me until I'm holding my healthy baby in my arms but hearing the doctor's words help to abate some of my fears.

Josie assures me that her continued morning sickness, which actually tends to hit at any time, is a good sign.

I watch the doctor set aside the ultrasound wand and hands Josie a tissue to wipe the residual jelly off of her stomach. She cleans herself and straightens her clothes while the doctor presses a few more buttons on his computer.

"I think we can start seeing you every month now that we've heard a strong heartbeat." He turns from us and turns the lights back on.

"You sure?" I hear the waiver in her voice and the doctor must too.

He steps close to her and places a comforting hand on her shoulder. "We were only monitoring your HCG levels until we could get a good heartbeat. The baby looks great, Josie. I'll see you in a month." He nods at me as he hands Josie a strip of paper and then he exits the room.

I can feel her sobs from my hand on her back. Turning my attention back to her I see her holding a black and white copy of our baby's very first picture. I pull her into my chest and cough having to clear the lump that has just suddenly appeared in my throat, along

*with batting my eyelashes from the burn that is registering behind
my eyes.*

"He's beautiful," I tell her.

*She sniffles and lets out a small laugh. "He or she looks like
a gummy bear, Kaleb."*

*I tilt her chin up and grin. "Most beautiful gummy bear I've
ever seen."*

*"Me too," she whispers and turns her attention back to the
printout in her hands.*

The memory reminds me about the pictures in my wallet. We
were given several different ones and Josie allowed, and yes I mean
allowed, me to have two of them after I was able to convince her to
scan them into the computer so we would have other copies of each
one.

I tug my wallet free from my back pocket and open it. I plan
to keep one in there always, but I grabbed two so I could keep one
on my desk at work. I run my thumb over the tiny black and white
baby and prop it at the bottom of my computer screen so it is within
eyesight whenever I'm at my desk.

Sensing I'm no longer alone I look up and see Jessica Riley
standing at the edge of my desk. She has a grin on her face that
doesn't reach her eyes. We haven't said much to each other since I
told her Josie was moving in before it was even official, a
conversation we had the day before she was abducted from her
school. I shake my head, hoping the memories and the pain of that
day and the weeks following don't take hold.

I wouldn't say that Jessica and I were very close. I mean we
had sex a few times, with both of us understanding it went no further
than that. At the time, I had no desire or inclination at all to look for

something other than a friend-with-benefits type of arrangement. All it took was seeing Josie for the first time and I was a goner.

I smile at the thought of Josie and watch her eyes light up. *Oh shit*. She must think I'm smiling at her. I drop my smile to a more professional acknowledgment.

"So you and Hernandez, huh?" I say to remind her of her actions in the parking lot just a few minutes ago and I know it's the wrong thing to say when her smile gets even bigger. I can tell her elation is not because of the man she had her lips all over.

She winks at me, "jealous?"

I'm unable to stop the huff that escapes my lips. I'm not trying to be rude, but the idea that I'd be jealous of her and some other guy when I have Josie is ludicrous.

I notice her bristle immediately. She begins to narrow her eyes in anger but stops. "We're not serious," she says with a nonchalant shoulder shrug. I raise an eyebrow at her because I'm not sure Hernandez is aware of this revelation with the way he was looking at her outside.

She leans forward on my desk. If I had any doubt about my love for Josie, it is cemented the second I see the swell of her breasts in the open V of her shirt and it doesn't even register with my body. I'm certain she could be stark naked right now and it wouldn't even matter, and that's saying something because I've seen her naked and her body is what I'd considered at the time, perfect.

Instinctively I lean back in my chair, increasing the distance between us.

"I mean," she says licking her lips, which now seems rather disgusting. "I'd cancel any plans I have with him if you wanted to hang out."

The only thing I can do is shake my head at her audacity. I've not gone around and advertised mine and Josie's relationship, but everyone was well aware of how I felt about her the minute she was abducted. Hell, I was suspended for most of the time she was gone for punching out a few patrolmen who weren't spending their time as wisely as I thought they should during the initial investigation. With how in everyone's business she is in, there's no way she doesn't know we're still together.

"Apparently you and Joselyne Bennett are still together." The snide way she says Josie's name gets my hackles up and is verging on seriously pissing me off.

"Yes," I tell her and continue just to piss her off for the nerve she has to throw herself at me and saying Josie's name as if it's the nastiest thing she's had in her mouth. "And by Friday evening she will be Joselyne Perez." I can't help but smile at the sound of her soon to be name.

She gasps and straightens her back suddenly at the news. "You're marrying her?" She's completely shocked which surprises me; usually she's the first one with the news around the precinct. She sneers at me. "What did you do? Knock her up?"

I've never wanted to clock a woman more than I do right now and I know my dad would be turning over in his grave at the thoughts running through my head. The mention of the baby has me cutting my eyes over at the picture below my computer screen.

She follows my line of sight. I've always said she was an incredible detective.

"Fuck!" She screeches. "You did knock her up! You'll never be happy, marrying a woman just because she's pregnant. You'll be miserable even if it feels like it's the right thing to do. She could never take care of your needs like I do."

I lean forward in my chair and lower my voice, my control teetering on nonexistent at this point. "I'm marrying her because I love her. I'm marrying her because she's the only woman who has *ever* had a piece of my heart." I close my eyes on an extended blink trying to do my best to reign in the urge for violence. Even though I have no need to justify myself, I add, "I asked her to marry me before we even knew about the baby."

"The *only* woman?" Her voice is a low growl and if I had to bet I'd say she's just as pissed at my revelation as I am at the way she's speaking about Josie. "You needed me, Kaleb. I gave you what you needed and you're throwing that away over some timid ass school teacher that's probably too afraid to even suck your cock?"

My laugh is low and maniacal and I inwardly smile at the trepidation in her eyes when she realizes she's pushed me too far. "You, Jessica," I say as I stand to tower over her, knowing the desk between us is a blessing at this point, "were an easy fuck. Don't try to convince yourself it was anything but that."

She takes a step back and I realize then that I've leaned further into her to get my point across. "Fuck you, Kaleb. There are any number of guys who would love a shot at me." She turns away and disappears down the hall.

"I'm sure more than half of the precinct has already had you," I mutter under my breath as I settle back into my chair and scrub my face with my hands. This is not the way I had anticipated my morning beginning. I'm grateful I got here early and the office is all but empty. I turn my attention back to my emails and begin counting down the hours until I can take Josie back in my arms.

***

My day passes uneventfully after my run-in with Jessica this morning, which for the most part is a good thing considering my profession, but it does make for an incredibly long day. I leave the office and make a beeline for our house the minute it's considered an acceptable time to leave.

"Josie, I'm home," I say with as much Puerto Rican accent as I can manage, knowing I sound just like Ricky Ricardo from *I Love Lucy.*

I make my way through the kitchen and realize the house is much quieter than it usually is in the evenings. A wave of panic hits me in the gut and my body is immediately covered in a sheen of sweat when I make my way into the living room and see Josie sobbing uncontrollably on the floor.

"Josie!" I slide beside her and take her in my arms. *Please, not the baby. Please, not the baby.* "Mariposa, what's wrong?" I hope she can't hear the tremor in my voice which would be a miracle since I can hear it myself.

"I can't do it." She rests her head on my shoulder and continues to cry, my shirt quickly growing damp from her tears.

My heart shatters. She's had time to think about it and now she's changed her mind. She can't marry me.

"We don't have to. We can wait as long as you like," my voice is pleading. I pray she just wants to postpone and not leave me completely. This has to be karma for the way I spoke to Jessica today. No woman deserves to be treated like a piece of ass and my words have led to this. "Please don't leave me," I whisper against her head as her sobs begin to settle down.

She lifts her head from my chest and her tear streaked face and red, puffy eyes nearly gut. "Wh…what?"

I release her long enough to wipe the tears from her cheeks and I notice the tremble in my hands. I'm seconds away from losing my shit and begging and pleading for her to stay. I swallow and try to choke back the emotion. I never once considered that she'd leave me again once I had her back in my arms after her abduction after she said yes and more importantly after we found out about the baby.

"You may not want to marry me, but please don't leave," I manage to say.

"Baby?" She grabs my face with both hands. "What the fuck are you talking about?"

My eyes go wide because never once have I heard her speak this way. *That* word, as far as I know, has never crossed her lips before.

"Why wouldn't I marry you? Why would I leave you?" I can feel the resolve in her voice.

"You're upset," I place my hand on her belly. "When I came in and saw you crying the first thing I thought was we'd lost the baby. Is the baby okay?"

She nods and places her tiny hand over mine on her stomach. "The baby's fine, Kaleb."

"Then you said you can't do it. Are you telling me you can't marry me?" I close my eyes, preparing myself for the worst but praying for a different conclusion.

I hear her chuckle like it's the most absurd question in the world. I open my eyes to see her using the back of her hand to wipe tears from her eyes.

"Josie?" It doesn't go unnoticed that she still hasn't answered me.

She turns her eyes to mine and softly kisses my lips. "You're not getting rid of me that easy Detective Perez."

I pull her to my chest and just hold her there, unable to release her until my nerves calm. The baby is fine and we're still getting married. The entire Earth could implode and I would care less because everything is right in my world.

"What has you so upset then?" I'm able to ask after several long minutes of just embracing her.

She shifts her weight and as much as I hate it, I let her pull away from my arms.

"Well after that it seems silly now," she says with a shrug. "I may have overreacted."

"Don't do that. Don't try to pass this off as hormones. The way you were when I came in here was much more serious than when I found you crying at the table last week because there were no pickle slices for your sandwich."

She giggles and it's the most beautiful sound I've ever heard.

"Mariposa?" I prompt her again. We need to get to the bottom of this so I can get her in my bed; my need to be inside her proving she's still mine is becoming almost unbearable.

"My contract from the school was forwarded here today." She points toward a stack of white papers sitting on top of a manila envelope that I didn't even notice until she pointed it out. "I can't go back, Kaleb."

I watch her eyes begin to fill with tears again and the tiny quiver of her chin nearly guts me.

"You don't want to go back to work?" My voice is soft and comforting.

She shakes her head no. "Just the thought of stepping foot back on a school campus makes me sick to my stomach."

I smile at her. "Then don't go, Mariposa. It's that simple."

"It's not *that* simple, Kaleb. I have to work." She's adorable when she's indignant. I love watching her stand up for herself or something she believes in and it's a relief from her demeanor a few minutes ago.

"You don't *have* to work, Josie." I rub her belly. "Stay home and have my babies." I grin at her because, honestly, it's the best idea ever.

"I'm not going to sit around the house and live off of you. I need to contribute." She pulls my hand from her stomach and stands up. I can tell she's gearing herself up for a fight.

"You're going to be my wife in five days, Josie. You're the mother of my unborn child. You wouldn't be living off of me." I watch her as she paces back and forth gnawing on her thumbnail.

Why is she making a big deal about this? A thought slams in my gut. Lorali has Ian, who is loaded and Alexa has Garrett, who is doing very well for himself and I'm a cop working for the city. It angers me to think she doesn't have faith in me.

I stand as well, walk towards her and hold on to her forearms to stop her pacing. I stare into her eyes.

"I may not be rich like Ian and Garrett, but I can provide for my family."

She raises her eyes to mine and I wonder how she'll read my determination.

"Baby," she runs her fingers over my cheek. "I know you can provide for us. That has never been a doubt." She kisses my lips and pulls away too quickly. "I'm saying I need to have something to do. I want to feel productive."

I can't really fault her for that. I know she loves teaching and has pride in her profession. I place my hands on her hips and lift her up so she can wrap her legs around my waist.

"I'll take care of you, Mariposa," I say against her lips.

We're both breathless by the time we finally come up for air.

"Can you take care of me in our bed now?" She pants against my mouth.

My shit day just got a whole lot better.

Chapter 14
Alexa

This is the life. I know I should feel ashamed for sitting in this chair being pampered by the spa staff of the Ritz, but I don't even feel a twinge.

I grin over at Josie and Lorali as they, too, are having what I'm sure is the best pedicure they've ever had. I'm the top manager at *Elite Spa* so one would think I should use them, but this is a girl's day; a gift to Josie to help relax and prepare her for her wedding the day after tomorrow. This hotel also holds a certain sentiment for me as well. Not counting it's the same place the 'threesome that shall not be named' took place; it's the hotel where I realized I had more feelings for Garrett other than the fuck buddy agreement we had. The beginning of the beginning if you will.

I'm sure, as all other girls days have gone, there will be gossip and story sharing. The last thing I need is for my staff to run the knowledge that I like to be tied up and have my ass whipped with a riding crop, or cane depending on how frisky Garrett is feeling, around the rumor mill at work. I'm not ashamed of what I do in my bedroom, but some things should be kept separate from work.

"So," I begin. "Garrett caught me masturbating the other day." I watch for a response from the lady massaging my calves. She doesn't even register my words; utmost professional. I'm sure she hears it all.

I turn my eyes to the girls and see the pink blush that has come over Josie's cheeks. There's a story there; I just know it. Lorali just shakes her head, not surprised at all. Why should she be? She was the queen of bean flicking before she met Ian.

I focus my attention on Josie mainly because she's so easy to toy with but also because she's just now able to participate actively in our sex talks and I have a feeling she actually wants to talk about it.

"Why the blush, Josie?" I taunt her playfully.

Her cheeks go from a light pink to a deeper crimson, but the smile on her face says it all.

"Has Kaleb caught you in the act?" I smile big at her and wait for her to spill.

She clears her throat and laughs at the same time. "Not actually." She's being vague and I know it has more to do with her shyness about the subject than her trying to be evasive.

"Well," Lorali interrupts. "Spill it."

Even though she lowers her head to speak, she's still smiling. "I may have done that once to try to force Kaleb into action."

She bites her lip at her own admission.

"And?" Lorali pushes harder. "Did it work?"

"No," she answers.

"No?" Lorali and I say at the same time. "What did he do?" Lorali continues.

She raises her head and looks at her sister. "He stood there and watched as he stroked his…"

She just lets the statement trail off. "Cock?" I answer for her.

She blushes again. "Yes, that."

"Fuck. That's hot," I say honestly, because seriously? Just the idea of that makes me wet.

Josie turns her head to me. "Well? What did Garrett do?" She asks brazenly now that she's shared her tidbit.

I laugh and shake my head. Love this girl. "He didn't just stand there and watch that's for sure." I lean back in my seat remembering how wild he was that day.

"Well?" Josie prods like her sister did to her just moments before.

"Garrett tied my hands behind my back and fucked my face," I tell her while watching the lady at my feet. She smirks this time at my admission. A fellow dirty girl I see.

"Sounds about right," Lorali says.

Josie continues to blush, but there is a wicked gleam in her eyes that tell me if I look at her internet history later I'd find some 'face fucking' research. I bet Josie is dirtier in bed than I am. It's always the quiet ones!

"It was how he was after that bothers me, though." They both sober and grow serious knowing I don't usually let things bother me.

"I was streaming video on the TV for…inspiration." I shrug, because who doesn't watch porn? "He told me he heard the sounds of the video from in the hall and he thought I was cheating on him. His head automatically went to the worst about me, like he couldn't even consider other possible scenarios."

Lorali opens and closes her mouth several times before she's able to form words. I can't tell if she's speechless or trying to find words that won't piss me off.

"Maybe his life experiences before you made his mind think of that first," Josie quietly adds.

I know she remembers what I told them about him and his ex, Jamie. I shake my head, pissed at myself for thinking this was about his lack of trust in me. I never considered for a second his past in all of this.

"Shit," I say and close my eyes. "I never even thought of that," I whisper.

Of course being tricked into marrying his high school sweetheart because she was pregnant when in fact it wasn't even his kid would have lasting effects on him. Hell, she almost ruined him for everyone. He never had a relationship with anyone since her, until I came along. Realizing he loved me and being able to admit it was the biggest uphill battle he ever fought.

"He loves you, but that level of trust is hard for anyone who's been through what Jamie put him through," Lorali adds.

"I didn't break his trust," I huff. I despise her more every second that I think about it.

"We know that, Alexa. He knows that. He has no control of where his mind goes in a situation like that. I'm sure he felt guilty about it himself," Josie says.

"I don't know if he'll ever trust me completely," I say more to myself than anyone else.

"He will," Lorali assures me. "Just prove to him every day that you love him and would never hurt him. Make sure you're everything he needs."

"More importantly," Josie adds. "Make sure he knows that he is everything *you* need. Leave no room for doubt."

I grin at her. "When did you get so smart about men?"

She shrugs. "I'm no expert. I just know it's the most incredible feeling knowing that Kaleb doesn't need or want anyone but me." She frowns slightly. "You guys will get there. It's just going to take more time. Kaleb and Ian aren't carrying around the baggage that Garrett has been saddled with."

"Lucky me," I groan. I can make light of it, but I know that Garrett is the man and lover that he is today because of what Jamie did to him. His passion and adoration for me are evident every time he touches me.

I close my eyes and picture the pain on Garrett's face the other day when he begged me not to go through some type of permanent birth control. How can he even be thinking about kids when the marriage conversation has never crossed his lips? Jamie seriously fucked him and any woman in his future.

"So?" Lorali says to Josie, thankfully beginning to change the subject. "Have you given any thought to how you want the nursery?"

Josie beams and if anyone ever had a doubt about her happiness over her current situation all they would have to do would be to look at her face at this moment and know that she's perfectly happy with where her life is heading, planned or not.

"Well," Josie begins as she pulls her phone from her pocket. "I've made a secret board on Pinterest and I can add you guys so you can see what I'm thinking."

Lorali laughs at the look on my face. I have to tell myself that I can be happy for Josie and look at baby shit for a bit even though my life is never going in that direction. Hell, I don't even want a dog.

Don't get me wrong I will love any child Josie and Lorali have. I'll even babysit them periodically if they need me to. I'm not a monster that detests children; I just have no desire to have one of my own. I'd much rather send them home at the end of the day; get my ass spanked, come, and go to sleep wrapped around Garrett. Not everyone shares my dreams and that's okay.

Josie is between Lorali and me so we both watch over her shoulder as best we can in our pedicure massage chairs to see what she's pulling up on her phone. I have to admit I like her taste. The rooms she's showing us are all neutrally colored, probably since she doesn't know what she's having yet, and are very modern.

"These are great," Lorali says showing more enthusiasm than someone would who is just admiring another woman's situation.

I raise my eyes to her and I know she knows I'm glaring at her because I see her cut her eyes to me and then back to Josie's phone. Normally I would grill her and make her admit to what I'm sure is Ian has convinced her to have a baby sooner than she said she wanted one the last time we were all together. I focus back on Josie's phone and leave it be for now.

"The room for the nursery is gray and I plan to leave it like that. I'm thinking either gender would look great in grays, yellows, and white." Josie explains as she flicks through pictures. It is obvious she's already put a lot of time and thought into choosing what she wants for the baby.

"I'm so sorry," Josie says to the woman painting her toes. "I thought I could wait, but I really need to run to the restroom." The woman dries her feet and legs and slides thin foam flip flops on to her feet.

Lorali and I both watch as she makes her way down the narrow hall in the back to the restroom.

"I thought we could set up the nursery while they're on their honeymoon next week," Lorali whispers to me. "As a gift of sorts so she won't have to worry about it."

I nod because it's a great idea as well an incredibly thoughtful gift.

"Well, you have a Pinterest account so we can pull ideas from there." I agree. "I think we should maybe do the type of furniture she wants but leave the detail stuff for her. We can take her shopping later when she finds out what she's having to get the rest of the stuff."

"Perfect," she says. "Shhh." She smiles as Josie slides back into her seat.

"Where's the honeymoon going to be again?" I ask because last we had talked nothing had been decided yet.

Josie gives me a soft smile. "The cutest little resort in Montana."

"Oh good!" Lorali says enthusiastically. "I knew you'd said Kaleb mentioned Reno. So glad you guys decided on something a little more personal."

Josie laughs. "He told me he was joking about going to Reno and didn't know what to say after I'd agreed with him."

I laugh too because Josie is so adaptable with the world around her it doesn't surprise me that Kaleb was shocked at her agreeing to something as crazy as a honeymoon in Reno when everyone knows full well Josie is not the type of girl who'd pick Reno for herself.

"So he picked Montana instead?" I ask.

"Kaleb wanted to do a week long beach vacation," Josie explains. "I'd love nothing more. I mean who wouldn't want to spend a week on the beach with Kaleb? I just didn't think it was a very good idea to spend that much money with the baby coming."

I nod my head knowing that it makes perfect sense and Josie has always been frugal even when she doesn't need to pinch as many pennies as she does.

I look at Lorali, but all she does is wink at me and begins asking Josie about her plans while in Montana. Seems my best friend has more than one secret she's not planning on talking about today.

Two hours later we are all buffed, polished, and waxed and settling into the limo for the ride back to Lorali's house.

"Game plan," Lorali says getting mine and Josie's attention. "Tomorrow night you stay with me so you can get ready Friday for the wedding. I know I said I'd drive you to the airport for your honeymoon but since I'll still have a house full of people I've had a car arranged to pick you guys up Sunday morning to take you instead."

"Kaleb is not going to like that, Lorali," Josie says shaking her head back and forth slightly.

Lorali huffs. "It's just a car ride, Josie. He'll get over it."

"Not that," Josie says. "He's not going to be very happy about having to spend a night away from me."

I grin because I know the type. I just so happen to have one of those at home myself.

"Well," Lorali says with a sigh because she knows Ian would have the same reaction. "It's just one night so he'll just have to get over it."

Josie nods in agreement, but the look in her eye says she's not so convinced he will. I don't envy her. There's a good chance Kaleb will sleep outside of her room and wear a blindfold so he can be around her but still not see her.

Anybody on the outside looking in may consider that absolute craziness. Kaleb is overprotective to begin with, couple that with Josie's abduction two months ago and the entire situation becomes clandestine. Hopefully knowing she'll be at the house with Ian and Josie's father will help him keep the tradition going and he will keep his distance, at least until she walks down the aisle.

Chapter 15
Josie

Turns out I didn't have to worry about Kaleb being upset that I was spending the night before the wedding at Lorali's; he actually insisted on it. Seems Puerto Ricans are even more superstitious than Americans when it came to the issue. Don't get me wrong he doesn't *want* to spend the night away from me and he made up for the time we would lose by spending most of the night in me, but he was pretty calm when he dropped me off at Lorali's house just a little bit ago.

I should be sleeping right now considering he wouldn't relinquish me until a quarter to midnight, but I can't turn my head off. There is not one single drop of doubt in my mind that Kaleb Perez is the man I want to spend my life with. Not one shimmer of shame that I'm ten weeks pregnant and getting married.

The only thing that worries my mind is that everything seems perfect right now and I'm waiting for the other shoe to drop. Things seem like a fairy tale and the last time my life seemed perfect I was stolen from the parking lot of the elementary school I was a science teacher at and held, tied up in a closet, for nineteen days.

After a few motivational mantras are spoken in my head, my nerves have settled enough for me to fall asleep. I'm anxious to get this one night over with so I can meet up with the most gorgeous man who has ever crossed my path at the end of the little aisle that's been arranged at our home.

***

I have no idea how long my knee has been shaking causing my foot to tap repeatedly on the floor of the limousine. I don't even notice I'm doing it until Lorali places a calming hand on my knee.

I smile at her impishly. "Sorry," I whisper.

"Nervous?" she asks softly.

"Excited," I explain. "It's like waiting to go downstairs on Christmas morning. Only better, because I know what's waiting for me."

She grins back at me and I can see the longing in her eyes that tells me she can't wait for her wedding day so she can do the exact same thing. I'm grateful to her for how she's been about the wedding and the baby. A lesser woman would have an issue with the little sister not only getting married before her but also having the first grandchild.

Lorali is an exceptional person and has been nothing but supportive of me since day one. She's never shown an ounce of disappointment or made me feel like I was stepping on toes being the first one to go through this. She's happy for me and it has shown through in each and every one of her actions as we prepared for my day.

Alexa has been the same way. She did my hair and makeup while Lorali and my mother watched in the room with smiles on their face. Well, Mom had tears shining in her eyes also, but she seems happy for me.

I was terrified of how my parents would react after hearing about the baby. My dad was a little skeptical at first about the engagement, but he settled after we explained that Kaleb asked for my hand before we even knew I was pregnant. He also bristled at the knowledge that Kaleb didn't ask him first. I'd like to slap Ian for setting that precedent and expectation.

"You ready?" my mom asks as I feel the car slow down and come to a stop.

I glance out the window and smile. Never in my whole life have I been so ready to do something.

With the way the house is arranged and the wedding arch is set up in the backyard we have planned for my wedding day to start once I get to the home. All I have to do is walk in the house, out the back door, and down the aisle.

My stomach flutters at the knowledge that in less than half an hour I'll be Mrs. Kaleb Perez, a married woman with a magnificent husband. Recognizing that fact makes me want to run rather than walk slowly to the wedding march that began playing the second the French doors on the back of the house were pulled open.

Less than twenty yards away the most gorgeous, sun-kissed man waits for me. The entire world falls away the second my gaze lands on Kaleb. He's dressed to perfection in a black suit and tie, and my mouth waters at the images I've conjured of how he's going to look when I divest him from each and every piece the second I get the chance.

His incredible green eyes match perfectly with the silk square in his front pocket and the tie around his neck. Coincidentally it also matches the tiny butterfly clip holding my hair in place. At some point green became our color. For me it was his eyes that made me love the hue; for him I'm sure it was the emerald panties I wore the same day we first made love.

I stop at the very end of the aisle and drink him in, my field of vision narrowing down and tunneling to only him. I don't see the couple dozen guests in attendance. My field of vision doesn't include Ian and Garrett standing beside him nor Lorali and Alexa across the aisle from him.

Kaleb. Only Kaleb.

I realize I'm taking too long when his face begins to lose color and the look of awe that was on his face the second he saw me begins to drop. The small step he takes in my direction and the slight lift of his left hand encourages me to move closer to him. It is then that I realize that I would follow this man through the gates of hell if he even hinted that he wanted me there. Kaleb, of course, isn't leading me into a life of sin and evil; he's my happiness and everything that is right in my life.

"You ready," my father whispers in my ear.

I look up at him and smile, giving my head a tiny nod. We begin our torturously slow walk towards Kaleb, the minister, and the rest of the wedding party.

I hear my dad as well as other guests chuckle. "Slow down, baby girl. He'll still be there even if we don't run."

My eyes go wide when I realize I've practically started power walking in Kaleb's direction. My eyes have never left his; his haven't left mine. The preacher says something; my dad responds.

My ears don't register anything but Kaleb saying "Mariposa" as he takes my hand from my dad's and kisses the top. Reaching up, he wipes a tear from my cheek and runs his finger down my chin.

"Kaleb," I whisper to him and lean in to kiss his lips.

The minister's cough and the audience's giggle remind me we are not alone and there are some things we are required to do up here in front of our closest family and friends before we'll be permitted to kiss. I blush, a wave of embarrassment washing over me when I realize that I just tried to sneak a kiss in front of fifty people.

I do my best to turn my attention back to the minister as he begins to speak. I'm grateful that we opted to keep with the traditional vows because I couldn't think at this moment to save my life. We kept with the traditions as much as we could. My something borrowed is a pair of earrings that Alexa loaned me and my something blue is the pale blue bra and panty set I have on under my dress; a little surprise for Kaleb later. My something old and something new is his mother's ring and the band we had made to match.

I repeat after the minister; Kaleb follows and it only takes minutes and a few spoken words to tie me to Kaleb Perez for the rest of my life. Finally, the preacher gives us permission to have our first kiss as husband and wife. Kaleb leans in first this time and places his hand on my lower belly, acknowledging the tiny life growing inside of me, and kisses me senseless. Thankfully he has enough wherewithal to pull back because I'm seconds away from climbing him like a tree.

We make our way back toward the house, passing all the smiling faces. We decided to have the reception at one of Ian's smaller hotels, but I insisted that we get married here at the house. This is where we fell in love and it just feels right to begin our marriage at the same place.

After almost an hour of pictures, we finally make our way to the bedroom so Kaleb can change out of his suit. I can't help but wonder how tacky it would be considered if we didn't show up at the reception at all. It will be a true testament of will if I can watch Kaleb undress and allow him to redress without consummating our marriage.

Just before I close the door to the room and shut out the entire world I hear Lorali say my name. I turn to face her, only holding the door open a crack and give her a pointed look.

She smiles like she's reading my mind. "I'll give you ten minutes, Josie, but then you have to get in the limo and go to the hotel."

"Cock-blocker," I hear Kaleb whisper with a laugh behind me. Seems he had the same ideas I did!

I acknowledge her with a slight nod and close and lock, the door behind me.

I pounce on him. When I say pounce I mean I literally run to him and jump in his arms. My dress is short enough that it hikes up and allows me to wrap my legs around his waist. My hasty actions slow the second I'm in his arms.

I calm my body and look in his eyes.

"Hi," I whisper.

"I missed you," he whispers before he lowers his mouth to mine.

By the time he pulls his mouth away, I'm panting.

"I need you." I'm practically begging and I'm hoping he gives in.

He releases the grip he has on my butt and allows me to slide down his body. If the sizeable lump he's sporting is any indication, he wants me just as bad.

My hands go to his shoulder and slide his black suit jacket off his shoulders. He catches it deftly as it clears his right hand and doesn't even look as he throws it with expert precision on the foot of the bed. He's wearing a matching vest that somehow manages to show the perfect narrowing of his hips but taking nothing away from the bulk of his shoulders.

He moans as I slide my hand down his tie and use it to tug his mouth to mine. Releasing his tie my hands begin working on the buttons of his black vest. He allows me to slide it off of his shoulders and I'm amazed that he's allowing this to happen; he's usually the one to put the brakes on when we are expected somewhere.

I slowly begin to sink to my knees as my fingers start working on opening his belt.

"No, Josie." His command sounds like more of plea as if he's barely holding on to his control over the situation. Knowing he's just as affected sends a wave of feminine satisfaction over my entire body.

"I want to taste you, baby," I whisper seductively.

"Stop," he says with more force than he had just seconds ago.

My eyes shoot to his as he reaches under my arms and pulls me up from my squatting position in front of him.

"We don't have time," he explains, the desire still evident in his eyes. "I'll be damned if the first time we join as husband and wife consist of you on your knees."

I roll my lips between my teeth to keep from grinning at how serious he is about this.

"The first time I make love to you as your husband will be just that, making love. It will be slow, sensual, and it will take a very long time. We don't have near enough time for that now."

I give him the cutest mock frown I can manage.

"Mariposa, I know you think it is okay to skip the reception now, but if we do you'll regret it." He's being reasonable and for once I concede without a fight.

A loud knock on the door kills any type of moment we were having.

***

A hundred years.

That's how long it takes to mingle, cut the cake, and throw the bouquet. I've chastised myself more than once for my ungrateful thoughts. Several of the families have traveled in from out of town to share our special day with us and all I want to do is go home and make love to my husband.

Making excuses because of my child has started early because by ten o'clock we're saying goodbye to everyone and telling them I'm exhausted. First trimester problems, you know? I am honestly completely exhausted, but I have no intentions of sleeping when I get home.

I snuggle against Kaleb in the back of the limo as it carries us back home. I can't get enough of the feel of his arms around me and the scent of his skin, both cologne and a certain element that is just him.

Apparently more tired than I originally thought, Kaleb has to wake me once we pull up to the house.

He scoops me up and carries me across the threshold, stopping only to close the door behind him and set the alarm. He only has to shift my weight fractionally and I love that he can carry me with ease. I feel protected and safe in his arms and if I could live there every minute, I would.

Even though I'm tired, I'm hit with another wave of adrenaline as he gently kisses my temple and sets me on my feet. This time, he doesn't stop me when I reach up to loosen his tie. I waste no time freeing the knot and throwing the emerald strip of fabric to the floor.

A riot of emotion is playing out on his gorgeous face. I can see passion, lust, and excitement, but the one that shines the brightest is love. If I ever have a doubt about how this man, my husband, feels about me, one look in his eyes is all the reassurance that I need.

I unbutton the front of his shirt while he works on removing his cufflinks, a gift from Ian and Garrett. He places them in the front pocket of his pants as I slide his shirt off, revealing incredibly sculpted arms and his golden chest and stomach. My mouth begins to water at the sight. Is it possible that he's even hotter now that he's my husband?

His belt and suit pants are next on my list. I get them open quickly and push them off his hips and to the floor. He reaches his thumbs into the elastic of his boxer briefs, but I stop him before he can push them down.

"Leave these on, for now," I tell him and smile at his groan. "I have a surprise for you."

This seems to appease him for now. I take a step back from him and he takes a step into me.

"Stay there," I tell him and increase the distance between us by a few feet. He looks pained and I watch him clench his fists as I increase the distance.

"I was so proud to stand before my family with both of my favorite guys earlier," I tell him as I inch my dress up my thighs.

"I don't want to talk about your dad while I'm standing here on my wedding night with a raging hard-on, Josie."

I bite my lip to keep from laughing and shake my head. "I'm not talking about my dad, baby."

He tilts his head slightly. "I know you're fond of Ian, but I had no clue you'd consider him 'one of you favorite guys.'"

He's so dense sometimes.

"Don't stop," he begs when my hands slow and stop the removal of my dress.

"I'm not talking about Ian either." I resume pulling my dress up, the bottom clearing the apex of my thighs and continuing to slide past my stomach. He continues to watch the slow ascent of my dress and doesn't respond.

Finally, the dress is completely off and I just toss it to the floor in the direction of his tie.

"You're beautiful, Josie," he whispers as his eyes scan my entire body.

"Do you like blue, Kaleb?" I ask referencing my pale blue, lace undies and barely there shelf bra.

He nods his heads excitedly. "I'd love it better on the floor." His voice is gravelly and rough.

"Don't you want your surprise?" I tease him again.

He groans in frustration as he takes a step forward and I stop him with an upturned hand.

"I was talking about my two favorite guys," I repeat. "Of course there's you and now, him," I say as I press the palm of my hand below my belly button.

His eyes flash from my stomach to my face, and back again.

"Him?" He whispers. "How?"

He rushes me and, this time, I don't attempt to stop him. He sweeps me up in his arms and kisses me feverishly as he spins us both around.

"A boy?" He asks, verifying once again.

I grin and shake my head up and down. "I had a Harmony test done and one of the things it determines is gender."

"You're sure? It's so early." His hand is resting on my stomach and his fingers are repeatedly flexing .

"The test is one hundred percent accurate on gender." The whoop he lets out is so loud I have to cover my ears.

"Best wedding gift ever, Mariposa," he says before kissing me again.

"You have one more to unwrap, Mr. Perez," I tell him hinting at my lingerie.

"With pleasure," he murmurs as his finger pulls down the front cup of my bra.

I hiss when his scorching hot mouth hits the tip of my breast. I was sure he'd attack me the minute I gave consent, but he doesn't. He laps at and licks my breast seductively, slowly, as if he has all the time in the world and wants to give them their due.

I reach my hands under his chin and open the front clasp of the bra letting it fall to the ground at my feet. I'm delirious as he suckles my breast and caresses the other with his hand, rolling the tip between his fingers. I'm not so far gone to keep from helping this along, so I hook my fingers in my panties and slide them off my hips.

His hand slowly slides from my breast and inches down my stomach, stopping just atop where his baby grows. His mouth leaves my breast and follows the same path his fingers made seconds before. He whispers something in Spanish to his son before lowering his head even further.

I grip him under his chin and stop his descent. "Nope," I tell him and waggle my finger. "You wouldn't let me earlier, so you can't either."

His eyes darken further, but he obeys and rises to a standing position. Without warning he picks me up and carries me to the bed. He places his knee on the mattress and lowers me slowly until I'm settled on my back, peering up at his vibrant green eyes.

He lowers his mouth to mine and I don't know if he's intentionally going at a snail's pace or if my brain has slowed things down on its own, but it seems to take forever for his lips to touch mine.

"I love you, Mrs. Perez," he whispers just before our lips make contact.

I know the whole situation of calling each other Mr. and Mrs. is a little cliché, but I dare you to have this man as your husband and have him say that to you and not melt. I don't know if it's possible for anyone and I know for a fact it's not possible for me because I just turn into a melty pile of goo when he says it.

I run my hands all over his body and down eventually making it down his back and inside the band of his briefs. I push them down as far as I can then raise my legs up and use my toes and feet to push them down to his ankles. I feel him shift his feet to remove them completely and his mouth never leaves my skin.

I whimper when I feel his hot breath against my neck and grow embarrassingly wet when he bites the junction where my neck and shoulder meet. I rotate my hips against his hot length. He groans which causes me to flex my hips again, my body searching and only finding a fraction of the friction it needs.

I squeeze the muscular globes of his butt cheeks and tug him closer. He needs no further convincing, within seconds he shifts his hips back and forward, slowly sliding inside.

We both hum our approval into each other's mouth, kissing continually as he rocks his hips back and forth. He fills me full and every inch of my core is encompassing every inch of his length.

It's heaven.

Kaleb slowly pulls his mouth from mine and peppers tiny kisses down my chin.

I bite my lip as his eyes meet mine and try to contain the emotion that is taking over every inch of my body.

"Mariposa," he says as he wipes a rogue tear from my face.

"I love you, baby," I whimper as all of the emotion and turmoil in my body begins to come together and focus where our bodies are meeting.

I pull my leg up slightly higher and he takes it even further when he sweeps his arm under my knee and pulls it to where my knee is almost touching my shoulder. He thrusts forward and I'm certain he's deeper than he's ever been, feeling thicker and filling me fuller than any time prior.

I'm useless at this point but can't help the greediness I'm feeling. I lift my other leg and almost like he reads my mind he scoops in behind the other knee. I'm practically bent in half under him and I'm amazed at the brilliant new sensations I'm blessed with in this new position.

And I thought it couldn't get any better. Married sex is awesome!

"Fuck, Josie. I need you to come," he pants in my ear and his words send me over.

I clutch at his back and over his shoulders as my body begins to shake under him and clench around his now pulsing cock.

I can't tell what he's saying into my neck as he comes undone and I'm not even sure it's in English, but it still brings a smile to my face.

He slowly withdraws from me and shifts his body so I'm lying on his chest. A whispered I love you is the last thing I remember before I drift to sleep.

Chapter 16
Lorali

"Holy shit!" Ian groans as his cock begins to pulse erratically inside of me.

I do my best to cover his mouth, but my arms are like Jell-O from the past two hours of acrobatic sex. I have been bent, twisted, and contorted into the craziest positions this morning and I loved every second of it. My only concern is the five other rooms full of family in the house. Ian assured me more than once that we are far enough away and the walls are thick enough that no one else in the house has any idea what we've been doing.

I set the alarm last night for earlier than we needed to get up. Ian had a few too many at the reception and was practically passed out before his head even hit the pillow. I did it to torture him but also to make him fulfill the promises he whispered in my ear last night as we slow danced, imagining our own wedding.

He's followed through with every spoken promise he muttered last night and then some. This man is like a machine, getting turned on and performing at the drop of a hat it seems. I can't wait for a lifetime of this. He touches, caresses, and makes love to me like it is the first and the last time every single time we come together. He's addictive and I can't seem to get enough of him, and I hope I never get complacent to the idea of making love to Ian Hale.

He kisses my neck and gingerly circles my nipple with the tip of one of his fingers. I would think nothing of it like he was doing it just to feel close to me if I didn't also feel him thickening against my leg as he catches his breath from the last orgasm. I'm swollen and I know I'll be sore all day long, but my body doesn't even take that into account as it tingles for more.

"We have to get showered." I groan as he pinches my nipple just barely enough to feel the tightening action. "The caterers will be here shortly for brunch."

"Sloan has the access code and she's very capable. She doesn't need us hovering over her to do her job." He lowers his mouth to my hardened point and licks it leisurely.

He's talking about Sloan Reynolds, the owner of *Party Panache*. She handles and caters every one of Ian's business and personal events. I knew I had no chance of helping with the wedding and keeping on top of today's brunch by myself so I didn't even argue when Ian scheduled her to cater this morning.

"We have guests, Ian," he grumbles incoherently with my breast in his mouth. "We have to get up."

I push him off of me and slide out of the bed, missing his grasp by mere inches.

He follows me into the bathroom as I turn the shower on, a half dozen jets coming to life and very quickly sending steam all around us. We can't seem to keep our hands off of each other. Honestly we never have been able to, but we do manage to get clean and dressed and out to the common areas of the house before our other guests make an appearance.

We have an eclectic group that opted to stay with us last night so they could join us for today's celebratory brunch. Alexa and Garrett stayed in 'their' room. Garrett drank as much as Ian did last night, but he was more lucid on the ride back to the house. I'm certain owning a club has aided him in building his alcohol tolerance.

Kaleb's mother stayed in the room that Kaleb and Josie use when they stay over and my parents are in another room. The remaining guest room is occupied by Kaleb's cousin Diego or Kincaid as his biker crew calls him. I'm forever grateful to him and his club for helping when Josie was abducted. He brought his girlfriend with him and I'm a horrible host because I haven't had the time to even learn her name much less had a chance to have a conversation with her. She seems a little skittish. They were going to stay at Kaleb and Josie's, but I insisted they stay here. Who wants to spend their wedding night worrying about guests in their home?

The other two rooms are filled with an aunt and uncle, one from each of my parents' side of the family. Needless to say, the entire house is full and I've spent the last two hours panting and screaming Ian's name like we are on a deserted island without a care in the world.

I shake my head and smile as I walk gingerly into the kitchen where, unsurprisingly, I find Sloane and several employees already setting up the food and getting the tables ready. Ian's house is huge but when you shove over a dozen people into it, logistics and choices become more difficult. For that reason we've decided on having a buffet style breakfast today.

The doorbell chimes and I smile as I walk to answer it. Josie and Kaleb are the only ones who are expected that didn't stay the night. I swing the door open as dramatically as I can.

"You're early," I say.

Josie swings her head and glares at Kaleb as she swats him on the arm. "I told you," she bites out.

He smiles and shakes his head at her. "Insatiable," he mutters to himself just before kissing me on the cheek and walking into the house.

"How was your evening?" I ask Josie as she slips past, her hand in Kaleb's.

"Wonderful," she answers as her eyes light up.

By the time we make it to the kitchen Ian, Alexa, and Garrett has joined Sloane's staff. She ignores them as the guys begin to pick and taste test the morning's offerings.

We circle around the granite-topped island in the center of the kitchen and I'm sure it looks like we're conspiring for something as if we're joining forces to determine how we will proceed with the day to include the interlopers into our world which normally includes just the six of us.

"I want to thank everyone for the wonderful gifts, the help with the wedding and reception yesterday, and all of the support and understanding you guys have had where Kaleb and I are concerned," Josie says as she makes eye contact with each of us.

We all respond simultaneously with 'of course,' 'don't mention it', and such.

Kaleb clears his throat gaining the attention of all of us. "I also wanted to say thank you." He reaches into his pocket and pulls out a handful of blue wrapped Starburst candies. "We wanted to share our news with you," he offers each one of us a piece of the candy.

The men and, of course, Alexa, stand there with the silly little blue candy in their hands with no clue as to what is going on.

Me?

I'm jumping up and down like an idiot and rushing to hug Josie.

"A boy?!?" I whisper-yell, because I feel like this is something they're only sharing with us right now.

I feel Josie nod her head yes as I squeeze her tight in my arms. Finally, the others catch on and Alexa joins us in the hug. She's a good sport at least. Kaleb must be ecstatic. Josie has mentioned more than once that a boy is what he was hopeful for.

I hear Garrett say "Damn straight" just about the same time Ian says "Fuck yeah, man." I pull away in time to see the man hugs and back slaps as the guys congratulate Kaleb. I release Josie so they can hug her and brush a kiss on her cheek.

I watch and smile as our group quietly celebrates the wonderful news that the very first baby to be born will carry on Kaleb's name. Unceremoniously I open my Starburst and pop it in my mouth. The second it hits my tongue I'm rudely spitting it back into my hand.

"Nasty right?" Josie asks beside me.

I hear a bold laugh from Kaleb. "Sorry. The starburst were the only blue candy we could find on such short notice."

I laugh when I see the guys throw theirs on the counter. I'm like a sweets and candy queen so the guys know if I don't like it there's not a chance in hell they will.

We stand around and chat until the other family members begin to join us. Eventually, everyone is up and we begin the line for the buffet.

We sit in various locations in the formal and informal dining area to eat because Ian's dining room only fits twelve. You can tell this is truly two families coming together because there is no segregation along familial lines. Everyone has split up to talk with the other guests.

Most everything is just how I figured it would be and only two things cause me to take a second look. Diego's girlfriend is sitting with her back to the wall in the furthest chair in the kitchen and her eyes are darting around the room constantly. I can't tell if she just seems really nervous, scared, or if she's high. I don't think it's the latter because she seems healthy, but what do I know about drug users? It's not something that's in my wheelhouse.

The second thing that doesn't go unnoticed is the way Alexa and Garrett are looking at each other and then the fact that ten minutes later when I look in their direction, they are nowhere to be found. I pray they found an alternative place for their nooner because their room is right in the middle between my parents' room and my Aunt Betty's. The plan is everyone is going to get packed up and leave shortly after brunch is finished. They better hurry their asses up!

The plan *was* for everyone to leave after brunch, but my parents and extended family decided amongst them that they will stay another night and head out first thing in the morning. Seems the pool looks too inviting and they want to lounge a bit. Ian, of course, graciously told them that was a great idea and pretended to ignore me when I kicked him under the table.

Ian and I excuse ourselves from the conversation Mom and Aunt Betty are having about the chances of bad weather in October for mine and Ian's wedding as we see Diego and his girlfriend rise from the table. I knew he wouldn't be able to stay long since he has such a long ride back to Farmington.

"Thank you so much for coming," I tell them as we, including Josie and Kaleb, walk him to the door.

"We appreciate the hospitality," he responds. He turns toward Kaleb and does the man hug thing. "Congrats, man. Best of luck." His attention is then turned to Josie and I watch as he reaches up and strokes the side of her face. "You look much better than the last time I saw you, Sugar."

Josie beams at him and kisses him on the cheek. She whispers something in his ear that I can't hear, but it causes him to wrap her in a big but delicate hug. She has tears in her eyes when he finally pulls away.

Kaleb opens the door and I'm startled at seeing two other leather clad bikes sitting casually in the driveway. They have similar patches on their jackets that Diego has and his lack of alarm at them being there causes me to believe that they are part of his club.

"Trouble?" Kaleb asks nodding towards the other bikers.

"Nothing we can't handle," I hear Diego say as he makes his way down the front steps.

Kaleb follows him, but Josie stays on the front stoop with me. Ian has already turned to go back inside, no doubt to see what Sloane will be able to do about breakfast tomorrow.

"What was that all about?" I ask Josie.

"What?" She says turning her attention to me but looking woeful at having to tear her eyes from her husband and his cousin.

"That little interaction with Diego," I offer.

She has a reflective look on her face and it is several long moments before she answers. "He's the one who found me in the closet." She smiles but it's a small sort of sad smile.

I nod in understanding, knowing that something like that would cause two of the most unlikely people to share an unbreakable bond. I'm dying to ask her what she said to him to get such a gentle yet impactful reaction from the seemingly scary biker, but I know it's not my business.

We leave Kaleb with the trio of bikers and head back inside to the remaining family.

"You guys planning to stay and hang out by the pool for a while?" I ask her as we make our way back to the dining room.

She doesn't answer so I turn to face to her and I know her answer without her saying a word. The look on her face tells me I'm lucky she got out of the bed to attend this brunch and she has every intention of getting back in it as soon as possible.

"I don't blame you," I say and nudge her hip with mine.

She starts making her way around the room telling everyone goodbye. I make my way down the hall to the powder room to check and make sure it's fully stocked after last night seeing as we will have guests again tonight.

I open the door and stop dead in my tracks at the sight of the back of Alexa's head bobbing up and down on Garrett's cock. The fact that this is what they're doing is not the shocking part; they are just as horny for each other constantly just like Ian and I are.

What shocks me the most is the fact that I stand there and watch for about ten seconds longer than I should at the sight of my best friend sucking off her boyfriend. When my gaze finally meets Garrett's all he does is wink at me and look back down at Alexa, who hasn't bothered to stop or turn her face to see who has intruded upon what should be a private moment.

That one tiny action of his eye snaps me out of whatever trance I was in and I gasp and leave the room, closing the door louder than I'd intended. My feelings, I realize as I make my way to the bedroom are twofold. On one hand I'm a little grossed out at seeing Alexa doing that. I'm also grateful that her head blocked the sight of Garrett's cock completely. I'm very close with Alexa and just about as close as friends can get with Garrett, we are so close that the sight is almost reprehensible.

On the other hand, I have to be honest and acknowledge that my body responded sexually to the sight of what was practically a live porno. I close my door, sit on the bed, and pray that the situation is never brought up again. I'll have to have a conversation with Alexa about locking doors later.

Chapter 17
Kaleb

We haven't left the bed much since we got back from the post-wedding brunch yesterday. My wife, I can't even keep myself from smiling when I think it in my head, and I have spent nearly every second of the past eighteen hours wrapped around each other talking, napping, and making love.

She made me the happiest man yesterday when she said 'I do' and the icing on the cake? She told me she was giving me a son, a Perez to carry on my father's name. Josie and I have had more than one conversation about the number of children we want. I've told her I want four, but she's more sensible and says we have to see what the genders are going to be since we only have so much room in the house. We'll see, I guess.

Josie grumbles as I tickle the skin over the womb where my son is nestled. She is not a bright and early girl. Thank goodness I like getting up early or we'd never get anywhere on time.

"Josie," I whisper in her ear. She smiles but she doesn't open her eyes. "Ian just texted that the car will be here in half an hour. We have to get up and get ready."

She rolls from her back to me, rubbing the creamy mess I left last night against my thigh. "Five more minutes," she pleads.

I'm regretting that I insisted we go somewhere for our honeymoon when she suggested that we just squirrel away in the house for a week.

"We have to get up, Mariposa," I smack her ass gently and wiggle my way out from under her. We will never get anywhere if there is a chance of skin to skin contact.

Twenty-five minutes and an orgasm each later, hey we are newlyweds, we are clean and ready to head out to Montana, just in time because I just buzzed the car service driver into the community.

"Got everything you need?" I ask as Josie sets her surprisingly small suitcase by my larger one.

"Yep," she says and she sounds almost giddy with excitement.

"You didn't pack much," I prod.

"I don't need much." Her voice is seductive as she slides up to me and wraps her slender arms around my waist. "I don't imagine we'll be wearing much."

I grin at her assumption and won't say anything to her now. As much as I'd love to spend every second of our honeymoon inside of my wife, she has to start getting out and letting go of some of the fear that she's been harboring since her abduction.

This isn't just coming from me. Josie mentioned that her therapist has said the same thing. I'm thinking there's no better time to do that than on our honeymoon. We'll be away from the town and people that the abduction occurred in so I'm hoping that helps her let loose a little.

I see the front of the car shadow the etched glass of the front door so I peck Josie on the lips and reach down to grab our bags. I may have to buy her more clothes, but I have no intention of telling her my plans; no reason for her to worry on the plane ride to Montana. I'll just spring it on her tomorrow or something. Less time to think, less time to worry.

I set the alarm on the house. I know Alexa and Lorali have plans to help set up the nursery while we are gone, but they have the code to get in. I'm leery of the plan, but they assure me Josie will be ecstatic about it. I've always thought that the mother-to-be wants to be involved as much as possible, especially with the first baby. Well, if Josie is upset it will be on them and not me.

I can't help but laugh when I step outside. Apparently 'car service' to Ian and me means totally different things. To Ian 'car service' means the stretch limo that's sitting in front of my house; to me 'car service' means maybe a town car or even a taxi. Josie is shaking her head as well at his excessiveness as she slides into the back seat. I follow her but feel out of place and can only nod at the driver who is holding the door open for us.

"Fucking Ian," I mutter as I settle beside Josie.

She ignores me and cuddles into my side as the driver closes the door and makes his way back around to the front of the car. Within minutes we are smoothly gliding out of our gated community heading to the airport.

The ride is spent talking softly to each other about our plans for the week. There are a few shops she mentions seeing online that she's hinted that she might like to go to and this gives me hope that she'll be okay with my idea to be out in public more.

I do my best not to give credit to the knowledge that literally our entire relationship has been spent with her being terrified of something and me protecting her. At first, it was the death threats and the break-in at her apartment, then the abduction, and now dealing with the aftermath of that. I pray she still wants me once everything gets back to normal and she no longer feels threatened by the outside world.

We've been paying so much attention to each other, it isn't until the car slows and stops that I realize we are not at the commercial airfield where we're supposed to be. Instead, we are parked beside a sleek, private jet.

Josie leans up to take in the sight of the irrefutably magnificent jet. "Well, it looks like we'll be going to Montana in style."

She's grinning from ear to ear and her excitement is contagious. The things I could do to her on a private jet are already taking up space in my head. *Thank you, Ian Hale.* I hope Josie is agreeable because I know the flight time will be even quicker now that we aren't flying commercial.

We make our way out of the car where another man stands with our bags already in his hands. The driver waves me off as I try to tip him. Seems Ian has taken care of everything. The man holding our bags inclines his free hand toward the plane so we make our way up the small flight of stairs into the cabin of the plane that is much more luxurious than I would've ever guessed.

A man, who is obviously the captain, makes his way from the front of the plane as we settle into matching leather chairs. He holds out two dark covered square pamphlets and hands them to me.

"You've already been cleared through customs," he says.

His words force me to look at what I realize now are passports in my hand and sure as shit it is mine and Josie's that I'm holding.

"How in the….wait. Customs?" I look over at Josie, who is just as confused as I am. "We're headed to Montana, why would we need to clear customs?"

"Mr. Hale expected this type of reaction." He reaches over to the table beside him and hands me an electronic tablet. "The video file on this may explain the situation better. We will wait for takeoff for your decision. I have no intentions on kidnapping a cop." He heads back to the front as I power up the tablet.

I tap the video file on the home screen as Josie and I lean in shoulder to shoulder so we can watch it.

The video begins to play and Ian and Lorali appear on the screen. She's sitting on his lap in what appears to be his office at their home, so they can both fit on the screen.

"Don't freak out," Lorali says. "We just wanted to surprise both of you with a dream honeymoon we know you'd never give yourself."

Ian interrupts. "First off," he grins at his fiancée. "I came up with the idea of the dream honeymoon." Just as I think that he's going to take credit for the entire idea he continues. "I want it known that I did not think that it should be a surprise."

So Ian understands my discomfort with not knowing what is going on. Well, he may be aware that I would be a little putout but I'm sure he could not understand the derision I'm feeling sitting here next to my pregnant wife not knowing what is going on.

Lorali smacks Ian on the shoulder and tells him he's being silly to even think we would mind. I think Lorali needs to be informed of just how much Josie has been affected by recent events.

"Anyways," Lorali says. "Kaleb, Josie mentioned you wanted to go to the beach and she told you no. Well, I could tell by our last conversation that my ever-sensible sister really wanted the beach but her practical side kept telling her no. Well, Ian is known for being impractical. Hence, you rode to the jet in a limo and you're sitting on the most luxurious one in his entire fleet. Enjoy the ride and you'll discover after takeoff that there's a cozy little bedroom in the back in case Josie gets tired on the flight to Playa de Amor in Cabo."

Josie hisses and starts to clap and bounce in her seat. It borderline pisses me off. If this is what she wanted, I would have given it to her in a heartbeat. The next time I ask her a serious question and she plays the 'it's-too-expensive' card I'll tie her ass up and tickle her until she tells me the truth.

My anger is more like a flash because she's so excited and happy. Her happiness conjures the same in me.

I realize that Lorali is still speaking. "There should be an envelope on the table there that has information on all the sites and activities. The vacation is one hundred percent inclusive so you guys won't need to pay for anything unless you leave the resort to do some shopping."

I feel Josie tense beside me at the mention of going off the beaten path.

"I know that scares you a little bit Josie and you'll be happy to know that we have also made arrangements for security in case you feel up to it. There is, of course, no obligation. That should alleviate any apprehension and I can tell you that Ramon is extremely happy to be in Cabo waiting to take you guys where ever you need to."

I feel like an asshole for even thinking that Lorali hasn't been receptive to the issues Josie has had. She's just as aware as I have been. So much so they've arranged for the one person outside of our group that Josie feels comfortable with to help us on our honeymoon.

"Not trying to step on any toes Kaleb," Ian breaks in. "We just want you guys to focus on each other without having to worry so much about security. Kaleb if you're wondering about the passports we commissioned your mother on that front."

Fucking Ian Hale thinks of everything.

"Your rooms should be stocked with appropriate clothes but, of course, call the front desk if you're missing anything and they know to send someone out to get it. Focus on yourselves because before long my little niece or nephew will be getting all of your attention. Have fun you guys. We love you!"

The video goes black. They must have filmed this before our gender announcement yesterday.

This next week is going to be incredible. A week on the sand in the sun with the most beautiful woman in the world. I have to be the luckiest man alive.

"Wow," Josie whispers beside me. "Are you mad?" She crinkles her nose up waiting for me to answer.

"Are you excited?" I raise my eyebrows up at her because as much as she's trying to keep her face passive her eyes are shining like two of the bluest sapphires I've ever seen.

She finally gives in, her face taken over by an incredibly beautiful smile.

"That's what I thought," I say and kiss her perfect nose.

Just then the man who carried our bags on appears with two glasses of champagne.

Josie holds her hand up to stop him. "I can't. I'm pregnant," she explains.

"Sparkling cider ma'am," he says and continues to hand her the long stemmed flute.

We sip on the cider as he carries over a tray of pastries, plates, and cloth napkins and places it on the table before us. Not that I would ever want to get used to this type of treatment, but I'm sure as hell going to indulge while the opportunity is here.

"Where are we headed, sir?" he asks as he settles a small plate of fruit beside the pastries.

I look over at Josie and grin. "Looks like we're going to Cabo." His grin is contagious.

"I'll let the captain know." He walks toward the front of the plane and within minutes I hear the rumble of the engines and feel the shudder under my feet. We both buckle up and settle in for takeoff.

The minute the captain comes over the speaker to inform us that we are safely in the air and movement within the plane is allowed we are out of our seats and making our way to the small room in the back.

We have nothing better to do for the next several hours so we utilize our time the best by joining a club. A mile high.

Chapter 18
Alexa

Worst day ever.

If we continue to lose accounts at this rate, I'll be out of a job before I even have a chance to decide on starting my own spa. We used to be the top of our game. A handful of viral videos later and now our spa services are what people are considering obsolete. It's not something I want for myself but if fish eating off of your feet, having snails crawl around on your face, or having your hair washed with bull semen is what's popular, we as a top spa in the Denver area should offer those services.

There are a few spas around town that have jumped on these new innovative fads and they are raking it in. The old money that owns and makes these types of decisions for my spa absolutely refuse to do anything now that may not be popular in a few years.

Normally that would make perfect business sense but right now the regular customers are not only going to these new spas they are canceling standing future appointments. We are sinking fast and it is all on my head as the manager. There are only so many things you can do to draw in new customers. Not only is that happening, but the existing customers are starting to deplete. It may be time to jump ship to keep from going down with it.

I'm vegged out on the couch in a pair of not so sexy pajamas by the time Garrett gets home at seven. I smile at him and wave him over. A night hanging out on the couch watching TV sounds like perfection to me.

He frowns when he sees me. I immediately bring my hand up and wipe over my face thinking maybe he sees something I don't realize is there.

"What's wrong?" I ask.

"Seriously? We have dinner reservations. I told you about it last week and reminded you about it yesterday." He complains but the tone of his voice is more disappointment than anger.

I frown at him. "I honestly forgot, Garrett. I'd rather just stay home." His face falls drastically which is a ridiculous reaction to something as benign as canceling dinner.

"You sure? There's still time." He grins slightly and I hate to disappoint him, but I'm just not feeling it.

"Can't we just cuddle on the couch? I'm already in my pajamas." I smile at him sweetly but honestly I want to kick myself because the next thought that comes into my head should never, ever be thought by a woman in her twenties. I've already taken my bra off is what I was going to tell him next. When did I get so lazy and complacent?

"Yeah, Angel. That's fine. Let me go get changed." This man is amazing. I know he doesn't want to be cooped up in this house, but he hasn't complained about my recent morph into a homebody.

"I ordered takeout. Should be here in a half hour or so." Garrett says twenty minutes later as he walks back into the living room.

He settles on the couch, lifting my legs and placing them on his lap. I know he's showered because his hair is damp and smells divine. I close my eyes and breathe in the rich manly scent of his body wash. He's in pajama bottoms and the dips and crevices of his pecs and abs call out to me.

"Bad day?" Ugh, why did he even have to ask? He begins to massage my right foot and it feels amazing. So much better than dinner in public.

"It's getting worse, Garrett. We lost eight more accounts today." I shake my head because it seems like every time he asks the bad news increases.

He gives me a look of sympathy because he knows how much I used to love my job. The decline hasn't been gradual. It is like how everything is nowadays. People see something, they want it right then, and there are always people standing around waiting to capitalize on it.

"I think it may be time to seriously start thinking about something else," I admit to him.

"Have you given any more thought to my offer?" He asks casually even though I know the question is anything but casual. He's wanted to back me for several months and I've always remained elusive.

"I have," I tell him. His grin is from ear to ear. "But," I hold my finger up to keep him from responding. "I don't need you to back me completely. I have a decent amount in savings. Maybe we could go in as partners."

He frowns again. He's been doing that a lot lately.

"After the business begins to turn a profit and I'm able, I'll buy you out." To me that makes the endeavor win, win.

"I have no expectation of being paid back, Alexa," he says, finally releasing my foot and angling his body more towards mine.

"That's not a very sound business practice, Garrett." He raises his eyebrow at my chastisement.

"Is that what you think I'm doing? That I'd offer to help get your business up and running as a business decision?" Usually, Garrett would turn something like this argument that I'm certain is about to start into a way to punish me and make me come at the same time, but right now he just seems hurt and surprised I would think he wanted to be my business partner.

"You're a business man, Garrett. Why would I think otherwise?" He's been acting so weird lately and it's throwing me off.

He closes his eyes and bites his bottom lip, almost like he's trying to get his thoughts together before he says something he'll regret. I wait him out because mildly upset Garrett is one sexy man and I could use a little of the aggressive side of him after the horrible day I've had.

I'm not going to purposefully push him because that's just not my style, but I don't back down or concede to him just because he thinks I should. Lately though he's been calmer, more affectionate, and leaning more towards passion than the haste and aggression that he used to come at me with.

I love it, don't get me wrong. Almost since the beginning of our relationship, he would go back and forth between what I consider his different sexual personalities. The past month? Nothing but soft and sensual, well except for that time he caught me masturbating. That was a fun day.

"I love you, Alexa. You are not business. What I offer to you is from me personally not as part of some business maneuver." He leans forward and sweeps me into his lap until I'm straddling him.

"That's a huge offer. You should benefit from it as well." I stroke my finger down his cheek lovingly.

"Oh, I'm sure I'll benefit from your gratefulness. Often I hope." He squeezes my ass cheeks and uses his grip to rub me up and down his growing erection.

"So essentially, I'm buying a new spa with my pussy," I smirk at him, but his ability to concentrate on my words left the minute my covered cleft put pressure on his cock.

"You know?" He says more to himself than to me. "I hate it when you cover my pussy." He tugs on the inside of each leg of my pajama pants and rips it up the seam at the crotch, exposing my bare flesh. "Much better," he praises.

"Ah," I moan as his thumbs sweep upward on either side of my clit. Just the promise of his touch sends a shiver over my entire body.

He keeps his fingers dangerously close, yet so far away from where I need him. I know better than to swivel my hips. Nothing keeps him away from me faster than trying to take his power and control of the situation away from him.

He edges closer to my body and strikes at one of my nipples with his mouth. My sensitive bud, which is easy to find in my tank top since it puckered the second I straddled his lap, stiffens further as he pulls his mouth away leaving a ring of wetness on the front of my shirt.

I hum my approval and jut my breast closer to his mouth. He doesn't take the bait but rather reaches inside my torn pajamas and rips them the rest of the way so they now hang separately on each leg.

"Shirt off, Angel," he instructs as he begins to slide his hands under my hips.

I obey immediately and while I'm busy lifting the fabric over my head he begins to lift me up so I'm almost standing over him.

"Pussy in my mouth," he urges and who am I to deny him?

He sweeps his hands inside of my legs and around the back of my hips. This has me almost sitting on his shoulders, my cleft against his hot, talented mouth. I do my best to hold some of my weight on my feet but a handful of licks and prods with his tongue and he's managing all of my weight. He's moaning against my tender flesh, so he doesn't seem too put out by it.

I have to put my hands on the back of the sofa to keep myself from leaning all the way over him. I want to come not smother him. One hand instinctively comes up to grip a handful of his messy hair.

"So good," I praise on a whimper as he nips at my clit with his teeth. I love his teeth. I love his tongue and the way his mouth is working over my body like his sole job is to bring me pleasure.

A hand leaves my hip and I feel his finger skate over the forbidden pucker he loves to tease so much. I gasp at the sensation, loving that too. A delicate touch is all he gives but the hand remains close, the dark promise still a possibility.

My hips begin to buck against him and his hands grip and move me, encouraging the motion.

"Garrett," I pant. "Fuuuccckkk," I moan and my body gives into him, convulsing and clenching; seeking out and not finding something to grip a hold of.

The orgasm was so powerful it exhausted me. Combine that with a rough, long day and I'm very near falling asleep.

"Stay with me, Angel. This won't take long." He kisses up my body as he lowers me back to his lap. "The taste of your sweet pussy always gets me half there."

I don't realize he's pulled his pajama bottoms down his thighs until he lowers me straight onto his waiting cock. I'm filled from tip to root and suddenly much more awake than I was seconds before.

"So tight," he says as I try to shift my hips to alleviate some of the mild discomfort at being filled without warning or preparation. "Fuck, Alexa. Hold still. I don't want to come *that* fast."

I close my eyes and will my body to calm. Eventually, after what seems like ages he begins to slowly lower me up and down his length, his strong arms doing all the work. The feeling is exquisite and I curve my back enough so I can kiss his mouth. I sweep my tongue against his and circle my hips on a downward glide. I swallow his moans as he does mine.

"God, I love you," he whispers against my mouth.

I'm amazed at how far he's come. Once he was able to accept that he loved me and spoke those words the first time, they suddenly became a part of his daily vocabulary. I'm a ridiculously lucky woman to have his heart.

"Shit," He says pulling his mouth from mine so he can look in my eyes. "Can you come again?"

I nod my head yes and begin to take over, increasing the speed and rhythm of my ride. I can hear his teeth grinding as he does his best to hold off on his own orgasm so I can come again. I wonder absently what he's thinking about to take the attention away from his cock which is buried over nine inches deep.

I'm very close and working hard to get there, but it's just out of my grasp. That is until that lone finger skates back over my back entrance. The effect is cataclysmic.

"Now," I moan, giving him permission to let go, and man does he ever.

My orgasm begins to seize him in pulses as his begins; my name on his lips as he reaches the apex. I collapse against his chest. If I thought I was drained of energy before, I was wrong. Now I can barely hold my eyes open.

"Bed," I beg against his chest.

He chuckles under my body, the action shaking me. "Give me a minute woman. You can't treat me to amazing sex and then expect me to walk again within ten minutes." I smile against his warm skin. "Go ahead and go to sleep, Angel. I'll carry you to bed in a bit."

The doorbell chime rings faintly in my head and I feel him lay me down on the couch as he goes to get dinner from the delivery person. I figure he just puts it directly in the fridge because he settles back on the couch and lifts me back into his arms.

I don't know how long we stay on the couch tangled around each other but Garrett, true to his word, eventually stands with me in his arms and carries me to bed. The jostling of his actions only waking me partially.

He places me gently on the bed and stretches out behind me, wiggling until he's flush against my back and his arm is draped over my stomach. Once again we are going to go to bed with no concern for the sheets and the mess we'll have to deal with in the morning.

"At this rate, Angel I'll never get to ask you." He whispers against my head and I'm certain he thinks I'm sleeping and he's said something he didn't intend for me to hear.

So much for getting any sleep tonight.

Chapter 19
Lorali

"This is not what I had in mind when you said you wanted to go shopping for the nursery," Alexa complains beside me.

We're sitting in the lounge area in Macy's and I'm thumbing through their catalog while looking at the pictures on Josie's baby board on Pinterest.

"They don't keep much in stock as far as baby furniture is concerned," I explain and turn the page in the thick book.

Alexa watches over my shoulder and points out the things she thinks Josie will like. I know she's not super excited to be picking out baby things, but she's a good friend to Josie and will do anything to make her happy.

"Their wedding was kind of perfect, right?" I say somewhat dreamily.

"I was thinking the same thing," she admits.

"The way he looked at her when she came out of the door." I sigh. "Perfect. I can't wait for October."

I look over at Alexa and see her face fall. "I'm sorry. I know weddings and babies aren't your thing."

She shrugs and I go back to flipping through the catalog. Now that we know she is having a boy we can select furniture that leans a little more masculine than gender neutral. I talked to Ian about the baby we hope to conceive soon. He's adamant that he has no preference on gender, but I couldn't ignore the shine in his eyes when Josie and Kaleb announced they were having a boy.

I of course just want a healthy baby, isn't that the wish of every mother, but I have no problem letting him know I want a boy first. A big brother to the second child is always a plus. Neither Ian nor I had one. Ian, as an only child, wants to have at least two children. He said his childhood was great, but it would have been better if he had a sibling to spend it with.

Alexa stays quiet for some time and even her minimal involvement with the selections have stopped. I close the book and turn towards her.

"Spill it," I say.

"What?" She says feigning confusion.

"Don't do that. Don't shut me out when something is obviously bothering you." I press her. "Are you and Garrett having problems?"

She huffs like that is the most ridiculous suggestion. "No," she answers. "Just the opposite in fact."

"So what's wrong? Work?" I sit quietly while she debates whether or not to answer me honestly. The time delay hurts; she's usually so open about what's going on.

"Work is shit, but that's not my issue currently." She frowns. "I think Garrett is gearing up to ask me to marry him." She scrunches her nose in mild distaste as if saying the words leave a bad taste in her mouth.

"Shit," I whisper.

"Yeah, shit," she agrees.

"You're going to tell him no if he asks?" I know she loves him and I seriously don't understand her aversion to marriage.

Alexa has lost just about everyone she's ever loved, her parents, her grandmother. She's suffered so much loss it's what turned her into the party girl she was until months ago when she and Garrett decided to make it official. She's always been afraid of getting hurt because she feels like she loses everyone she loves.

Garrett is one hundred percent dedicated to her. He has made a complete one-eighty turnaround in regards to relationships because of Alexa. He's all in. I can see him wanting to marry her. He's watching all of his friends getting married and sees their level of happiness; it's not a far reach that he wants that with her.

"I honestly don't know," At least she's being truthful. "I can't see myself without him. Just the thought turns my stomach. I sure as fuck don't want anyone else."

"Then why the apprehension?" I bend over and place the heavy catalog on the table in front of us.

"Why the rush?" She counters.

"Well, he hasn't asked yet so the timetable is still growing. Honestly? It doesn't seem rushed. It's more like a natural progression." I tell her.

"He wants to buy me a fucking spa, Lor." She pushes herself further back on the couch and slouches.

I can't help the laugh that escapes my lips. "He wouldn't be a Hale if he didn't offer something exuberant like that."

She nods in understanding. "I know he loves me and I love him more than I ever thought I could love another person aside from you girls and my grandmother." She closes her eyes, gathering her thoughts.

I reach out and take her hand in mine.

"But all of it is scaring me. He may be getting ready to ask me to marry him. He told me he may want kids with me one day. I never wanted any of this." I watch as a tear runs down her cheek. She's really upset at all of this.

"Honey," I say and scoot closer to her. "You never wanted any of this or you never allowed yourself to imagine you could have it?"

There is a huge difference in the two and I'm thinking it's the latter that's tearing her up so much. As if admitting that she wants the fairy tale with Garrett will bring her world crashing down. If she doesn't say the words or allow her mind to dream and think of what marriage and family with Garrett would be like, then she won't be destroyed when her inevitable history finally realizes she's happy and shows up to destroy her.

She's plagued by her past and it's keeping her from being completely happy.

"I don't think marriage and kids are in my future," she answers sadly.

"What if that's what Garrett is offering you? Do you want it?" I ask softly, but I'm not just going to give up when she clearly either needs to just talk this out or a nudge in the direction I can tell her heart wants to take her.

She releases a small pitiful laugh. "Do I want to spend the rest of my life with the most magnificent man I ever had the pleasure of meeting? Of course, I do. Garrett says I'm it for him and I feel exactly the same way. Kids? Well, I can't even think of them right now." She squeezes my hand slightly. "But do I want to puke when I picture myself pregnant with his child anymore? No. The trepidation on that subject has dulled a little."

"Well until then, at least, the sex is still hot, right?" She has a lot to think about and I think I've involved myself as much as she'll allow.

She smiles. "The sex is amazing." Her smile isn't completely meeting her eyes.

"I feel a 'but' with that statement," I grin at her.

"He is amazing, Lor. But lately, he's been so passionate and attentive. I mean, he's always attentive. I guess I mean the aggressive edge we've always had has been absent recently." She admits.

I remember the red striped skin on the back of her thighs a month or so ago while they were at our house for a pool party. Ian assured me that she must like that kind of thing and that Garrett would never do something like that to her if he wasn't sure she wanted it.

"So he hasn't spanked you recently," I say with a mild edge of embarrassment.

She throws her head back and laughs and the red flush that comes over my face. I know she thinks I'm probably embarrassed about talking about spanking, when it is actually because I'm afraid she'll realize that I, too, like it when Ian swats my ass on occasion.

Eventually, her laugh dies down. "You can say that," she agrees. "He's more of a 'pain until I squirm, pleasure until I scream' type of guy, but the last month or so it's more about passion and softness." Lines knit her brow as she continues. "I think it's because he's getting ready to propose so he feels like that's how he should act."

"It's sweet that he wants to be super loving before he asks you." I mean it is pretty sweet.

"You don't get it," she says quietly. "I need both sides of him. I need the side of Garrett that ties me up and whips my ass with a riding crop."

My eyes go wide and she laughs again.

"What if he thinks that's how he has to be if we're engaged? How he plans to be if we marry?" She shakes her head no. "I don't want that. I don't want the dynamic to change between us. It can't change." She emphasizes that last part and I know this scares her more than the actual marriage.

She's afraid she'll say yes and when everything is said and done, she will be locked into a marriage with a different man than the one she fell in love with.

"Have you said anything to him about it?" I ask.

She shakes her head no. "I don't want him to know I have suspicions about the marriage thing."

"You can talk to him about your sex life without it going towards the discussion of marriage."

"I'm scared if I mention it the conversation will end up with the question, and I'm not sure I know what my answer will be," she explains. "I won't say yes unless I mean it and I'm afraid we'll start to crumble unless I give him the answer he wants."

I nod my head because I'd feel exactly the same way. I wouldn't agree to marry someone if I wasn't sure that I wanted to. I'd never agree to something like that just because I was afraid of the fallout if I said no, or even not right now.

"Okay, then try to get him to respond the way you want him to," I grin at her. "You're creative. Give it some thought and come up with a sure-fire way to make him spank your ass."

"What do you suggest?" Her grin is devious.

"Go to his club while he's there and dance and flirt with another man," I offer.

She shakes her head no. "Remember the conversation about getting caught playing with myself? I don't ever want him to question my faithfulness to him."

I can understand that. She was pretty torn up that he automatically thought she would cheat on him.

"So take him to one of those kinky clubs and demand he spank your ass in front of a group of people," I say off the cuff, not actually meaning it.

Her smile is from ear to ear. "You are a fucking genius. Lorali Bennett!"

***

The nursery came together perfectly and just in the nick of time. We had the furniture delivered all on the same day and Alexa and I worked all day yesterday getting it just perfect.

Josie is grinning from ear to ear as I open her front door to welcome her and Kaleb back from their week long honeymoon in Cabo. She looks wonderful, sun-kissed and unapologetically happy. Kaleb has a look of apprehension on his face and I know he's worried Josie will be upset that we've overstepped our boundaries by working on the nursery. We've left all of the personal touches and such for her to do herself, or with our help when she's ready.

"Welcome home guys," I say and hug Josie.

"What are you all doing here?" She asks looking around at our entire group.

"We just wanted to welcome you home. We've missed you," I explain.

"Have a good time?" Ian asks shaking Kaleb's hand and giving Josie a quick hug.

"It was wonderful, man. Thank you," Kaleb answers.

"Don't mention it," Ian assures him. "Glad you guys had a good time."

"We actually have a surprise for you," Alexa cuts in and grabs Josie's hand, tugging her gently and forcing her to walk down the hall.

Josie smiles politely and allows herself to be pulled toward the nursery. We all follow behind them and stop as we reach the door to the nursery. This is the room Kaleb had told us she wanted to use for the baby and we have transitioned it into hopefully the perfect beginning to her dream nursery.

Alexa turns the doorknob and pushes the door open dramatically then steps out of the way so Josie can take it all in.

She gasps and brings a hand to her neck as she shifts her eyes and looks at every corner of the room. "I love it," she whispers as she steps further in and turns slowly in a full circle.

The joy is evident in her smile as she reaches for a yellow and gray pillow on the gliding rocker in one of the corners.

"I love the darker wall," she admits pointing to the deep gray accent wall that the crib is on. She lovingly runs her hand over the edge of the crib. "The furniture is perfect. Kaleb, isn't it wonderful?"

He grins and steps near her, every ounce of doubt wiped away at her reaction. I know my sister and I knew she'd be excited about us getting a jump on her furniture. She technically picked it out because we got the exact furniture from the picture she pinned most recently and wrote 'this is perfect' in the caption.

"We only got the furniture and a few accent pieces because we knew you'd want to personalize the rest yourself for the little guy," Alexa tells her.

"Thank you guys," Kaleb says wrapping his arms around his wife, keeping his hands protectively over his son. "You have definitely gone above and beyond with the nursery and the wedding. We've definitely been blessed."

We all smile at him. They deserve all the happiness in the world with what they've been through.

"Well," Ian begins. "It's been way too long since we've all gotten together just the six of us. What does everyone think about getting together soon for dinner at our house?"

We all nod in agreement and promise to check schedules to see when they all match up. It seems all of our lives are absolutely perfect.

I never would have let the thought cross my mind had I known that thinking it was only inviting the worst possible demons in our lives. Demons that would destroy us and possibly alter our lives in a way that we'd never fully recover from.

Chapter 20
Ian

"Hey, guys. Come on in," I tell Josie and Kaleb as I step aside and let them walk by.

"Are we late?" Kaleb asks.

"Nope," I answer. "Alexa and Garrett just got here themselves."

It's been over a week since they got back from their honeymoon and the first time everyone's schedule was clear to get together. Monday night is not the most ideal day of the week, but I know everyone's excited to see each other.

I kiss Josie on the cheek and shake Kaleb's hand as we make our way back to the others who are having drinks in the living room.

I head to the kitchen and grab Josie a cold glass of chocolate milk. Lorali has told me all about her cravings and the nausea she suffers with all day long. Chocolate milk seems to be safe so we made sure we had it in stock.

I hand the glass to her and she takes it graciously. "Kaleb, beer? Scotch?"

He holds his hands up. "I'm on call, man nothing for me. Thanks, though."

"That's awesome, Josie," I hear Lorali says to her sister. "Which one did you pick?"

"I went with the Montessori online school," she answers and takes a long sip of her milk. "I liked their principals and learning style most. It will get me as close to what I had in the public school."

Kaleb squeezes her hand in solidarity, showing her she made the right decision. It's apparent that they struggled with this in some form or fashion.

"So you'll be working from home then?" Alexa asks. "Won't have to make any trips to the office?"

"All from home," Josie says. "The home office for the company is in Utah. I even did my interview over Skype. They have no expectation of ever seeing me in person."

"Man," Garrett says. "If I could work from home every day, I'd never wear pants!"

We all laugh until Josie's stomach makes a rude sound, reminding us all that we are here technically to eat dinner.

"Hungry?" I joke with Josie.

"Seems that way," she answers.

"Well, let's feed the pregnant lady," Lorali says standing from the couch so we can all head to the dining room.

Lorali made chicken parmesan, Italian being her favorite food to make. We also had breadsticks and salad. Dinner was delicious and the conversation among the group was awesome. Loads of laughing and joking around and periodic innuendo because clearly we are all very sexual people.

"Did you see the highlight reel from last night's game?" Garrett asks me.

I shake my head no. What I won't say in mixed company is that Lorali offered to shave me last night and there was no way I was going to watch TV over having her hands on my sack.

"I didn't, but I know the Rockies got their asses handed to them." I did see the score and just by that I have to assume the game was brutal.

"They did, but the Mariners were on fucking fire," Garrett counters.

"We can head down and watch it if you want," I say to the guys.

"Good," Lorali cuts in. "I want to show the girls my dress. Kaleb, Garrett, please keep my fiancé downstairs."

The guys look confused. "Lorali won't let me see the dress," I explain.

"Don't ruin it, man," Kaleb says with a huge smile then turns his attention to Josie. "There's nothing better than seeing your bride in her dress for the first time on your wedding day."

I look at Lorali and laugh at her smug face. "See? I told you. Listen to the man. He's the only one who's done it."

My eyes dart to Garrett and she winces immediately at her faux pas.

"Shit, Garrett," she says softly. "I wasn't thinking."

He tilts his head at her, like her being concerned over his prior wedding was ridiculous. He chuckles. "It's fine, Lor. Jamie's ass rode in the truck with me to the courthouse." He looks over at Alexa, who for some reason, is studiously examining her fingernails. "My next one is the important one."

No one responds, but there's no way to miss the immediate stiffness in Alexa's spine at his declaration to the group.

"So," Lorali says as she stands from the table. "You guys head down to the cave. We'll be upstairs."

"She keeps that dress under lock and key," I tell the guys as we head out of the room.

"That's strange," Kaleb says.

I can't help but laugh. "Not really. She's caught me twice trying to get a peek at it."

Kaleb laughs. "Seriously, man. It's worth the wait."

"Speaking of weddings," I begin as I close the door to the basement behind us. "What the fuck was that shit upstairs, Garrett?"

He just shrugs, like he's not going to eventually spill the beans. "Not like I'll ever get the chance to ask her." He settles into one of the leather recliners and tips his glass of scotch to his mouth. "I've made plans more than once that have been ruined."

Kaleb's phone goes off with a text notification and he pulls it from his pocket. He reads the text silently and frowns.

"Hey, guys. Sorry, I have to cut this short. Duty calls." He shakes both of our hands.

"Hope it's nothing too serious," Garrett says.

"Another day another dollar," Kaleb explains. "Some business burned down and they found a shit ton of cocaine in the guy's office."

"Well, somebody's night just went to shit," I say.

"Hey," he says turning around at the door. "I'll be back to get Josie. Hopefully, it won't take that long."

"Let the girls know you're heading out," I tell him. The last thing I need is Josie freaking out even for a minute wondering where he went.

"Where were we?" I ask as I grab another beer from the mini-fridge. Garrett ignores me, postponing the conversation as much as he can. He hates 'shop talk' as he calls it. Says that Kaleb and I sound like a couple of women when we start talking about our girls.

I settle in the identical recliner beside him.

"You pretty much said you made plans to ask Alexa to marry you and they were… ruined?" I raise my eyebrows, encouraging him to speak.

"Pretty much," is his non-answer.

"You're thinking of marriage?" I can't believe it. I would've bet one of my kidneys that Garrett, no matter how much he loved Alexa, would never go the marriage route again.

He grins at me and nods his head yes.

"Seriously?" I'm dumbfounded.

"Bought the ring and everything." He offers.

"What made you change your mind? You always said never again?" I'm not toying with him. I'm seriously at a loss here.

"I never imagined I'd meet someone like her. She's a game changer man." This I can understand perfectly. Lorali was my game changer.

"I was already thinking about it. It's been in my head for weeks, but then I saw how Kaleb and Josie looked at each other at the wedding." He shakes his head like he's clearing it of the image. "That's what I want, man. I want that with Alexa."

"You feel like that's something Alexa wants?" I know she's been just as 'anti-commitment' as Garrett has been in the past.

"I think so. I've been being really sweet to her. Doing my best to show her how much I love her." He scrubs his hands roughly over his face. "I mean I haven't spanked her ass in forever."

I can't help but laugh at the dynamic of their relationship. "So being sweet entails no spanking huh?"

He shrugs, not making any excuses as to how he handles things in his bedroom.

"So how have your plans been ruined?" I've gotten over the shock that he actually wants marriage.

"Let's see," he starts counting off on his fingers. "My bar manager has had some type of strep shit, so plans had to be canceled so I could go work the bar in his place. Once, Alexa completely forgot about our dinner plans and she's been having such a horrible time at work I didn't push the issue. Johnny came back to work, but he's still not up to par. Hell, *Ampere* is closed tonight because he needed some time to rest after the busy ass weekend and the assistant bar manager had to go back home for a few days due to a death in the family. We had tonight scheduled with you guys and there was no way we were missing that. So I just posted online that we would be closed on Mondays now."

"Business is good enough to do that?" It's an honest question from one businessman to another.

"Business is fucking excellent," he says with a smile. "Line around the block every time the doors are open. But my staff needs a break. I run a tight ship and I haven't found anyone else good enough to start training to help Johnny out. It would mean I'd have to be up there more until they were adequately trained and I want to be at home with my girl."

I nod in understanding.

"It was never an issue before Alexa. Now? I want to be home when she's at home," he explains.

"I get it, man. I've had to make tons of adjustments at work so I can have the extra time with Lor." I pat him on the back as I stand from the recliner to grab another beer.

The conversation shifts back to sports and we settle in and watch ESPN for a while so I'm able to catch the highlights from last night's clusterfuck of a Rockies game.

Garrett yawns beside me before saying, "want to go up and see if the girls want to watch a movie or something?"

I smile at him. "You need your girl huh?"

He smiles back at me. "Me too," I tell him.

They must have had the same idea because just as we are walking towards the stairs to get them, Alexa and Lorali are making their way down.

"Where's Josie?" I ask.

"She was tired so she decided to lie down while Kaleb's gone," Alexa answers.

"You ladies want to watch a movie or something?" Garrett asks.

They both shrug and turn towards the living room.

We argue for at least fifteen minutes on what to watch before settling for *A League of Their Own* on AMC. We were going to lose the battle so we might as well watch one with hot chicks and baseball.

Almost two hours later I stretch under Lorali, who's sleeping with her head on my lap. The end credits have started to run. I glance over at Garrett, who also has a sleeping Alexa on his lap and watch him softly stroke her red hair as if she's the most precious thing in the world to him. If I were a betting man, I'd say she was.

"You guys going to stay over?" I whisper ask him.

He gives a huff. "Might as well." He wiggles his hips and scoots to the side so he can get out from under her.

I do the same thing with Lorali and look down on my beautiful, honey-haired, sleeping beauty. Fuck I can't wait to marry this woman. I can't wait to see her stomach expanding with my baby. I can't wait to start the rest of our lives together.

The sound of the doorbell cause both of them to stir on the couches. They both sit up, hair wild and eyes sleep filled.

I make my way to the door, knowing it's Kaleb coming back to either get Josie or crawl into bed with her. I feel Garrett behind me as I make my way to the foyer.

Chapter 21
Kaleb

The address texted to me on my cell phone was familiar, but I didn't know why until I pulled up outside of the very familiar business.

"Fuck," I mutter under my breath as I get out of my car and walk towards the group of officers and a man recognize as one of the city's arson investigators.

"Mike," I say and reach out and shake his hand. "Must be pretty evident if you're out here already."

"I've got to draw it up still, but there's no guess as to what started the fire and where." We begin walking towards the front of the burned out building. "The fire burned hot and fast. The front's a complete loss and the back's completely destroyed with smoke damage."

We clear the front of the building, my sneakers crunching over charred debris.

I know my night just went further in the toilet when I see Stan Rhodes walking toward me from the back of the building.

"Tell me you were just in the neighborhood and you were bored so you stopped by?" I ask the homicide detective. I'm practically begging him.

"I wish, Perez." We shake hands and I follow him to the very back.

He pushes a door open into a space that is clearly marked as an employee break area.

"Son of a bitch," I groan as he steps out of the way and the body of a young man, I'd guess in his early twenties, comes into view.

He's on the floor face down, dressed in jeans, no shirt or shoes, and a blanket tangled around his feet. There's an empty bottle of vodka beside him. From the looks of it, he passed out drunk on the couch and wasn't cognizant enough to get out of the building before he succumbed to smoke inhalation.

"Poor fucker," I say.

"Yeah," Stan says beside me. "Looks like smoke inhalation, but we won't know for sure until the autopsy report."

"So at a minimum we're looking at negligent homicide and that's only if the fucker who started the fire didn't know this poor fella was back here," Mike adds.

"Well, Stan this trumps me so that means you're in charge," I look at him.

"Yeah. Joy," he says sarcastically.

"Show me why I was called in," I turn and head back out into the heavily damaged area.

"You were called in before we found the DB. They never would've bothered you otherwise," I nod in agreement.

I don't know if me being here and involved in this situation is going to be for better or worse. So much shit is going on right now I haven't had time to filter it all and compartmentalize.

"We hit the office first after we saw how extensive the place was wired for security. Figured we could access the video feed and get our answers before the smoke even cleared." Mike says as we make our way to the very back corner of the building.

We clear the door to the office and I look around. The place is untouched by the flames that incinerated so much of the front. Smoke damage was evident on the walls and in the layer of soot that covered every surface.

"We called one of our IT guys in and he was able to access the cameras." Mike points toward the computer on the desk. It's the only place I've seen so far that the soot has been disturbed.

"He looked in the desk," Mike angles his head to the open drawer. I walk around the desk and see two bricks of cocaine just sitting there. "He was hoping to find the passwords for the system; he found that instead."

"Motherfucker," I mutter and they both look at me oddly. "The security feed?" I ask in an attempt to get them back on track.

"He didn't find the password, but he was able to work his magic and gain access." Mike frowns.

"And?" How do I know shit is about to get worse?

"The entire day's feed has been erased," Mike says. Just as I think that's the worst of it, he keeps fucking talking. "We called the security company. Only one person with access and that is who logged in tonight from this computer."

I don't even want to ask, but I do anyways. "Let me guess? The business owner?"

Mike nods. "He accessed the computer and not only deleted the day's feed, but he also powered down the system so it wouldn't record anything at all. No video since six this morning."

"He accessed the video at four this afternoon, but just erased back even further. The first call came in to dispatch at a quarter after four. Citizen reported smoke coming from the roof. Looks like he cleared the security feed, lit the match, and left." I look at my watch and run the timeline through my head.

This doesn't look good at all.

"Who in their right mind would burn down their business and leave bricks of coke in the desk?" Mike asks no one in particular.

An idiot.

"An idiot," Stan says from the doorway.

I nod in agreement and scrub my face with my hands.

"If he wanted it to all go up in flames why no accelerant back here?" That part doesn't make any sense. If he wanted to burn it all down, he would've gassed the entire building. Especially the area where the drugs were. These are all questions that will come out in the wash in the full investigation.

Right now our job is to look for probable cause, enough to make an arrest. A businessman with means and money makes him a flight risk and that is something we always try to avoid.

"Prints?" I ask anyone who may be listening.

"The crime scene techs just showed up, but the DB has precedence. They'll make it in here eventually." Stan says.

We all know we can't touch shit until CSI clears the scene, so I can't even start my part of the job until they're done. Mike walks past me and out the door of the office. Stan and I turn to follow him.

"He poured what I'm sure is gasoline all over the counter over there. I'm sure he thought the other liquids would aid in the destruction of the rest of the building." We look to the left where the most damage was sustained.

"Hard to go unnoticed with anything more than a small can of gas," Stan explains. "Especially on a Monday afternoon around the time people would start getting off of work and heading home."

I look at my watch. "I've been here almost two hours. Has the business owner been contacted?"

Stan shakes his head no. "With what was found in the office we were holding off. Mike just found out the info from the security company before you got here. With that info, notification is going to be in the form of his arrest."

"That means you, Perez," Mike says and slaps me on the back as he walks away to talk to a couple of his guys that are taking measurements and pictures of the fire damage.

I give Stan a fuck you look. "Sorry, Perez. My scene and I can't leave. Grab a couple of the unis with you since you're out of the bag." He nods towards my plain clothes. "We need to keep this as official as we can."

"Got it, man," I say and turn toward what used to be the door. "See you back at the barn."

I wave over two of the uniformed officers that have congregated in front. These are the types of officers that are never going to promote. They aren't even trying to look like they're working. There's a dead body inside and these fuckers are joking outside in clear view of any reporters that may be present, along with every other citizen who's carrying a news camera in their pocket in the form of a damn smartphone.

My mood is total shit and it's only about to get worse. Two of the officers stop before me, waiting for direction. "You guys follow me."

"Arresting the perp?" One asks.

I nod.

I get back into my unmarked police car and drive across town to the one of the most affluent neighborhoods in Denver. Twenty minutes. That's all I have to wrap my head around what my job is about to force me to do.

I pull up in front of the massive home and exit my vehicle. My heart is pounding along with my footsteps as I climb the handful of steps to the front door.

I press the doorbell and think of my beautiful, pregnant wife. I cringe knowing our world is about to blow up.

The door is pulled open. "Hey, man. Josie's up…" Ian stops talking when he sees the look of resolution on my face as I step aside and the two uniformed officers behind me come into view. "What's going on?" His face is full of innocent confusion.

"Fuck, Ian. I'm sorry to have to do this man." I turn my attention to Garrett. "Garrett Hale." The uniformed officers take a couple of steps closer to Garrett. "You are under arrest for the unlawful possession, distribution, and sale of a controlled substance, arson, and homicide."

Garrett raises an eyebrow at me like he's waiting for the punchline to a horrible joke. Movement behind him catches my attention briefly and I see Alexa and Lorali come around the corner and enter the foyer.

I force my attention back to Garrett and pray that my wife is asleep or at least occupied and I'll be gone before she realizes what's going on. This may destroy us.

I continue to Mirandize Garrett as one of the other officers pulls his handcuffs loose and clasps them to one of his wrists. Garrett is cooperative and I'm sure he's in shock. I know the initial evidence points to him, but a lot of it doesn't make any sense. Once he's hooked up in the cuffs, he's turned back towards me.

"Do you understand your rights as I have read them to you?" I finish.

He glares at me. It's understandable. Just two weeks ago this man stood before my friends and family as a groomsman in my wedding. His cousin, who I consider my best friend is drilling holes in me with his eyes.

"Arson? Homicide? Drugs? What the fuck is going on, Kaleb?" I can tell he's trying to stay calm, but his worry is betrayed by the tremor in his voice.

"I'm not lead on the case. I can't discuss it with you," I say. I want to distance myself, but I know that's not even possible.

"Tell me what the fuck is going on, Kaleb. Don't treat me like some fucking criminal." He's beginning to get frantic.

The officer begins to walk out of the house with him. "Don't say a fucking word, Garrett. I'll have an attorney there as fast as I can." He nods at his cousin.

"Garrett!" Alexa has come out of her shock seeing Garrett being walked out the door in handcuffs. Ian grabs her around the waist. "What the fuck are you doing, Kaleb?"

I look at her and I'm suddenly pained at the anger, hate and rage that she's staring at me with. "I'm just doing my job, Alexa." I turn my attention to Ian and I hope he can see how much I don't take pride in what I've just done. "Get the attorney there as soon as possible, man. It's pretty fucking bad."

He nods at me and I can tell that he's torn. Not between Garrett and me, because that is a given. Family first every time; he's torn between accepting that I have to do this as a police officer and accepting that his best friend just arrested his cousin. Either choice could mean the end of the bond we've formed over the past few years.

"Please keep Josie safe. Tell her that I love her," I beg of him.

Alexa is a sobbing mess by this point and Ian is barely able to keep her on her feet.

"Please, Kaleb? Don't do this," she pleads. Her alabaster skin is splotchy and her eyes are already red and puffy from crying.

I have to clear my throat to keep my emotions in check. This has to be one of the worst days of my life, only coming in second to the day I woke of from being shot. That day I was informed my father was dead. That day ties for first place with Josie's abduction.

"I'm so sorry," I say, and it's aimed at the trio of people still standing in the foyer.

I nod to the other officer and follow him out the front door, closing it softly behind me. I squeeze my eyes shut when I hear Alexa begin to wail on the other side.

Chapter 22
Garrett

I can't think of another more humiliating time in my life than climbing out of a police car while under arrest for drugs, arson, and murder. Even the entire fucking situation with Jamie didn't come close to this level of degradation.

I guess I should be thankful I'm handcuffed in front and not behind my back. They did give me that allowance at least. I've been transported back to Kaleb's precinct and even though I have no level of guilt in any part of this situation I hang my head as I exit the car. The patrol car -Kaleb didn't even transport me himself- pulled into a garage like area and they didn't open my door until we were sealed inside.

I tried speaking with the two uniformed officers while in the car, but they were adamant that they could not give me any details about the case and I would have to ask the detectives once we got back to the station. Although this pissed me off to no end, they remained professional for the most part; only speaking to each other about normal guys shit like my world had not just been thrown off its axis.

The booking process takes much longer than I thought it would; the entire system is more of a hurry up and wait for the next person to do their part. First, I had to sit while the patrolman filled out paperwork. The wait for my mug shot wasn't very long, but the wait for prints was the problem. I waited I know half an hour before the line was cleared and they were able to get to me.

I've been placed in a holding cell with less than desirable people. I can't help but look at them and wonder what they've done. I also have to keep a keen eye and make sure I don't end up in some trouble. A few of them are apparently here for either drug charges or offenses stemming from their drug issues. I inwardly chastise myself for my judgments by outwards appearances of the other men in the holding cell. Seems they could be in here and completely innocent just as I am.

I'm sure they're watching me the same way, trying to figure out what I did. The patrolmen took all my property so I have nothing other than my clothes to speak for the type of man I am. With the way the scraggly man in the corner is watching me, I'm thankful I'm not wearing my Rolex, certain I'd have to fight to keep it.

My stay in the holding cell ends faster than I thought it would with how long the book-in process was but still not fast enough. A uniformed officer, who I've never seen before, calls my name as he opens the cell for me. As he cuffs me I hear the other guys in the cell mention 'judge' and 'detective,' speculating where I'm heading. The officer is close-lipped so I have no clue where I'm heading until I'm taken through several very thick doors and down a long silent hallway.

I'm escorted into a room labeled 'Interrogation 1' where the uniformed officer roughly shoves me into a chair at the table and proceeds to handcuff me to the ring connected to it.

"What the fuck is your problem, man?" I'm not one to disrespect authority but this guy has no reason to shove me like he just did.

"Shut the fuck up, asshole," he says as he backs out of the room. *Hernandez.* I commit the name on the front of his uniform to memory then try to calm my nerves, because seriously? What can I do? Not like I would ever attack a cop, but this guy on the fucking street would be a whole other situation.

Before I can revel in my anger and hatred over the entire situation Kaleb and another very tall, burly man walks in.

"Fuck," Kaleb mutters. "I told Hernandez you didn't need the cuffs." He pulls his key ring from his pocket and begins to release me from the cuffs.

Once free, I circle each of them with the other hand, not realizing how tight they were placed on me until the circulation was allowed back into them.

"Yeah, well," I begin. "The guy's an asshole so no wonder he didn't listen to you."

"Sorry about that, Garrett. We can't help the book-in process, but you weren't supposed to be taken to the holding cell." Kaleb apologizes to me.

The other cop in the room shoots daggers at him, like being cordial is against the rules during an interrogation. Then I narrow my eyes at them; my anger from my arrest as well as the way Hernandez treated me for no other reason than the guy is a douche, coming to a head.

"I have no interest in whatever fucking good cop; bad cop scenario is playing out here." Kaleb leans against the wall with his arms crossed over his chest and has the nerve to look affronted by my statement. "In no way, shape, or form am I involved in any of the shit you guys are saying I did, but I'm not saying a fucking word until my attorney shows up."

Big guy nods to Kaleb instructing him to do God knows what and Kaleb turns and walks out of the room. The man, who I assume is also a detective, sits in the chair across the table from me.

"My name is Randall Holt. I'm not the lead detective, but just filling in for Stan Rhodes until he can get away from the scene." He clears his throat and leans back in the chair crossing one leg over the other at the knee. "Detective Perez just went to go check on your attorney," he explains.

"Who...who died in the fire?" My throat is dry and dread sits in my stomach waiting for the answer. Johnny and the lead waiter are the only ones who have keys to the place beside me. I'd never wish such a death on anyone, dying in a fire is horrendous, but I find myself praying it's not him.

"You've asked for your attorney, Mr. Hale. I can't give you any information on the case until that person arrives," he says with no inflection of his voice.

Detective Holt just watches me from across the table for what seems like hours until the small phone on the wall rings and the person on the other end informs him that my attorney has just checked in at the front and is being escorted to the back.

A few short minutes later the door swings open and Kaleb walks in behind a tall, sophisticated man whom I've never seen before. He's carrying an expensive soft leather briefcase and wearing a visitor sticker badge.

"A moment with my client, please detectives?" He asks and waits for them to stand and leave the room. He narrows his eyes at Holt. "Please don't forget to turn off the cameras, Detective."

Holt looks shocked like he would've never even attempted to record a confidential conversation. It gains him a little respect in my book. Holt nods at the attorney with a mild look of contempt and exits the room.

When I start to speak, he holds his finger up and points to the camera in the corner and waits for the light to go from green to red.

"Mr. Hale, I'm William Prince. Ian Hale called and told me to get here quickly, but it seems he's as in the dark as to details of the charges. Have you gained any knowledge of what your charges are?" He pulls a pen and legal sized yellow tablet and occupies the seat that Detective Holt just left.

I scrub my hands over my face. "What time is it?" I ask because there are no clocks in here and they took my watch when they brought me to the jail.

He flips his wrist and looks down at his arm. "Just after two. The charges?" He prompts again.

"They told me I was being charged with arson…" It literally just dawned on me that Kaleb was called into work because a business burned down and there were drugs inside. "Did my fucking club burn down?" I hadn't even considered the arson charge. It's kind of hard not to get pushed to the back of your head when you're handcuffed and the charge of murder is mentioned.

He nods solemnly. "Ian told me that *Ampere* was where the fire occurred. They haven't shared any news with you?"

I shake my head no. "They've been pretty tight-lipped. I don't even know who it was inside that burned up."

"I didn't do this. I have no involvement with drugs and I sure as fuck didn't set my club on fire." I tell him and even though it's not his job to believe me, I pray that he can see my innocence in my eyes, ensuring he will fight for me and not just for the extensive amount of money he will make from a case like this.

"Where were you today?" He asks.

"I decided to keep the club closed today. We've had staffing issues the last few weeks. Business is good enough we don't really need to be open and many of the other clubs are closed on Mondays." I have no idea why I'm giving him all of this information. I sigh. "I was at home most of the day. Left to grab my girlfriend Alexa from her work and then headed to Ian's."

He's writing all of this down so I wait until he's caught up. "When did you leave your place?"

"Fuck I don't know. I wasn't really on a time schedule. Maybe three forty-five?" I answer.

"Don't ask me. Tell me," he prods.

"Fuck!" I slam my hands on the table. "I didn't spend my day logging my actions. I didn't anticipate needing a fucking alibi!"

"You went straight from home to the girlfriend's work?"

I nod.

"How far is that?" His pen is poised ready for my answer.

"Fifteen minutes maybe."

"How far is your club from her work?"

"Fifteen minutes or so," I respond. "Why are we going over this?"

He writes down what I said and then lays his pen down on the paper. "The detectives are going to ask you the same questions. I just need you to be aware of what your answers are going to be. There is a fire and a dead body. They will know a very good estimate of when the fire started by the nine-one-one call that was placed. So they have a timeline. Now they're going to want to know what the timeline of your day looks like."

"That's all well and good, but when can I get out of here?"

"After you see the judge and you're arraigned," he explains.

"And then I what? Post bail?"

He nods.

"I've asked Ian to procure your passport. With your means the judge will be more accepting of a bond request if they know you can't leave the country." He pauses. "It's going to be hard enough as it is with the murder charge."

"Want to bring the detectives back in so we can tell them no comment?" I chuckle at his nonchalance.

"Is it that easy?" I ask.

He gives me a slight grimace. "Not really but I'll advise you on when to answer and what is safe to say. You say you're innocent so I don't imagine anything you tell them will hurt your case."

"I *am* innocent," I ground out. "Yeah, bring them in I guess."

He stands, walks to the door and knocks on it. Less than a minute later Kaleb and Holt walk back in.

I glare at Kaleb. "Does he have to be in here?" I nod toward Kaleb; his face falls, but he looks resigned and turns to leave.

"Detective Perez," Holts says in a booming, authoritative voice, "is involved in this investigation. Since this is an interrogation, you as the suspect don't get to pick and choose who's in the room."

He settles in the chair across from me and sets a thin folder on the table in front of him. Kaleb stays on the wall, looking uncomfortable and I can't tell if it's because he's been put in a position that puts us on opposite ends of the criminal justice spectrum or if he's disgusted with me as a person.

William settles in beside me. "What are the charges?" He asks as he readies his pen again.

Holt looks at me as he answers his question. "Possession of a controlled substance with intent to deliver, arson, and homicide." His eyes never leave mine and I do my best to hold his gaze but hearing those words officially in this room after just being booked into Denver City Jail make it hard to do.

"Type of drug?" William continues.

"Cocaine." Holt answers.

I wish this man could have been a fly on the wall any number of times I've kicked people out of my club when they've been caught with the shit. I don't even let my VIPs get away with that shit and I know for a fact that at most clubs in the city the owners overlook it.

"I don't use or sell drugs, Detective Holt. Feel free to drug test me or check the cities records. Every time I've caught people using in my club I call an officer out to issue a criminal trespass warning so they can't return." I explain to him.

Holt doesn't respond to me and William continues. "Amount?"

"Two bricks. Hasn't been unwrapped and weighed yet. My estimate is around two kilos."

William continues to write. "The deceased?"

At this, Holt opened the folder and slides a paper across the table. I don't even know why I glanced down at it, but one look and my stomach turned suddenly; the sight of one of my valued employee's lifeless body brings a wave of nausea up my throat. The trash can that caught the contents of my stomach right beside the table tells me they either intended to show me this picture and anticipated my reaction or people puke often during interrogation.

"That wasn't necessary, Detective," William chastises.

I wipe my mouth with the back of my hand and watch as Holt just shrugs his shoulders and places Darren's picture back in the folder.

"Deceased is Darren Davies, waiter at *Ampere*," he answers the question William asked prior to me getting sick.

I swallow roughly. "Darren was a good kid. I have no idea why he would even be at the club. We were closed today."

Once William is done asking questions about the charges, Holt begins asking his own set of questions. I answer each one honestly.

I told him myself, Johnny as my right-hand and Darren as the lead waiter had keys to the building and the alarm codes. The only other person is the boss of the cleaning crew I outsource to.

He asks about the security feeds and I inform him I'm the only one with the ability access it, which makes him smirk a bit. Just as William said he would, he grills me about my whereabouts all day and I answer him as honestly as I was able to answer my attorney.

Holt asks questions for what seems like hours, but he's very calm and mostly professional about it all and I have to wonder if he would behave the same way if I didn't have counsel present. Eventually, he grows weary of asking the same questions or he's run out of ways to alter them to get me to slip up.

It's daytime by the time we are done and we're informed that the judge is on the bench and ready to begin. As I'm walked, back in handcuffs, to the small courtroom in the jail, I realize that I didn't ask nor was I offered a phone call. I'm hoping I won't need to make one and I will be heading home shortly, but if things don't go my way I'm hoping they will allow it after this hearing is done.

More than anything in the world I need to hear Alexa's voice right now.

Chapter 23
Alexa

Hours. He's been gone for hours. Not only has he been arrested but I somehow allowed Ian to talk me into not going up there. I had him bring me home to get his passport and I stayed so I can be here when Garrett calls or gets to come home. I made Lorali promise me that she will go to the police station with Ian since I'm at home.

She's texted me constantly so I know his attorney made it up there quickly. She did tell me that the attorney walked to the back to meet with Garrett and the detectives and she hasn't seen him in hours. Five to be exact. I can't even imagine the hell he's going through.

I don't know policy and procedure as far as the police are concerned, but I'm certain the local news anchors have much more news than they should. They release the name of the man who died in the fire. Darren Davies. Doesn't ring a bell to me but I haven't been to the club but a few times since being shot and that was just to visit with Garrett or hit him up for an after work quickie if he wasn't going to be home until late.

I had to stop watching the news. After a while it just became repetitive. *Police have someone in custody.* They haven't said Garrett's name yet, but it's only a matter of time. *Several kilos of cocaine were found in the building.* How would they know that shit?

The stress of it all hit full force a couple of hours ago and that's when the drinking started. I know that drinking while upset and stressed out is the worst thing to do, but my nerves can't handle this situation without a little help.

By the time Lorali texts me to tell me that the judge relented and is allowing Garrett to be released, I'm drunk to the point of not even getting off the couch. I immediately regret my decision and the two bottles of wine I emptied solo while waiting to hear about the situation. Now I'll be a mess when Garrett gets home and he doesn't deserve that.

I don't know how much time has passed between Lorali's last text and when I'm jostled awake on the couch. I'm engulfed in the delicious scent of Garrett as he scoops me up from the couch and carries me to our room.

"I need you, Angel," he whispers in my ear, but I'm still clouded in the haze of alcohol and don't wake up fully. I've failed him when he needed me the most.

***

I slowly wake from unconsciousness. I say that because I wasn't sleeping, I was passed the fuck out. My alcohol tolerance is apparently low since I hardly drink anymore; that coupled with the fact that two bottles of wine would put almost anyone in a stupor.

I groan as I turn on my back, missing the feel of Garrett. If he's in the bed, he's normally spooned against me or vice versa. Turning over on my left side I see that he is in the bed, but he's sitting up with his back against the headboard. I take notice that I've been stripped and I'm naked in the bed. Even with everything going on Garrett undressed me last night, knowing I hate to wear clothes.

"Hey," I whisper, my voice gravely. "I'm so glad you're home." I admit and run my hand up his thigh.

He looks down at me dismissively and I'm hit with shame. I wince knowing I never should've drunk last night.

"Did you get any sleep?" I trail my fingertips against his abs hoping I can seduce him and make him forget about yesterday.

I see his cock twitch in his pants so I'm surprised when he grabs my hand and keeps me from stroking it.

"No," he says with no emotion.

I gape at him. The anger I can work with, the frustration I can even build on; but no hint of any emotion shows on his face as he looks at me. His blank expression sends chills down my spine. The man I love and the man who I thought was gearing up to ask me to marry him is not the man that's in this bed with me.

That man, I'm sure, was lost the second the handcuffs were clicked onto his wrists last night at Ian's house. I pray he's only missing and not gone forever.

Garret swings his legs over the side of the bed and stands never taking his eyes from mine as I plead for forgiveness, not completely sure the number of sins I need to be forgiven.

"Alexa," he says pointing the floor at his feet. "Knees."

Even though I'm uncertain of the situation because of his aloofness, I scramble off the bed and kneel at his bare feet. I drop my head submissively, still having complete faith that even if he's upset with me, or the situation he's facing in general, he would never do anything to hurt me. He may be mad, but I'll never doubt his love for me.

"Clasp your hands behind your back and keep them there." I hear the rustle of fabric and see his boxer briefs pool at his feet. I follow his command as he kicks them absently to the side. "Unclasp them and I'll keep you tied up all day."

My sex grows slick at the delicious threat, but I have no intention of disobeying. I know he'll make this good for me as well but more importantly if this is what he needs right now, then I'll give him anything he asks for. *Or takes.*

"Suck," he grunts and I feel the heat of his cock on my cheek.

I open my mouth and lick him from root to tip just how I know he likes it, peering up at him as I do. He's staring straight ahead and other than the sharp burst of precome I'm blessed with, no other emotion registers on his face.

I suck voraciously on the tip of his thick length repeatedly until the surfeit of sensation causes him to grip a handful of my hair and he pulls me off.

Finally, he peers down at me but the smirk or heavy-lidded eyes are not what I get. On his face instead is a flat if not mildly maniacal look of mild contempt.

"Suck it right or I will tie you down and fuck your mouth until you pass out from lack of oxygen." I whimper and nod my head in understanding.

He's upset and I know that is the only reason he's acting like this; however, I feel slightly twisted because my reaction to his threat is beginning to seep down my legs.

He keeps his hands tangled in my unruly bedraggled hair and rather than fuck my mouth he uses his hold on me to push and pull my mouth down his length. I gag slightly each time he presses me down his full length, yet I try to take even more on every downward slide knowing he loves the sound of me struggling with his cock in my throat.

I want to reach up with my hands and cup his heavy, swaying sac and I also have a sudden urge to lick a finger and slide it inside of him, but I don't. He was very clear about his expectations and I know with the mood he's in, testing him would not benefit me.

A whisper of a grunt is the only warning I get before he explodes down my throat. I drink every last drop of him and continue sucking, hoping for more. He may not be able to verbalize his pleasure, but the mildly salty thickness that just slid down my throat is proof enough to me that he enjoyed it.

He briskly pulls his unflagging cock from my mouth and tugs me up. Keeping a commanding hold on my hair he leads me out of the room, down the hall, and into the guest bedroom. I have no idea when he did it, but the bed has been shoved to the side and a leather covered saw horse is taking up space in the room, cuffs and various tie-downs connected to each of the four legs.

I stare at the leather covered contraption in both awe and trepidation. His intentions are perfectly clear.

"What...?" Before I can finish the thought, his hand lands solidly on my bare ass, causing me to take a step forward.

"Keep your mouth shut, Alexa or I will ball gag you." I snap my lips closed.

Apparently I'm on a need to know basis and I don't need to know when he added this contraption to the guest room. It's going to be rather hard to explain should we ever have overnight guests.

He tugs gently on my hair and leads me the rest of the way into the room until my hips are against the end of the implement. He releases my hair and I obediently lay my stomach on the top, and spread my legs, lining them up with the legs of the saw horse, and dangle my hands near the other cuffs at the front.

"Good girl," he praises as a finger drifts down the full length of my spine.

I smile at his words; happy to be pleasing him but, even more, thankful that he's finally verbalized something other than delicious threats.

I close my eyes and try to settle my nerves, anxious at not knowing what he's going to do. As he ties my legs and arms down, I begin to criticize myself for being upset with the soft side of Garrett that I've had for the last month. I told Lorali I wanted more and I'm getting what I asked for tenfold.

Once I'm secured to the bench, he places a thick blindfold over my eyes, successfully blocking out any and all light. Next comes the noise canceling headphones, making my shallow, uneven breaths the only thing I can hear.

I whimper when my inner thigh is stroked with cold leather. The anticipation of his assault is exquisite and sends goose pimples over every inch of my heated, exposed skin.

The initial slap of what I can only assume is a riding crop is hard enough to make me cry out. The heat radiating from the point of contact outward. I wiggle my hips, my body begging for the next bite of pain. Garrett does not disappoint.

He didn't ask me to count the hits like he has in the past when I've done something that required 'punishment,' so I do my best to stay quiet, but I end up begging him. I beg him to stop and then beg him for more.

I don't know which end is up and it seems like it will never end. What I do know is my ability to sit comfortably was taken more than a dozen hits ago.

He must grow weary of the begging because less than a minute after his last swat my jaw is tugged open and the taste of rubber hits my tongue as he straps a ball gag around my face. I begin to tremble as every one of my ways to safe word is taken from me. I'm beginning to question the whole situation and my safety, never having been at anyone's complete mercy before. This wouldn't bother me as much if I was certain that the man in this room is the same man who professed his love for me yesterday.

Just as total panic begins to set in, I feel him place a tiny metal jingle bell in my hand and force my fingers to clasp around it. He strokes my cheek gently and I think my Garrett is back but before I can take a second breath, he grips both of my tortured ass cheeks in his hands.

I scream around the gag and then whimper as he slams into me. My body does its best to accommodate the sudden intrusion. Garrett doesn't even slow his brutal thrusts when I erupt around him, my orgasm gripping him repeatedly; instead he smacks my ass in the very spot that he caused the most damage setting off another climax right on the heels of the first one.

He hammers into me until he suddenly and without warning pulls free from my clinging core. I expect the sting of his hot come on my ass, but instead I feel his essence dripping from me and down my thighs. He powered through his own release.

Immediately he uncuffs my legs and wrists and removes the headphones. I lie on the bench trembling, trying to calm my raging pulse. I can hear him leave the room but he hasn't said I can get up so I wait. It isn't until I hear him walk down the hall and close the door to his office, shutting me out completely that I realize he's finished.

I stay on the bench a while longer and let the blindfold covering my eyes catch my tears.

***

Garrett stays in his office for the rest of the evening. I don't know exactly how long our scene lasted, but it was after six in the evening when I finally managed the courage to pull myself up from the bench and get a shower.

The tears continued to flow in the shower, in part to the sting of the welt marks on my ass as the hot water sweeps over them, but largely because I've never felt so alone in my life. Not when my parents deserted me, not even when my grandmother and only living blood relative passed away from breast cancer.

Garrett is right down the hall and he couldn't be farther away right now if he was across the pond in England. I can't call Lorali and tell her about what happened and what I'm feeling because I just told her not too long ago that I missed this side of Garrett.

Well, sort of. This side of Garrett I've never seen before. Even when we had agreed to a one-night stand months ago, he didn't treat me so dismissively. That's the part that hurts the most. He wasn't there to tend to me after the most in-depth scene we've done. The biggest thing I'm concerned over is I don't know if it was punishment for being intoxicated when he got home last night or if this is what he needs from me with the situation of his arrest.

I can be who he needs me to be, for now, but I won't be able to handle him not ever touching me with gentleness. Imagining him not telling me he loves me is enough to cause another round of tears.

"Mr. Thomas," I say after the voicemail beeps indicating it's recording. "I have some personal issues I'm working through and will need to take some time off. Once I have a better grasp of how long that will be, you will be the first to know."

He calls back almost immediately, obviously screening his calls and chastises me for needing so much time off so often and how it is unprofessional and how the spa can't handle the salaried employees taking off when some hourly employees had to be laid-off because sales were down.

I lost it.

Right then and there I quit my job with no notice and no other plans for my future. I never took my future into consideration. After the day I had, I was not going to let someone who I did not respect talk to me the way he did. I gave him every piece of my mind that I'd been filing away over the last several months and then hung up on him. Let *Elite Spa* crumble; I had other things to worry about.

It's close to midnight when I get a text from Garrett. *Office.* That's all it says, so I comply because I've already told myself I will be what he needs for now.

He's sitting in his office chair and watches my eyes as I step in closer to him; the same blank look on his face as I step closer to him.

"Knees," he commands.

Here we go again.

An hour later, I'm a panting, sticky mess. At least, this time, he opted for nipple and clit clamps, leaving my sore ass alone. My body is completely sated, but my heart has been further damaged by his lack emotional involvement.

I haven't felt his lips on mine for over twenty-four hours now; the longest we've ever gone since getting back together after my shooting. The closest thing I get to affection from him is the tender touch to my clit as he fills my ass with a butt plug, which he does *after* he comes, so I know he's not done with me yet.

Chapter 24
Lorali

It has been weeks since Garrett's arrest and things could not be worse. Not that anyone even wants to get together but we haven't all been in the same location since Kaleb knocked on our door with two uniformed officers and took him away in handcuffs.

I managed to convince the girls to get together for some wedding stuff. I feel guilty for even asking, but Ian assures me that things are under control as best they can be and we should continue to do what we need. He's certain the case will be dismissed and we should live as if it will happen any day.

I pick Josie up from her house first. She seems a little more laid back and I think her honeymoon and time away to relax has helped. We grab Alexa next. She insisted I pick her last, refusing to go to Josie's for fear of running into Kaleb-even though I assured her he's at work. She wasn't taking any chances.

Alexa makes her way out of her apartment building less than a minute after I sent her a text letting her know we were here. I'd never say it to her, but she looks horrible. Her hair seems flat, she's more pale than usual, and she has bags under her eyes. There is no way to ignore her wince when she sits gingerly in the backseat of the car. I want to ask her what's been going on since Garrett was released from custody, but I'm honestly afraid of her answer.

I stick with what I hope is a safe subject as I catch her eyes in my rearview mirror. "What's Garrett up to today?"

I watch as she cuts her eyes to Josie like she's afraid to speak candidly in front her, in fear that Josie might tell Kaleb what she says.

"I think he had planned to call and see if Ian wanted to work out or something," she finally answers but then doesn't offer anything else.

I'm at a loss at how to get us back to the relationship we had before. I do know that Alexa doesn't blame Josie for what's going on, but I'm sure she despises Kaleb. Personally, I'm torn. I know Kaleb is only doing his job but at the same time I'm extremely upset over the entire situation.

"What are the plans today?" Josie asks and I can tell she's trying to lighten the mood.

"We're meeting with the caterer and baker today," I tell her.

She smiles, but it doesn't reach her eyes. I know she can feel the heavy tension in the car. I pull up outside of the business that *Elisabel Elite Events*, my wedding planning organization, recommended.

"I've had it," I say, putting the car in park and not turning the ignition off. "We just need to put all the shit on the table so we can start getting passed it. I can't handle all the stress and I know it's not good for the baby."

"What's going on with the case, Josie?" Alexa just dives right in. I shouldn't have expected any less.

"What do you mean?" Josie asks turning in her seat so she can see Alexa better.

"What has Kaleb said to you?" Alexa prods.

"Kaleb hasn't said anything to me specifically about the case," she answers quietly.

Alexa huffs and I see her cross her arms over her chest and sits back further against the seat. She winces at the contact and sits up straighter, keeping her back from touching the seat back.

"I don't deserve that, Alexa," Josie says with a little more fire in her voice. "Kaleb won't say anything about it. And if I'm being honest I haven't even had the chance to ask him. Kaleb is *always* working on Garrett's case."

"What is he hoping for? The fucking death penalty?" Alexa asked heatedly.

"Are you kidding me?" Josie asks affronted. "The only thing he has said is things don't line up. He makes it sound like he's doing his best to prove Garrett is innocent and the only way he can do that is to find the guy who did do it so he can clear his name."

I watch in the rearview mirror as a tear rolls down Alexa's cheek. "Sorry," she apologizes.

"Please don't jump down my throat, and if it's not too much to ask, please don't bash my husband. We've hardly seen each other and we've not made love in weeks." Josie admits. "We're newlyweds; we should be going at it like rabbits."

Alexa smirks at her. "Watch what you wish for," Alexa says and then turns her head to my line of sight. "I never should have complained about the softer side of Garrett."

"Uh, oh," I say and wrinkle my nose at her admission.

"Yeah, I haven't seen that side of Garrett since before all of this shit blew up."

"I noticed you wince when you got in. How bad is it?" I say to her.

"Physically? Nothing more than I can handle. Emotionally? That's a whole other story." She looks out the window, breaking her eye contact with me. "He's been very detached lately."

"Have you talked to him about the charges?" I ask because I'm concerned about his well-being including his mental health.

Alexa shakes her head no. "He won't talk to me. He pretty much just stays in his office until he's ready…," she pauses briefly. "We have hardly seen each other. The only time it seems he wants to be around me is to fuck."

"I'm completely in the dark also," I admit with shame. Ian has always been upfront and honest with me. "Ian won't tell me anything either. He just acts like it hasn't happened and refuses to answer questions with any specifics."

We all sit quietly for a minute, reflecting on each other's situation.

Alexa's circumstances continue to bother me as does her physical condition. She's normally so put together. "So you work all day and then when you get home, you service him until he's had his fill?"

She lets out a weak laugh. "Forgot to tell you guys about that I quit my job. Right after he was arrested. The past several weeks it has been nothing but Garrett and me at home. I haven't been to the salon," she says and gives a half-hearted fluff of her hair. "Haven't had my nails done." She holds her hands up to reveal the damage to her manicure or lack thereof.

"He's abusing you," Josie whispers my thoughts out loud.

She glares at her. "He is *not* abusing me," she says icily but doesn't defend his actions any further.

"Alexa," I say softly, hoping that my love for her comes across as just that rather than an attack on Garrett. "Your back and bottom are so sore you can hardly stand the touch of the seat on them, and he's not communicating with you other than to have sex with you."

She tries to hide the tear that manages to sneak down her cheek. "I love him. If this is what he needs right now, then this is what I'll give him. He's dealing with so much more than we are right now. I'm glad he needs me right now. I don't want him to keep all that shit bottled up."

"Kaleb admitted to me that he feels guilty for being the one to arrest him," Josie whispers from beside me. "I think that's why he's working so hard to figure out what happened. He didn't ask to be the one to arrest him. He did say he hoped things would be easier if someone was there that he knew. I know you hate him. I just wanted you to know that."

Alexa sighs deeply from the backseat. "I don't hate him, Josie. I hate this entire situation."

"Thank you," Josie says. "I just hope when all of this is over things can go back to normal."

"I feel like shit for keeping up with the weddings plans," I offer.

"You shouldn't," Alexa says. "Life has to go on. We can't let this rule our lives anymore than it already is."

"Plus," Josie says rubbing the tiny little bump on her stomach. "I could go for some food right now."

We all laugh. "Morning sickness gone I take it?" Alexa asks and I can tell she sincerely wants to know.

"For the most part," Josie says. "Now I get heartburn from everything."

"Ugh, no thank you," Alexa says holding up her hands, her view of having children standing tall.

"Well let's go in here and stuff our faces!" I tell them turning off the car and opening my door.

It seems we've resolved the issues within our little group of girls, but it's the group as a whole I'm concerned we may never be able to heal.

Chapter 25
Josie

"We have to get together again soon," Lorali says as she's dropping me off from our outing to the caterer's.

"Anytime," I agree. "School doesn't start for another few weeks. Just let me know."

I wave and watch as she drives away. We dropped Alexa off first and Lorali has some event she has to go home and get ready for.

For the first time today I realize that I had no fear about my safety. I was so nervous about what it was going to be like around Alexa since it's the first time we got together since the arrest that I never even gave weight to the fear that has been clinging to me since my abduction.

Thinking of it now does make me move up the driveway quicker, though. My fear only increases when I see a big red envelope on the front porch with my name on it. I don't want to touch it and I also don't want to leave it, but, more importantly, I don't want to be outside the safety of my home.

I scoop it up and unlock the front door, deactivating the alarm as I walk past the system on the wall on my way to the living room. I sit down on the couch and convince myself that I'm being silly and I shouldn't be fearful of an envelope. There is no blood oozing out of it and there are no lumps, only what feels like paper.

Against my better judgment, I open the sealed tab at the top and pour the contents on the coffee table.

Worst mistake ever.

I'm faced with picture after picture of my husband in various compromising, sexually explicit situations with another woman. My world comes crashing down around me.

I try to tell myself that Kaleb would never cheat on me but can't keep my mind from thinking of all the time he's been gone recently. How closed off he's been.

I begin to sob and it doesn't even stop when I hear the front door open informing me that Kaleb is home from work.

I feel his warm arms wrap around me. "Not again, Mariposa. What has you so upset?" He coos in my ear.

I tug free of his arms, my stomach beginning to turn at the feel of his arms around me; the one place I never wanted to leave is now the place I can't even stomach to be.

He tries to wipe my tears from my face and I pull out of his reach.

"Josie?" he pleads.

I can't manage words so I just point at the black and white pictures that have gone untouched on the coffee table. As I glance at them again, they seem grainy like they've been pulled from a video. *Just great, now there's video proof my husband is cheating on me.*

"What the fuck," he says with a gasp, picking them up and flipping through them. "I can't believe Jessica sent this shit." He says and begins cussing in Spanish.

I narrow my red, puffy eyes at him. "Well, it seems Jessica is no longer happy with being the other woman."

"Other woman?" His eyes go wide. "No! Josie, these are from a long time ago. How could you ever think I'd cheat on you?"

"Oh, no you don't!" I raise my voice at him. "You're not pushing this back on me! How could I ever think? You're never home Kaleb. You've hardly touched me the past few weeks."

"Who is she?" I ask bitterly. "What is she to you?"

"Her name is Jessica Riley. She works at the PD." I hiss and he holds his hands up in surrender.

"What is she to you?" I ask again.

"Nothing," he says so convincingly I almost believe him. "We had sort of a friends with benefits thing going on long before I even met you."

"Had?" I say in disbelief.

"Mariposa," he says calmly and holds the pictures in front of him. I angle my head so I don't have to stare at him. "How hard did you look at these pictures?"

"Long enough to see my husband cheating on me with a stacked brunette." I fire back at him.

"Look at the pictures, Josie." The one on top is of him with his eyes closed, bare chest and the back of *Jessica's* head. Clearly he's enjoying the blow job if the way his eyes are closed and his head is thrown back is any indication.

"What do you see?" Is he trying to torture me?

"Besides my husband getting sucked off by some whore?" I raise my eyes to his.

"I wasn't your husband then," he says slowly and calmly. "Have you ever seen me without this?" As he says this he brings his hand up and rubs the short stubble on his face.

I glare back at the pictures and back at him. Grabbing the pictures from his hands and flipping through them; his beard missing from everyone.

"I had to shave to make entry on a house with swat. They used tear gas and I had to wear a facemask. I don't get as good of a suction to my face with the hair." He explains. "These are from February, Mariposa. Months before I ever laid my eyes on you."

"Kaleb," I whisper unable to find the words to say. The only thing worse than not trusting someone is finding out you're wrong and them knowing you questioned their dedication. I begin to cry again.

"No, Josie." He scoots closer to me on the couch and touches my face. "Please don't cry. I hate it when you cry."

"I'm sorry I jumped to the worst possible conclusion," I say on a sob.

He doesn't gloat, he doesn't get mad at me for questioning his faithfulness; instead he kisses me, passionately.

"I've missed you so much," I mumble against his lips between kisses. "I've been so lonely."

"Shhh," he says and holds his finger against my lips. "Can I make love to you?"

It kills me that he feels like he has to ask. I resolve myself to getting a few things off my chest, but first I need him as much as he needs me right now.

"Please," I whisper past his finger on my mouth.

He stands and sweeps me up in his arms, kissing me the entire way to our bedroom. He undresses me slowly and then insists that I do the same to him. I run my hands over every inch of his golden skin I can reach.

Once naked he lifts me and places me in the center of the bed never taking his mouth from mine. He cups my breast, kneading it and rolling the tip between his skilled fingers. Before long his hand is skating down my side and over my mound.

He groans when his fingers slide easily through my desire. "So ready for me," he says huskily.

"Kaleb," I whisper pleadingly as I rotate my hips on his working hand.

He lines his body up with mine, the thick head of his cock nudging my lips open, begging for entrance. I close my eyes and wait for bliss but once they are shut the pictures of him with another woman flash in my mind. I squeeze them shut even harder and try to will the images away.

"Josie," Kaleb whispers and almost like he's reading my mind he continues. "Please open your eyes. Look at me, Mariposa. Watch me; see how much I love you." He strokes his hand down my cheek delicately as he slowly slides inside. "There is only you. I've already forgotten anyone who came before you."

He slowly begins to slide in and out of me and my eyes flutter begging to close, but I keep them open. I'm no expert on relationships, but when Kaleb is looking at me, I've never doubted his love and devotion.

I score his back with my nails on a particularly masterful stroke and he groans against my neck. He fills me so completely body, mind, and soul.

He rotates his hips on every down stroke, teasing my clit, torturing it slightly before withdrawing. By the first hint of my orgasm, I'm wound so tight, I'm afraid of the devastation it will leave behind.

Kaleb reads my body like a book. "Come with me," he commands softly.

My body obeys; the first pulse of his orgasm giving mine permission to begin. I moan uncontrollably and he swallows my cries as he kisses me deeply. His hips continue to move slowly for several more minutes as he milks every tremor from my body. I smile against his mouth as he whispers words of benediction and promises against my lips.

Eventually, he settles in beside me with his eyes closed and his fingers ghost over my overheated skin. He tickles and traces over the entire front of my body, leaving goose pimples in their wake.

He settles his hand over my lower belly on the tiny bump that is there. Something he used to do before chaos broke out in our world.

"Josie!" He sits up abruptly and his eyes dart down to my stomach. He's just now noticing the little-raised hill below my belly button. "The baby?" He asks in amazement. I nod and smile. "Can you feel him move?"

"Still too early for that the books say." His happiness is infectious.

He settles back down beside me but never removes his hand from my stomach; his fingers flexing against it periodically.

He sighs loudly like it's the first time he's been able to release his breath in ages.

"Bad day?" I ask and place my hand over his.

"Bad couple of weeks," he answers. "I'm sorry I've been gone so much these last couple of weeks. This case is not producing the results I was hopeful for in the beginning."

"Just the case has you frustrated?" I know I shouldn't prod and I'd never tell anyone if he disclosed something to me and asked me not to tell, but I've been in the dark with my husband's life for weeks.

"I wish," he says softly. "We had a jail sergeant shove Garrett around while he was in custody. His attorney has asked for charges to be filed against him. I don't really like the guy but I watched the video and he did what Garrett says he did. Marco's career could be over from something almost every cop has done out of frustration."

My blood runs cold at a memory from my abduction. "Marco?" I whisper.

I feel him nod against the top of my head.

"Not a very common name is it?"

"Not around here," he answers. "Josie," he pulls away from me. "What's wrong? Why are you shaking?"

"When," I have to clear my throat and start over. "When I was in the closet," I swallow around a lump in my throat I can't seem to clear. "When I was in the closet, I heard them talking about being lucky Marco called and gave them a heads up about a raid on another house."

His eyes go wide, but he stays silent for a few minutes likes he's trying to work something out in his head. "Are you sure that's what you heard?" He eventually asks.

"Certain," I answer truthfully. "They said he worked at the police department. One of the reasons they said they kidnapped me was because the 'kitchen' was raided, which I find odd because, what's the big deal with someone raiding a kitchen?"

His eyes narrow and I'd be fearful for Marco's safety if he were in the room with us.

"They're referring to a meth lab, Josie." He stands from the bed and begins to get dressed. He pulls on a shirt, boxers and tugs his pants up his legs.

I watch as he reaches into his pocket and pulls his cell phone out, selects a name from his contacts and holds it to his ear.

"Holt," he barks into the phone. "Let me tell you about some pillow talk," he begins. I hear him growl. "If you ever say something like that about my wife again, I'll forget you're my superior."

He pulls his phone away from his ear and I can hear laughing from the other end.

"This is fucking serious, Randy," Kaleb tells his boss. "My wife said she remembers the people from her abduction mentioning that a man named Marco gave heads up on that raid out on Old Post Oak Road."

He pauses as Detective Holt speaks on the other end.

"I don't know, but how many Marco's could there be out there?" He listens. "How about we proceed with the charges against him for police brutality, we both saw the video. See if we can't get Anthony in with him. People seem to love talking to him."

Another pause. "No, I don't think he started working until after we last used him."

Kaleb grows silent once again. "I appreciate that man. You know I can't take the lead on this because of Josie, but I'd like to be able to get more answers on her case. The other seems like a dead end at this point."

I wince, knowing he's talking about Garrett's case.

Chapter 26
Kaleb

"I hate that I'm leaving you again," I tell Josie and trail my fingers down her cheek and run my thumb across her kiss swollen bottom lip. "I don't want to leave you alone."

"I'll be fine," she says not quite convincingly.

I look at my watch. "Mia will be home in about an hour. I already made arrangements for a uniformed officer to bring her here as soon as she gets back to the station from her training."

Her eyes light up and I love that she loves Mia as much as I do. I know that she is a police K9, but that doesn't make her any less part of the family.

"I'll text you," I promise as I kiss her at the inside door leading to the garage. "Check to make sure its one of my guys before you answer the door." I bend down and pick up my utility bag from the floor at my feet. I don't really need it, but I didn't want Josie to see me carrying out the envelope with the pictures Jessica sent. I have more than one person to deal with tonight.

She nods at me and steals one last kiss before I leave. The kiss turns into more the second her lips are on mine. We've both been deprived and I hate that I've been away so much.

Her hands roam my body as her mouth explores mine. I unbuckle my pants and push them down, the weight of my firearm dragging them to the ground. I lift Josie so her legs are tangled around my waist and slowly inch us to the wall as she hovers right over the head my throbbing erection.

"Is this okay?" I ask against her neck.

"Are you asking me if it's okay to make love to me?" she giggles and bites my ear.

I groan. "I'm asking if it is ok for me to fuck my wife against the wall instead of making love to her in our bed." I qualify.

"Yes, please," she answers and I slowly lower her onto me, coating myself in her wetness.

I spend the shortest five minutes of my life pounding into my petite wife against the door leading into the garage. By the time I'm done, she's so pliable that I have to carry her to bed.

"Sleep well, Mariposa," I whisper and kiss her forehead as she snuggles deeper into our bed. The same bed I've hardly seen recently.

Less than two hours after getting home I head back to the precinct which is beginning to seem more like home since I've spent so much time there recently. For the first time in my life, I'm starting to regret becoming a cop and not a banker like my mother had wanted.

When I get to the precinct, I head straight to Holt's office. It's late enough in the evening that the place is all but deserted, which is a good thing considering we are dealing with one of our own in this situation.

Holt is sitting at his desk as I walk into his office and close the door behind me.

"What's the game plan?" I ask as I sit down.

"We have to process this tomorrow. That gives us time to get Anthony in place. If we pick him up tonight, it will look suspicious." Holt explains. "I drove by his house on the way back up here and there were no cars in the driveway."

"He's probably at Jessica's," I mutter under my breath.

"What's that?" Holt asks.

"He's involved with Detective Riley," I inform him. "She was wrapped all around him in the parking lot a few weeks ago. I don't know if they're still together."

He leans back in his chair and steeples his fingers under his chin. "Really?" He asks as if this changes things.

"Yes. Does this change our plans?" I have no idea why their relationship would change what we need to get from Hernandez as far as him informing on the raid.

"Detective Riley was in my office when I got the call about Trina Gilbert being connected to Alexa Warner's shooter, Blake Evans. She sat in here while I made the calls to set up the raid." He says in a low tone that grows in anger with each word.

"Fuck," I collapse back in my chair. "You think she's involved." It's a statement, not a question because the answer is obvious.

"She's the link to the raid; she's the link to Marco. I can't think of another way for Marco to get the information as quickly as he did. Can you?" I shake my head no because it's so apparent.

"I think I need to recuse myself," I tell him.

"Because your wife is connected to Trina Gilbert," he provides as reasoning.

"Full disclosure, sergeant," I reach down into my bag and pull the envelope out with the pictures of Jessica and me. I hand them to him. "I was in a brief sexual relationship with Detective Riley earlier this year."

He slides the pictures halfway out of the envelope and pushes them back in. "Fuck, Perez."

"Yeah," I say in acceptance.

"This pile of shit just keeps growing, doesn't it?" He tosses the envelope with the pictures back to me.

"What do we do now?" I know what he has to do because he's a by-the-book type of cop.

"We need Riley out of the precinct before we can even think about getting information out of Hernandez," he says. His eyes light up with an idea and from the looks of it, it's going to be one I won't like. "How do you feel like taking one for the team?"

***

I'm steaming fucking mad by the time I leave Holt's office. The plus side is I know I'll never have another issue with workplace bullshit keeping me from doing my job. I've never regretted fucking someone as much as I do Jessica Riley.

I sit patiently at my desk and wait for her to get to work. There's no way she's going to get away with sending these damn pictures to my wife, purposely upsetting her and making her doubt my commitment to her. I love her more than life itself, but our marriage is still brand new; hell our entire relationship is still new by normal standards. I can't have some petty, vindictive woman trying to destroy that. It's absolutely unforgivable.

Knowing she gets to work just a little before eight, I sit at my desk and fume until closer to nine. I can't concentrate on work at this point so I don't even try. I do my best to calm down and normally looking at the black and white photo of my tiny son helps, but today the sight of if angers me even more.

What would I have done if the pictures were harder to prove that they happened in the past and not recently? Without that evidence I could have lost my wife, my son. I place the picture in the top drawer of my desk. I shouldn't be looking at it while this upset.

Unable to wait any longer I get up from my desk, grab the photos, and make my way to Jessica's desk.

She smiles at me as I make my way to her until her eyes drop to the bright red envelope in my hand. I can't help but to sneer at her, but inside I'm taking pride in the fear and trepidation in her eyes as I watch her eyes dart around, making sure others are near.

Her smile returns once she's knows she's not alone. I specifically waited to make sure others were around. Without them I don't know that I'd be able to control my temper enough not to pin her to the wall by her fucking throat. Sorry Dad.

"What the fuck do you think you're doing," I say in a much louder than conversational tone and toss the envelope in front of her.

She places her hand on top of the offending envelope. "Your bride is not too happy to find out about us, I take it?"

"There is no us," I bite out.

"Well, she doesn't know that does she?" She stands behind her desk, trying to gain more even footing in the argument I know she can tell is going to happen. "If your bed is cold and you apologize for treating me like shit, I might consider helping you keep it warm."

"Treating you like shit?" I snarl at her. "I never treated you like shit! And your stupid fucking ploy didn't work. Josie and I are just fine. Stronger than ever actually!"

"You used me!" she yells.

"I fucked you, Jessica. You knew from the beginning that's all it was!" I run my hands over my buzz cut, trying to gain some composure. "Shit, you've fucked over half the guys in the precinct!"

The entire office is staring at us by this point; many of the men turning their heads away from us in shame at my declaration.

She ignores my last words. "You'll pay for how you treated me!"

"How I treated you? You're pissed because I fell in love with someone else besides you. Can't you see how fucking crazy that is?" I scream back at her.

"Your sins include so much fucking more than breaking up with me!" Her scream is high pitched and hard on the ears.

Just as I was about to tell her there was no relationship to end, I'm interrupted.

"Enough!" I turn my head toward a red-faced Randall Holt. "My office. Now." I turn from her desk and begin making my way to his office. "You too, Riley."

I can hear her stutter and begin to try to talk her way out of it. She stops talking and I know that Holt just gave her a don't-fuck-with-me look which stopped her words.

Once in the office, Jessica sits primly in the chair in front of Holt's desk. I opt to stand against the wall because even being this close to her may be harmful to her health.

She begins to talk as soon as Holt closes his door. He holds his hand up stopping her once again as he takes his seat behind his desk.

"I have no fucking clue what that shit out there was about, and I have too much else going on to even fucking get into it." He glares at both of us. "Badges and guns." Jessica starts to argue, blaming me for the altercation in front of the entire precinct. "Both of you are on administrative leave until Monday."

I unclip my holster and badge from my belt and place them on his desk in front of him.

Jessica does the same only she more slams them down.

"I'd like to file a complaint against Detective Perez for harassment," she states calmly.

"Are you fucking kidding me?" I yell. I turn my attention back to Holt. "If she does that then I'm filing one against her as well. I won't be the only one with a write-up in my jacket for this shit!"

"On what grounds?" She asks.

"For sending those pictures to my fucking wife!" I declare.

She narrows her eyes at me and then turns back to Holt, who's watching the whole thing play out with his eyebrows raised.

"Were you aware that Garrett Hale was not only a groomsman in Detective Perez's wedding but his cousin Ian Hale paid for his honeymoon?" She informs my boss.

"How the fuck would you know that?" It's apparent she's been either stalking me or at the least checking into my personal shit.

"Why are you so concerned Detective? Afraid people will find out about you working on Hale's case or altering evidence to get your friend off?" Her voice is low and accusatory.

"Stan Rhodes is lead in that case and there has been no impropriety on my part." I hiss back at her.

Holt clears his throat. "Was he in your wedding? Did his cousin pay for your honeymoon?" He turns his attention to me.

"Yes, sir," I answer honestly. I have nothing to hide and have no control really over the case since I'm not the lead on it.

"You didn't think that was something to inform me of!" His voice is harsh. "Do you understand what this means?"

I shake my head no because honestly I don't.

"I have to call internal affairs in to make sure you didn't fuck up the case!" He explains.

I watch Jessica's eyes go wide. "I don't think that's necessary, Sergeant. I shouldn't have said anything. I was just angry."

"Too late now, Detective. Riley, you're on admin until Monday. Get your shit together and calm the fuck down. Perez, you're on admin until I.A. says you can come back." I nod at him. "Now get the fuck out of my precinct I have work to do."

I don't say a word as I turn and leave. I collect my things from my desk and head home. I could never be upset with spending time with her, even if it means my job is being threatened and my work ethic and integrity are being questioned.

I hit the grocery store for a gallon of chocolate milk and then head home to my wife.

Chapter 27
Garrett

Fuck I think to myself as I come inside Alexa for the second time today. My fingers tingle to touch her, to run down her beautiful back.

I pull out with a grunt and leave the room, heading to the en suite in our master bedroom. I know I'm an asshole. I know I don't deserve her. I know she deserves way better than what she's been getting from me lately. But I need her. The only time the racing thoughts and my demons are calmed is when I'm deep inside of her.

It's been like this for weeks. I do my best to stay away from her but when the shadows start to creep in, I seek her out. She's tolerated everything I've given her. She's not once said no or used her safe word to stop a scene. I went too far the very first day after the judge arraigned me and cut me free.

Free.

Like that's really the case. Free means Ian put up two million dollars as collateral so I didn't have to go back to a jail cell. Processing out and having that Hernandez prick shove my head into the wall was bad enough. I couldn't imagine having to sit in there any longer.

Alexa hasn't left the apartment more than a handful of times and when she does leave she's only gone for a few hours tops. I'm certain she quit her job, but we haven't really spoken since all this shit started. Well, I'm not in a very talkative mood. I know she'd love to sit down and have a conversation with me, but I just can't stomach to be around anyone right now.

I've practically closed myself off in the office at the penthouse and kept to myself. The police haven't called me back to the station to ask more questions and my attorney tells me that they have been unusually quiet. A gang war in L.A. has pulled most media attention away from Denver so my name has never been mentioned in relation to the charges. I should count my blessings I guess; hard to do facing murder charges.

I have been leaving the office door open the past couple of days. I don't have a reason behind it, maybe I do want Alexa to come in and insist I talk to her, but I'm afraid I've broken her. I'm certain I've ruined any chance to fix our relationship. A relationship I valued more than anything else in the world. A relationship I single handedly destroyed during my grief and anger over losing my business, a man I would consider a friend and being arrested.

I didn't even go to Darren's funeral. My attorney thought it best to stay away from the situation altogether. I sent flowers, it was the least I could do.

Small amounts of information have trickled through. Police discovered Darren was at *Ampere* because he and his partner Chase Phillips had a huge fight and Darren ended up there getting drunk at the bar because Chase kicked him out. It was just a stroke of terrible fucking luck that some motherfucker decided to burn the place down.

Johnny calls at least every other day to check in on me. I have to admit that it's beginning to get on my nerves, but the man is out of a job and I feel guilty as shit about that and my other employees, so I haven't put an end to it. He's staying at a low rent motel because he couldn't make rent on his apartment. I offered to pay until he could find another job, but he shut me down. His pride won't allow him to take money from anyone and I understand the pride thing completely.

Pride is what keeps me from walking through the penthouse and making love to my girl.

I can't fathom why she hasn't just walked out on me yet. I've used her as practically nothing more than a sex slave for the past few weeks and yet she stays. She comes running when I call for her. She comes repeatedly every time I'm inside her even though I haven't done anything specifically to her to make it happen. My cock appears to be enough.

I miss her and she's no more than twenty yards from me at any given time. I miss her taste. My mouth hasn't been on her in weeks and what I'm able to lick off my fingers when she's blindfolded hasn't even come close to being enough.

I scrub my hands over my face and step out of the shower, toweling off as I walk into the bedroom. Alexa, who recently has been staying out of my way until I go back into my office, is walking out of the closet. She has clothes in her hand, but she's just as naked as I left her in the living room fifteen minutes ago.

My cock jumps at the sight of her flushed skin and even more so at the red, irritated marks around her ankles and wrists. I didn't break the skin, even at my worst I've never taken it that far with her, but the welts from the rope haven't had time to go away.

The urge to take her in my arms and kiss her senseless is strong. Knowing that when I do, when I allow that emotion back into my head I will break, keeps me from doing it.

Her eyes go wide at seeing me walk into the room then her gaze darts lower and she sees my straining cock. With a devious grin, like I haven't been inside of her twice today, the last time less than an hour ago, she slinks up to me. She lets the clothes in her hands fall to the floor and sinks to her knees at my feet.

I wasn't expecting her to do this and the fact that she's trying to take control almost has me taking a step back. She's quicker and before I can react I'm tunneling into the hot wetness of her mouth.

My knees almost give out. To say that Alexa gives the best head is an understatement. This woman's talented mouth should be given a Nobel peace prize for physics. Not once has she taken me in her mouth and it not elicited an explosion.

I know she wants to get fucked and that's why she's sucking so voraciously on me. She's well aware I'd rather go off inside of her than any other place. I wish I had the restraint, but honestly I need her like that again as well. My orgasms are the most rewarding when I feel her come on my dick before going off myself.

"Enough," I bite out and shove her shoulders until she's sprawled out on her back on the soft carpet.

Her heavy-lidded eyes gleam at me. It's the first time since my arrest that I've faced her this way without a blindfold. I can see the pain at my distance in her eyes and it guts me. She deserves so much better.

The scene has already started so I'm committed and she brought this on herself. I lift her legs high on my hips and kneel between her legs. This raises her lower body off of the floor giving me complete control. I raise my eyes to the ceiling and slam into her, repeatedly.

I can never seem to get enough of this woman. The best times of my life have happened when I'm inside her. I bite my lip when I remember her telling me she loved me as I came inside of her all those months ago. That was the day I was set free. It was also the day I reacted poorly which sent her away and she was shot.

I'm destroying her again, but I'm terrified that she'll leave and I won't have her anymore. I'm too selfish to do the right thing by her.

"Garrett," she pleads.

I look down at her and she smiles softly.

"You want my eyes, Angel?" I say in a harsh tone she doesn't deserve. She nods. "You think you can suck my cock anytime you want without asking?" She whimpers. "I own you," I say sliding my hand up her body and settling my grip around the base of her throat, squeezing her beautiful neck slightly.

"Yes," she pants.

I don't know if she's agreeing to my ownership or if she's turned on by my grip on her delicate neck. The closest we've come to breath play is when I force her to choke on my dick. I squeeze tighter and she moans, her eyes rolling in the back of her head.

Less than thirty seconds of restricted breath and Alexa is coming like a freight train on my cock, sending me over the edge with little to no warning. *This woman. Perfect.*

I release my grasp on her throat and nearly come again at the sound of her first full breath. Fuck, she never disappoints. Sated and completely exhausted I pull out of her and crash on the carpet beside her.

I glance at her and notice her eyes are closed as she continues to pant, calming from her explosive orgasm. I don't know if the tear rolling down her cheek is from my treatment of her or the result of her obstructed airway. I die a little more inside as I watch it meet her hairline.

This time, she's the one who eventually gets up and leaves, walking to the bathroom and shutting the door behind her.

"I love you, Angel," I whisper as I hear her turn on the shower.

I don't know how long I lie on the floor wallowing in self-pity but I scramble up and grab some sweats when the shower cuts off.

My phone rings in my office as I'm tugging my shirt over my head. I quicken my steps even though I know it won't be any good news from my attorney. I've just about given up hope that the charges are going to be thrown out. We go for discovery next week and from what my attorney has been told by the Colorado State Attorney General's office the evidence is pretty damning.

William seems to think I've been framed, but I'm certain I've not made any enemies; not ones that would go to this extreme to retaliate against me for something. He asked about Alexa and her shooting. I assured him that wasn't it. All of those fuckers, including her shooter Blake Evans, are dead; Evans was murdered in the jail and the others were killed during Josie's rescue.

I grab my phone off of the desk and answer it.

"Hale," I grunt into the phone.

"Hey, man." Ian.

"I haven't skipped town," I tell him as a sick attempt at a joke. He doesn't laugh. "What's up?"

I hear him sigh. "Lorali is pestering me to get everyone together." I can tell by his tone he knows what my answer will be and he's only going through the motions to get her off his back.

The Strange thing is I know Alexa will want to go and since I can't give her the happiness she needs, maybe visiting with her friends would be a consolation.

"Sure, man. What time?" I ask looking at my watch. It's only three in the afternoon.

Three in the afternoon and I've already taken Alexa three times today? She has to be sore and I know leaving the house would be in our best interest. If anything a deterrent to keep me from trying to get inside of her again.

"Huh?" He's confused since I gave him an answer he wasn't anticipating.

"What time?" I repeat myself.

"Anytime," he says. "We're here. Do you have to wait for Alexa to get off work?"

"Alexa hasn't been to work in over three weeks," I inform him with no further explanation, mainly because I'm not sure why. Maybe she's taken vacation time or some shit. "See you in an hour or so."

We say our goodbyes and I palm my cell phone and walk back into the bedroom. Alexa is at her vanity blow-drying her hair. I busy myself by getting dressed, waiting for the noise to go away so I can speak to her.

She turns the dryer off and watches my reflection in the mirror without turning her head to face me. Distance. She seems so out of reach.

"We're going to Lorali and Ian's," I inform rather than ask her if she wants to go.

She smiles at me and nods her head but the affection is muted and I know it's only a matter of time before I lose her completely.

Chapter 28
Ian

Opening the door for Alexa and Garrett, I realize just how long it's been since I've seen them. Garrett called not too long ago to see about hitting the gym, but I was busy and couldn't make it. The last time I saw him was when Lorali and I dropped him off at home after seeing the judge weeks ago.

Today he's sporting a full beard and I'm certain he hasn't shaved since his arrest. I notice Alexa also looks less that her normal put-together self. She gives me a weak smile when I peck her on the cheek and I know instantly that things at home aren't how they used to be, both of them look broken.

I follow them as they head into the living room.

Lorali gets up off the couch and gives Garrett a hug. He allows it but doesn't hug her back as Alexa sits down beside Josie on the couch.

"Josie," Garrett says in acknowledgment. She tells him *hi* but doesn't move to get off the couch.

Garret turns from the women and makes his way toward the door to the basement. I shrug my shoulders at Lorali, kiss her on the cheek and follow behind him.

I close the door behind me and as soon as I clear the last stair I make my way to the mini bar. I pour two glasses of scotch because the conversation I'm sure to have with Garrett will not be covered by beer alone.

I hand him a glass and sit in the leather recliner I always sit in when we hang out down here. The TV is on, Sports Center, of course, but the sound is muted. Garrett doesn't sit; instead he paces back and forth like a caged tiger, looking for a way to escape.

"I'm ready when you are," I tell him and sit further back in my chair, crossing one leg over the opposite knee.

"Where's Kaleb?" He asks. I don't know if he actually cares or if he's checking to see if there's a possibility that he may show up tonight. "Working?"

"Josie said he's hanging out with a friend tonight. I got the feeling that he doesn't feel welcome over here," I tell him. Who blames him; last time he was here he was treated pretty shitty just for doing his job.

His grunt tells me Kaleb's assessment is right. Garrett's in a rough position no doubt, but Kaleb is as well.

"He's not working because he's been suspended for not letting his sergeant know about his connection to us." Garrett stops pacing and turns to look at me. "He can't go back to work until Internal Affairs clear him for his involvement in your case."

I watch him gage his reaction to the news. "Fuck," he puffs out. "He doesn't deserve that shit. Why didn't he tell them?"

I shrug. "Lorali thinks that Kaleb was trying to work every angle to clear you. He knew if he was pulled from the case he wouldn't have access to the information and tips that were coming in."

He begins to pace back and forth the length of the room, stopping periodically to refill his tumbler with more scotch.

"You going to tell me what's going on with Alexa?" He doesn't stop pacing, but his step falters a bit at my question.

"What are you talking about," he finally asks.

"It's apparent that there's trouble in paradise." I set my empty tumbler down because I have to work tomorrow and it will be impossible if I have a hangover for the all-day video conferences I have scheduled.

"Is it?" He asks and finally stops the pacing and sits in the leather recliner beside me, hanging his head in his hands. "I'm fucking losing her, Ian."

"Has she said she wants to leave?"

"No, but I'm pushing her away at every turn." He scrubs his hands over his face. "Fuck!" His voice booms and reverberates off the walls.

"Why?"

"Why what?" He turns his head to me.

"Why are you pushing her away?" He laughs but not in a way that makes me think I said something funny. It's more of a laugh that says the situation is apparent and I shouldn't even have to ask.

"She deserves better than me." He sounds resigned as if he's accepted his fate and he's just waiting for the hammer to drop.

"Bullshit, Garrett. You're a good man. All of this shit will eventually be over." I hope he can hear the truth in my words and know I'm not just trying to placate him.

"And if it doesn't?" He sneers at me. "You think she's going to stick around and come visit my sorry ass in prison? Fuck, I'd never even ask her to do that."

"It won't get that far and you fucking know it."

"You don't know that!" He jumps up from his chair and starts pacing again.

"They can't convict you if they don't have evidence. They can't have evidence if you didn't do it." My tone is flat because I need him to see that he's overreacting.

"Innocent people go to prison all the time," he says.

"You need to calm down. The case hasn't even gone to the grand jury. Do you remember how quick Alexa's case went before the grand jury? A couple weeks that's all. There has to be a reason they haven't gotten to that step yet." His pacing begins to slow as he mulls over my words.

"What the fuck am I supposed to do in the meantime?" He leans against the wall with his arms crossed, seriously waiting for his response because I'm at a loss for the answer.

"Lay low, but live your life how you would've before all this shit went down," I say to him.

"It's not that simple, Ian," he whispers.

"It is that easy, Garrett. You sit at home with your girl, watch TV, fuck like bunnies, and you wait until you hear anything different on your case. Anything else and you will drive yourself mad." *If you haven't already,* I don't verbalize.

"I have ruined everything with Alexa. I've gone from being within two steps of asking her to marry me to treating her like a piece of ass that's only around to fuck me at my every whim." I cringe because I know that Garrett loves that woman to death so he must be in a super low place for this to be going on.

"Make it up to her," I shrug because the woman is here. She's stayed so she must feel like he's worth the fight.

"How the fuck am I supposed to do that? I haven't even kissed her since I was arrested." I watch him clench his fists open and closed, angry at himself for his actions.

"You start by going upstairs, wrapping yourself around her and watching a movie." I grin at him.

He laughs shallowly. "I'm pretty sure she's about ready to cut my nuts off," he says.

"But she won't. She loves you; it's not too late to work yourself back to her." I tell him. "Be the man you were before; she fell madly in love with that man. She still loves that man."

"Start with a movie huh?"

I shrug. "As good an idea as any." I look at my watch then grab my cell and fire off a text to Lorali. Within a minute she responds. "Lorali says Josie has already gone upstairs to lie down and plans to stay all night. She won't feel like a third wheel."

He nods in understanding. "And if Alexa attacks me?" He gives me a half-hearted grin.

"We'll make sure to call an ambulance before you bleed out," I say jokingly. "And if things go the opposite way there are fresh sheets on the bed in your room upstairs." I waggle my eyes at him and stand, walking toward the stairs.

He follows behind me mumbling about waiting too long to come over and that he's sure she hates him by now. We make our way up the stairs and into the living room where the girls are watching some stupid chick flick, of which I could care less. I can never pay attention to movies when Lorali is near.

Alexa notices our approach and her eyes go wide darting from the glass of wine in her hand and back to Garrett. She seems like she's been caught doing something she shouldn't.

"Ladies," I say walking toward Lorali. "Can we join you?"

Lorali grins and holds her arms open to me. I sit down beside her and watch Garrett's more cautious approach to Alexa. She tries to lean forward and place her glass on the table, but he stops her movement by gently clutching her wrist. She watches with unsure eyes as he reaches for the bottle of wine and refills her glass.

He kisses her on the temple and sits beside her. Her body is rigid and she continues to cut her eyes at him like she's waiting for him to morph into someone else. He has a lot more work to do than I had initially thought, but when I see her eventually settle and lean into him, I'm certain it will all work out.

An hour later and he's grown balls big enough to at least put his arm around her shoulder, trailing a gentle touch up and down her arm. He probably thinks she's fallen asleep with her head on his shoulder because he can't see her face, but the tiny smile on her lips tells me she's just enjoying the affection.

I get Lorali's attention and angle my head towards them. She squeezes my hand letting me know she sees it too. I hope this calms some of her worries.

The doorbell chimes and I get a sinking feeling in my gut, suddenly hit with a feeling of déjà vu.

Chapter 29
Kaleb

I hate lying to my wife. Well, I'm not exactly lying it's more like a lie of omission. I told her I was hanging out with a friend tonight. She didn't ask me who, I'm certain it's because she still feels guilty for the way she responded to the pictures, and I don't offer.

Sergeant Holt is kind of a friend, but I did leave out the part about working. Ok, not technically working but Holt said he had some things he wanted to share with me and he could only do it after the other people in the office left for the day since I am still on suspension.

I park my truck in the parking lot after dropping Josie off at Ian's. I text Holt to let him know I'm here and wait by the side entrance for him to give me access to the building. Before long the heavy metal door is swinging open and not only Holt but Detective Stan Rhodes is in the doorway. I narrow my eyes because I don't like being surprised by shit and Holt should have mentioned him planning to be here.

Suddenly I'm hit with a wave of panic. Garrett sure as shit isn't guilty yet he's been charged with very serious offenses. Is it possible they have found something and misconstrued it as illegal on my part? I'm like a deer caught in the headlights of an oncoming car, not sure if I should join them or run, which is crazy because I'm not guilty of shit.

It reminds me of the first time I saw the red and blues flashing behind me when I was seventeen and my first instinct was to run. Not because there was a cop behind me and I was guilty of speeding, but knowing my father was going to find out sent sheer terror through my veins.

Rhodes smirks at me reading my mind. "Get your ass in here Perez, we don't have time for this shit."

His slap on my back when I walk past him and into the precinct is brotherly. We make our way through the various corridors until we get to Holt's office. We all settle in and wait for Holt to begin.

He's grinning at me but doesn't say anything at first.

"Well?" I ask eventually.

"It seems Anthony and Marco know each other from the streets," Holt says with a flat affect.

"Fuck," I mutter. "So we got burned?" I sit back roughly in my chair knowing without him confessing we're screwed.

"Just the opposite actually," Holt says with a grin. "Hernandez started talking the minute we put him in the cell."

"Fuck yeah!" I want to give him a fist bump, but he's really not the type so I stay in my seat.

I watch him click his mouse and turn up the speaker on his computer. "There were some pleasantries, but I'm just starting at the meat and potatoes."

I hear Anthony's very distinguishable laugh. It's more like a hyena cackle than a sound that should come from a human.

Anthony: That's fucked up man. You gonna tell me what your ass is in here for?

Marco: I fucked up man. Let my anger at this prick get to me.

Anthony: You beat somebody's ass on the street?

I hear Marco chuckle.

Marco: Naw, man. I shoved some assholes head in the wall. They caught me on camera.

Anthony: Shitty luck, bro.

Marco: Yeah, but he'll get what's coming to him.

Hyena cackle.

Anthony: You got some plans then. I like it!

Marco: This shit has already been set in motion. I just couldn't handle myself seeing that motherfuckers face.

Anthony: The guy you slammed?

Anthony pauses before continuing. I presume Marco nodded an affirmation to him.

Anthony: What's the beef with him?

Marco: You heard about Shelly right?

Anthony: Yeah. Heard about that shit. Pretty fucked up what happened.

Marco: No lie. My girl calls me and tells me that Shelly and her old man's operation is about to get lit up. So I do what any cousin would do and let them know.

Anthony: Of course man. Family first.

I hear some slapping noises as they commiserate with what sounds like some hand slapping.

"So we have him for informing on the raid," I say. "Perfect."

"We got him on so much more," Holt angles his head back to the computer. "Marco loves to talk."

Anthony: So you roughed up one of the cops?

Marco: This guy wasn't a cop. Shelly started hanging around that Trina bitch. That stupid whore went fucking nuts after Evans was arrested for knocking over that liquor store.

Anthony: Shit, Marco. I didn't hear about any of this shit! I did hear that Evans got shanked in the fucking latrine, though. I fucking hated his ass. Glad that fuckers dead.

Marco: Yeah, well. He started running his fucking mouth and I couldn't have that shit.

Anthony: Fuck yeah, man.

More hand slapping.

Marco: You'd be surprised what some of the crackheads in here will do for a hit.

"Holy shit," I whisper as Holt stops the tape. "Did he just fucking admit to having Evans killed?"

Holt nods. This clears up two cases because they never determined who shanked Evans in the bathroom right after Josie was abducted.

I turn to Rhodes. "You here because of Evan's death?"

"Partly," he says and smiles.

"It gets better," Holt says.

"There's more?" I ask incredulously.

They both nod.

Anthony: I'm confused as fuck, bro. What did this have to do with cracking that guy's head?

Marco: The bitch that Evan's shot? This guy is her man.

Anthony: Sorry, man. Still not following.

I hear a frustrated sigh, surely from Marco at Anthony playing dumb.

Marco: It's a big clusterfuck, but try to keep up. Are you high? What the fuck are you doing here?

Anthony: Got busted with a few grams. Three strikes for me, dog. I'll be sent down for sure this time.

Marco: Shit man I'm sorry. I don't ever usually get my hands dirty with the drugs. I lucked out a while back and ended up with a couple kilos of some prime shit.

Anthony: I got a cousin that can move that shit for you.

Marco: Thanks, man but I used it for this fucker I was talking about. If it hadn't been for that mother fucker's girl, Shelly would still be alive. I'd kill Trina my fucking self if she wasn't already dead.

Anthony: Sounds like the whole situation is fucked.

Marco: I may lose my job, but I'm taking that fucker down with me. Money is the only reason he's out and didn't get the Evan's treatment.

I hear Anthony's hyena cackle again and, this time, it sounds strained and forced. He's well aware of the shitstorm Hernandez just confessed to.

I just glare at Holt, silenced by disbelief and shake my head from side to side.

"What's the next step?" I query.

Holt sits up straighter in his chair and opens the desk drawer to his right. He pulls out my holstered glock and my shield and slide them across the desk to me.

I stare at him as if he's tricking me in some way. "I haven't spoken to I.A. yet."

"Why would you need to? There wasn't an investigation." Holts pushes my belongings closer to me and I take them off the desk. "Great show with Jessica Riley though. She had no clue we set her up."

I nod at him.

"How has your time off been?" Holt asks with a devious smirk.

"Really good. Just what I needed, especially after that bitch sent those pictures." I say.

"The tape we just listened to happened two days ago. Marco was brought in and interviewed earlier today and he sang like a fucking bird. The Attorney General's office opted to not seek the death penalty if he gave a full confession." Holt pauses. "He implemented Riley. Seems she's the mastermind behind all of it. We don't have all the details, but he gave us quite a bit."

"He hinted that Riley was somehow involved in Josie's abduction. He doesn't know exactly how because she didn't share all of that info with him, but he says she hinted at it often." I bristle at the knowledge. "She wanted her out of the way so she could have you," Rhodes says.

"When do we bring the bitch in?" I hiss through clenched teeth. I knew Jessica had a thing for me, I knew she was upset that I backed out of our fuck buddy agreement, I knew she was vindictive when she sent those fucking pictures to Josie. I never would have imagined her doing this shit. Almost since day one that she knew about Josie she'd been out to get her.

"We," Holt says pointing between him and I. "Don't do anything. Rhodes and I will handle this."

I glare at him. "Sergeant," I begin and he holds his hand up to stop me.

"We're talking about bringing in a Denver PD detective and a sheriff's deputy. This shit is going national when it busts open. We have to keep everything above board."

I start to argue. This has to do with my fucking wife and the people who were involved in her abduction. I could have lost her and our child over this shit.

"Now, I'm not saying you can't ride along, but you have to stay out of it. I can't have anything called into question." He explains and it does nothing to abate my absolute abhorrence towards them.

"My fucking wife." The more I think about it, the angrier I grow.

"Is safe," Holt says in what he thinks is a calming tone.

"Why am I even here?" I spit out.

"We knew you'd want to know. We don't want you on the outside; we just can't have you in the middle of it. We can't take the chance the case gets thrown out." His words calm me a bit. "Plus," he adds. "We figured you'd like to let your friend know the charges against him will be officially dropped tomorrow."

"I heard Marco admit that the drugs planted were his, but what about the arson?" There is so much shit going on, I'm beginning to get confused.

"Marco said in his interview that Riley convinced some young bartender or some shit to plant the coke and light the place on fire. My guess is the arson is the bar manager Johnny Hill's doing." Holt says reminding me of what Garrett said. Johnny had access to everything at the bar, practically had free reign.

"No shit?" I raise my eyebrows.

"Like I said he sang like a canary once he started talking," Rhodes says with a smile.

"You remember Felipe Espinoza?" I nod at him. I'm still pissed the feds had pulled the 'higher jurisdiction' shit on that cartel fucker. "He convinced Marco to go to his hotel and clean it before we could get over there. That's how he scored the kilos of coke."

This day just gets better and better. Marco Hernandez will be spending the rest of his life in prison. Worst thing? They hate cops and dirty or not he doesn't have a fucking snowballs chance in hell of surviving.

"We actually do need you for something," Rhodes says as he stands from his chair and stretches out his back. "We can't find Riley or Hill. My bet is Garrett Hale knows where his bar manager is. Think you can find that out for us?"

I huff. "I don't know that Garrett is going to be talking to me anytime soon. He was pretty fucking pissed the last time I saw him."

"Maybe the news you share with him may help a bit." Holt stands as well and looks at his watch. "If you could go to his penthouse and find out that'd be great. SWAT started gearing up an hour ago."

"He's not at home; he's at his cousin Ian Hale's house." They narrow their eyes at me and I hold my hands up in surrender. "I dropped Josie off over there before meeting you guys. I'll call you if he tells me anything."

"You call us either way so we know what steps to take next." Holt demands.

"Yes, sir." I shake both his and Rhodes hand and make my way out of the building and back to my truck.

Chapter 30
Josie

I'm always amazed at how quickly I got used to sharing a bed with someone. It's nearly impossible to sleep when Kaleb isn't in the bed with me. I haven't told him this because he already feels guilty for being gone so much. I make my way back down the stairs to the living room to join the others because tossing and turning in bed is only causing me more stress.

At the bottom of the stairs, the doorbell rings. I smile because it can only be Kaleb this late. We had agreed that I would stay the night here, but I knew he'd never be able to stay away from me.

Ian passes me making his way to the door and I follow him. I can feel someone else behind me and I turn my head to see Garrett walking in that direction as well.

Ian opens the door and Kaleb is on the front step, a small smile on his face. It grows bigger when he sees me. Ian tilts his head and looks around Kaleb and my guess is he's checking to see if there is anyone else behind him. Things weren't so great here the last time he rang the doorbell.

He's alone. "May I come in?" He asks and I see Ian turn his head toward Garrett, gauging the situation. He opens the door further when Garrett just shrugs his shoulders.

I notice his badge and gun on his belt and my steps falter. He's no longer on administrative leave?

"I'm actually here on official business," he says.

"Fuck," Garrett says and rubs his face with the palms of his hands. "What now?"

"My sergeant asked me to come by and let you know that all charges against you will be dropped tomorrow." I grin and I hear Alexa squeal.

"Don't fucking play with me, man," Garrett says as he reaches out to the wall to steady himself.

"I'd never do that," my gorgeous husband says.

"How? Who? What?" Garrett begins to stammer.

"I can't go into detail right now because it's an open investigation, but we have enough evidence that proves you weren't involved."

Before Kaleb finishes his sentence, Garrett falls to his knees on the floor. Immediately Alexa is by his side and wrapping her arms around him. Overcome with the emotion and stress from the last couple of weeks Garrett begins to sob.

Ian looks at each of us and tilts his head to the living room, asking us silently to give them a few minutes to wrap their heads around this incredible news.

Kaleb sits on the sofa and I climb in his lap. "You have some explaining to do," I whisper in his ear.

He laughs lightly but nods his head acknowledging that we'll talk about everything later.

"Can I get you a beer, Kaleb?" Ian asks from the bar across the room.

"I'm actually not done working just yet. I need to talk to Garrett about something. Hopefully, he can give me some information that we need to proceed with the case." He says this as his lips trail down my throat.

Ian laughs because we just can't keep our hands off of one another. "Let's just give them a few minutes. They've had a couple of bad weeks."

"I wanted to tell you," Kaleb kisses my cheek. "I got an email from Child Welfare Services. They were finally able to locate a relative for Gracie."

I beam at him. "Really? Who?"

"Her Aunt Diane lives in Tennessee and is driving in to get her." He kisses my lips again. "Just a few more days in state care and she'll be heading to Huron to live with family."

We sit and chat for a while longer and eventually Garrett and Alexa make their way back into the living room. Garrett's face is still red from his emotional break, but he has a smile on his face.

He walks toward Kaleb, who gently eases me off his lap so he can stand. We watch with bated breath until Garrett extends his hand to my husband.

"We good?" Garrett asks.

"Yeah, man. We're good. Sorry about all this shit." Kaleb apologizes as he shakes Garrett's hand who then pulls him into one of those manly backslapping things.

"You had a job to do. Don't imagine it was any easier for you than it was for me." Kaleb sighs and shakes his head agreeing with him.

Garrett grabs a seat across from us and Kaleb sits down as well.

"Is there anything you can tell us?" Garrett prods.

"I was hoping to get some information from you and I can't do that without giving some information away." He looks around the room and makes eye contact with each one of us. "I need to know that what I say doesn't go any further than these walls."

We all verbally agree.

"I need to know if you know where Johnny Hill took off to." I watch as Garrett's eyes go wide.

"Why the fuck are you looking for him?" Garrett stares at Kaleb. "No." He shakes his head emphatically. "There's no way."

"We have it on good authority that a woman who has manipulated him into thinking they are together, convinced him to plant the coke and start the fire. We don't think he knew Darren Davies was there." Kaleb explains.

"He mentioned meeting a girl at a coffee shop," Garrett says in recollection.

"Did he tell you her name?" Kaleb asks.

"I think he said her name was Jessica or something like that." Kaleb hisses and even I can tell that is exactly who he believes is involved.

"Hold on. Jessica?" I interrupt. "Is it the same..."

"Yes," Kaleb answers me before I can even get my question out. "But it goes so much deeper than the pictures, Mariposa."

"Pictures?" Lorali says.

Kaleb laughs. "I'll explain it all when I can, but right now we need to find Johnny." He turns his attention back to Garrett.

"He told me a few days ago he was staying at some shitty hotel off of Vine. He didn't give me a room number and I can't remember the name." Garrett says and I can see his frustration growing. "He made me feel like shit for weeks. Feeling sorry for his ass since he lost his job. I offered to pay his fucking rent until he could get another job and you're telling me he set my ass up?"

"That's where the investigation has led us," Kaleb says shaking his head. "Shit, Garrett. I hate that you even got brought in on this. They made sure all of the evidence pointed back to you."

"Fuck," Garrett says sitting back further on the couch. "I'm just glad this shit is over."

"Well, it's not quite over. The charges will be dropped, but you need to get with your attorney and start working on your expungement. The arrests will show until a judge orders them to be deleted." Garrett crinkles his nose, obviously weary of the whole process. "Sorry man," Kaleb says again.

"Well, at least, there's light at the end of the fucking tunnel now," Ian adds.

Kaleb turns to me and cups my cheek gently. "I hate to leave you again, Mariposa, but I have to see this through."

"When will you be home?" I ask and lean into his warm hand.

"As soon as Jessica and Johnny are arrested. They hurt you, Josie." He turns his attention to the group. "They hurt all of us. I have to make sure they're in custody."

I kiss him and allow him to stand. I hold his hand and walk with him all the way to the door, reluctant to let him leave; knowing he may be going into a dangerous situation.

"Please, be careful," I beg him.

"I don't actually get to be involved since I'm too close to this case, but I need to be there to see them brought in," he explains. "Will you be here or at home?"

"Is it safe at home?"

"Stay here for tonight," he says. "I'll grab you when I'm done and all of this is over."

"I love you, Kaleb." I lean in for a kiss and he obliges.

He kisses me like he did the first time when I got home after being abducted. He kissed me with everything that he has like he felt like he was close to losing me again.

"I love you, too."

I close the door behind him and start counting down the minutes until I get my husband back. I have so many questions and I expect him to answer each and every one.

Chapter 31
Alexa

When Garret came back in the room and joined me on the couch, I knew then and there that Lorali had said something to Ian, who in turn said something to Garrett. For the first time in weeks, his touch was gentle and he held me and let me touch him back.

When Kaleb showed up again, I could feel the dread rolling off of him and I knew the little glimpse of my old Garrett was gone. I never would've expected the news Kaleb came to share. We left Ian and Lorali's house shortly after Kaleb did.

The drive back to the penthouse is spent in total silence. I don't know what to say or if he even wants me to speak so, I spend the time watching out the window until the familiar sight of the subterranean parking garage comes into view.

I climb out of the car and begin walking toward the elevator, mimicking his actions in reverse from earlier. I have no expectations of how things will be now, only hope that eventually the man I love will make his way back to me. That hope shines a little brighter when he comes up to my side and takes my hand in his and doesn't let go the entire ride up to our home.

He opens the door quietly and I walk past him into the penthouse. I'm nervous and it's evident by the slight tremble in my fingers. I cross my arms and wrap them around my stomach to try to control my nerves or at least not let them show. Garrett has managed to exploit every weakness I've shown lately and I'd like for tonight to not be more of the same.

I begin to walk to the bedroom when I feel the heat of his body on my back. I close my eyes at the sensation I've missed with every cell of my body. I want to cry when his strong arms wrap around my waist and he pulls me back against his chest.

"Angel," he whispers in my ear.

I melt into him. One word spoke with true love and I'm able to push aside any apprehension I had about what's in store for tonight.

I lean my head back against his chest and close my eyes.

"Alexa, I want to…" I turn in his arms and lift my finger to his lips preventing him from speaking.

"No words; we don't need to talk." I smile weakly at him then focus my eyes on his kissable full lips.

I hear him growl as he watches me lick my own lips, wanting nothing more than to lick his.

Then he says the words I've been waiting weeks to hear. "Kiss me," he begs and I love him even more for allowing me the chance to move in first.

He's letting me decide what I'll take from him when he's been the one to take everything he's needed and wanted recently.

I shift up onto the tips of my toes and ghost my lips ever so slightly against his. He moans softly against my mouth and the sound shoots straight to my core. I can't stop the whimper that bubbles from my own.

His hand reaches up and cups my cheek softly as I put a few inches of space between us. He closes his eyes and gently shakes his head back and forth, struggling with what I don't know.

"I love you so fucking much," he eventually says in a broken tone.

"And I you." I lean in again and take his beautiful mouth.

My hands go to his unruly, over long hair and the soft skin of my face registers the rough feel of his beard. An idea hits me, but I want to make sure tonight is not just a fluke. Being honest with myself I know if things continue the way they have after we got the news the charges will be dropped, I don't think I'll stay. It will break my heart, but I'm at the end of my rope.

I cup his cheeks in my hands. "Are you back?" I ask hopefully.

His eyes are sad and I can see he too regrets his actions the last couple of weeks. "If you'll have me."

I kiss his lips softly and tug on his hand pulling him toward our bedroom, straight through the room, and into the bathroom.

He stands and watches me without a word as I get out the razor and shaving cream. I set the supplies on the bathroom vanity and turn my attention back to him. I walk to him purposely, reaching for his shirt. Maintaining eye contact, I slowly unbutton his shirt and push it off of his shoulders. I trail my hand down his pecs and abs as I bend over and retrieve it from the floor. I toss it in the direction of the laundry hamper.

He closes his eyes at my touch and his breathing grows erratic. My hand slows as it inches toward the top button of his jeans. I sweep my finger just a fraction of an inch inside and sweep it toward his hip. His muscles bunch and he hisses.

I'd love to tease him for the next couple of hours and I probably will, but we're in here for a reason. I withdraw my finger and work the buttons of his fly free. Leaving his black boxer briefs in place, I push his jeans over his hips and let them pool at his feet. He groans when I run my nose down his straining length as I reach down to collect his jeans and again on my way up to a full standing position. I, too, toss them near the hamper.

Just as he reaches his hands up to touch me, I step out of his grasp.

"Sit," I say and point to the end of the bathtub near the shaving supplies.

He obeys with a smirk.

I squirt shaving gel in my hands and rub them together until they are both filled with thick, creamy foam. As I apply it to his cheeks, chin, and neck he rests his hands on my still clothed hips, sneaking his hand under the very bottom of my shirt. His soft hands on my overheated skin almost cause me to lose focus on the task at hand.

Slowly and methodically I do my best to shave his multiple weeks' worth of growth. I grin inwardly, grateful to have mastered the skill in my continuing education classes while working at the spa.

When I'm done, I hand him a towel to get the remaining shaving cream off. Pulling the towel away, he smiles at me and I smile back. I've missed his joy, I've missed him.

I grip his neck and trace my thumb down his cheek, loving how he fractionally tilts his head into my touch. He mimics my embrace and places his large hand against my face as he bends his head down, angling his mouth so it fits perfectly over mine.

The first hot sweep of his tongue inside nearly melts my panties and I know without a doubt if he checked he'd find me slick and ready for him.

I reach for the hem of my shirt and begin to pull it up and off but his hand on mine halts my actions.

"Let me," he hums against my panting mouth. I raise my hands and allow him to pull my shirt free of my body. His finger lightly traces the curve of my breast where it meets the satin of my bra and I roll my head on my shoulders. With the flick of his fingers, my bra is open and sliding down my arms to the floor. He doesn't give it a second thought as it lands at our feet on the tile.

Greedy hands heft the weight of my ample breasts and broad thumbs graze the tightened tips. A taste of his touch and then his hands are moving on, slowly gliding down my body to the front clasp of my jeans. In less than a breath they, along with my lace panties, are at my feet and Garrett is lifting me up.

I tangle my legs around his waist and lick the raging pulse in his neck as he walks us out of the en-suite and to our soft, king-sized bed. With one knee on the mattress, he catches our combined weight with an outstretched hand, lowering me gently to the fluffy duvet.

I raise my feet up and use my toes to push down the remaining piece of clothing he's wearing. The ability to get my legs up that high is largely due to the yoga I've been doing to work out my sore muscles after one of our sessions.

I groan at the feel of his hot, thick length as it settles on my pubic bone and lower stomach.

On his elbows, he pulls his head back and peers down at me. "If you're too sore from earlier…" I quieten him with my mouth on his and grip his firm muscled ass in my hand, squeezing the flesh and pulling him closer against me. "I want to taste you," he admits, licking over my neck and shoulder.

"Later," I promise and reach down to line him up at my entrance. "I need you inside of me like this." I nip at his lip. "Soft and sweet."

He groans when I shift my weight, forcing myself around the head of his engorged cock.

"Angel," he moans and slides his full length in.

My eyes flutter closed and my head flexes backward at his invasion; my back arching. Pure bliss.

"Garrett!" I pant when he reaches under my hip and angles my body so each one of his deep strokes is hitting that tender bundle of nerves only he's been able to find.

His mouth covers mine just as my body begins to clench uncontrollably around his rigid erection. His hips slow gently milking every last constriction of my rippling muscles. Several delicious minutes later he grunts into my mouth and begins to spurt thickly inside of me.

The kissing, touching, and caressing continues until his only slightly softened cock is solid inside of me again.

"More?" I tease with a smile.

"So much more, Angel," he promises. "Marry me, Alexa."

My world fucking stops. The question I never thought I'd want to hear. The question I was certain I would never hear from Garrett after his arrest and the way he's acted since. The question, at this point in time, I don't have the answer to.

"Garrett." I move myself out from under him, immediately missing the warmth and protection of his body.

"I know I've been an asshole. I know I don't deserve you and I sure as shit know you deserve better," he pauses and swallows roughly as I climb off the bed. "But I will give you any and everything your heart desires."

I cover my face with my hands still in shock from his sudden declaration. It's beautiful and perfect, but I can't forget it comes on the heels of the most emotionally damaging couple of weeks of my entire life.

"I'll do anything, Alexa. I swear." Garrett slides off the bed and slowly walks toward me.

"Anything?" I whisper softly.

I look into his gorgeous whiskey-colored eyes and see every word is spoken with every ounce of truth in his body. This man will cherish me for the rest of his life. *You're it for me.* The sentiment he spoke what seems like a lifetime ago comes to mind.

"Anything, Angel," he vows

I take a step back from him and point to my feet. "Knees," I command.

Chapter 31
Ian

The second I kissed my wife for the first time I knew no other woman would ever get more than a cursory glance from me. She's beautiful in silk and satin, but, more importantly, she's mine. There are hundreds of people at our wedding and if I'm honest some of them I know are here from my side of the guest list, but I have no clue who they are.

None of this concerns me when Lorali is near. We glide around the dance floor as if we're the only people on the face of the Earth. I can't keep my hands off of her and since we're in mixed company dancing is the safest bet right now. I'm expected to have her flush against my body, hiding the throbbing, hard erection only she and I are aware of. We've only been married for a few hours so no one is surprised when my lips brush her neck or when our mouths meet almost constantly.

The beautiful tinkle of Lorali's laugh makes me turn her in my arms so I can see what caused the reaction. I see Garrett holding Alexa hard against his body and chuckle myself at the strained look on his face.

I know your pain, man.

The gorgeous solitaire on Alexa's left-hand catches the light from the chandelier and sends fiery prisms around the room. We were all shocked when she showed up for a Labor Day cook-out with that rock on her hand. Even Lorali and Josie, who know her better than anyone, never guessed she would say yes. Answering the question is only half the challenge; now Garrett has to get her to the altar and it's been a month and they have not even talked about a date yet.

Everything stemming around Garrett's arrest two months ago has been settled and his record remains untarnished. He and Alexa have been collaborating on some type of spa retreat they plan to build east of Denver. The whole thing is very hush-hush, but I get the feeling that it will require a very exclusive membership and some kinky predilections. To each their own, I guess.

Kaleb and Josie spin around the dance floor, pulling my attention from Alexa's hand. They seem blissfully happy. Josie's stomach has expanded just a tad more. She's just a little over half way through her pregnancy and every report from the doctor has been great news. I smile down at Lorali and picture her stomach swollen with my child and it brings me pure joy. I. Can't. Wait.

So much has happened over the last ten months. Garrett and I both found the loves of our life; a feat on its own considering our previous train of thought regarding relationships. Josie also found her partner and other half, a man I consider a close friend.

So much tragedy has also tried to tear us apart. First, Alexa's shooting which snowballed all of the other events. Josie's abduction was emotionally devastating to everyone. None of us wanted to give up hope in finding her alive, but nineteen days is an awfully long time to go without considering it. Garrett's arrest was enough to tear any small group apart and somehow we managed to battle through and come out mostly unscathed.

After we complete the customary tasks involved in every wedding reception: bouquet toss, garter throw, and cake cutting, I spend the rest of the evening on the dance floor with my amazing wife. I can't even describe how light I feel now that I know that Lorali is mine for the rest of our lives. Totally cheesy, I get that, but never in my life have I felt this content. I vow to spend the rest of my life making sure she's happy and completely spoiled, well to the extent she will allow.

***

After what feels like a hundred years, we are finally back home as our jet doesn't take off for the Maldives until first thing in the morning.

"I have a gift for you," Lorali smiles mischievously.

"Is that so?" I slide my tuxedo jacket off because I hope her gift includes us both being naked.

"Well, two actually," she amends.

"Let's get started then," I tell her and begin to unbutton my shirt.

She laughs. "Not so fast Casanova." She places her hand on the center of my chest to halt my undressing. "Have a seat." She points to the seating area of our bedroom suite.

I oblige her even though I can think of nothing more than getting her out of her spectacular wedding dress.

I stalk her with my eyes as she disappears into the walk-in closet, only to return a minute later with a flat box wrapped in white, silver embossed paper with simple but elegant purple bow.

Please let it be kinky lingerie.

She hands it to me and bites her lip. She's nervous it seems, which only piques my interest even more.

"I hope you like it," she whispers as she releases her hand from the box. I watch her sit gingerly on the edge of the bed I, no doubt, will be taking her on very shortly. My cock is hard just at the anticipation of imagining what my bride would consider an appropriate wedding night gift.

I slowly untie the bow without breaking eye contact with her. She fidgets on her spot on the bed.

"Why are you nervous, Baby?" I tease her.

She gives me a bright smile but doesn't answer me.

I turn my attention back to the box in my lap and pull the top of it off and fold away the purple tissue paper, revealing a black, leather-bound book. I nearly come in my pants when I flip the front cover open and see a picture of my beautiful wife wearing nothing but a long string of pearls, looking seductively into the camera.

"Lorali," I gasp and run my fingers over the image of her flawless skin.

The picture is erotic without being pornographic. I run my finger over her delicate neck and trace the pearls down between her breasts. The picture cuts off right where I know her pert nipple starts. I lick my lips and envision my finger lightly teasing her hardened bud.

"There's more," she promises from across the room.

I don't take my eyes from the book as I turn the page and groan at the sight before me. Lorali is strategically positioned so her breasts and the heaven between her legs don't show, but she's wrapped in the same veil she wore when she became my wife just a few short hours ago. I'm breathless.

It is then that I recognize the signature of Jody J placed stealthily in the corner. This knowledge doesn't make things any easier in my pants. Not only am I now picturing her naked but I can also taste her on my lips. Jody J is the spectacular artist who took the pictures for the private showing I enticed Lorali with on our first official date. I somehow managed to seduce her into letting me slide my fingers into the beautiful pussy of hers and lick her essence off of her neck. My cock is throbbing.

I groan and look up at her because I know where this is going. Just like the *Orchid* showcase we attended back in January, I anticipate these pictures gaining speed and increasing in seductiveness with each turn of the page. I don't know if the zipper holding my erection back will be able to tolerate the strain; the tux is Armani so hopefully the workmanship is top notch.

I close my eyes and turn the page, waiting a few breaths before opening them again. Two things happen at once. First, I start to drool at the sight of my wife standing in nothing but a pair of purple stilettos, facing out over the skyline of Denver. I trace her gorgeous naked back and down her toned thighs with a shaky finger.

Secondly, I smirk when I realize she's had this picture taken in my office at work. This sneaky minx managed to fly under the radar and have boudoir pictures taken in my place of business. The same place I hold business meetings and try to woo other businessmen into my way of thinking as well as the same office where I've had to fire and take the upper hand of a situation countless times before. Now, when I walk in here, the only thing I'll be able to picture is my naked wife in fuck-me heels. I'll have to remember to thank Susan, who undoubtedly played a part in helping make this happen.

I turn page after page, looking at picture after picture of Lorali like I've never seen her before. The best part? I'll have these pictures forever. Not only are the images seared into my brain but I can pull this bad boy out anytime I feel the urge to ogle my bride.

The last picture is the pièce de rèsistance, just how I knew it would be. Wearing her long flowing veil, she's sitting with her legs spread-eagled and her knees bent. Her right arm is crossed over her front, hiding her perfect pink nipples but doing nothing to disguise the lower curve of her supple breasts. Her left hand is cupping her sex softly. Her eyes speak of passion and erotic promise. I close my eyes and try to will away her hands from covering her magnificent body needing desperately to see her wholly.

I lick my dry lips and close the book softly. "Best fucking gift ever, Lorali," I praise her.

She slides seductively off of the bed and prowls toward me. "Hold that thought," she offers as her hands reach behind her and she unzips her designer wedding dress. I swallow roughly when she releases the fabric and it crumples at her feet, revealing the sexiest purple lingerie I've ever seen.

"Baby," I pant as she unclasps the bra barely holding in her perfect breasts and allows it to join the dress at her feet.

I want to get up and go to her; I need her fiercely, but I know she's running this show. She's left standing in only her stilettos, the ones from the photo shoot, and a pair of lacey purple underwear.

She turns, giving me her back, runs her hands down her sides, and slips her thumbs into the waist of her barely there panties. She glances back over her shoulder as she slides them down, bending at the waist until she's folded in half.

Looking at her perfect pussy, I notice the light reflect off of a violet gem that's situated right where her… holy shit.

I jump up from my seat and quickly make my way to her. With her still bending over, I run my hand down her delicate back, between her cheeks, and cup her glistening sex, my palm applying pressure to the jeweled butt plug my devilish wife has been wearing for God knows how long.

She moans at the sensation.

"So fucking naughty," I taunt as I palm her breast and force her to stand. "Something you want to tell me, baby?"

She whimpers as I begin the push and pull of my middle finger into her tight heat, pleasing the pussy that I now own.

"Your," she moans. "Your second gift."

"What's that?" I ask playing coy.

"My ass," she promises. Then back peddles slightly. "Well, I want to try anyways."

I pull my finger from her swollen sex and tap it on the plug lodged in her.

"Oh God!" she proclaims at the sensation as she reaches behind me and deftly begins to open the fly of my tuxedo pants.

Unable to resist her any longer I start working to get my shirt unbuttoned and off. Fumbling hands urgently undress me, both mine and hers. Eventually, I'm standing stark naked, every sweet curve of her back fitting perfectly against every hard inch of my front, but it's not what I need right now.

I turn her in my arms so I can manipulate her beautiful breasts with my hands. I lower my head and take one tight bundle in my mouth and sweep my thumb over the other. She grips my head with unrestrained violence, pulling me closer against her.

I honestly don't know how much foreplay is considered acceptable on your wedding night, but I'm about maxed out. Releasing her full breast I reach down and stroke my rigid cock, taking notice of the precome already leaking out of the tip. If I don't get a better handle on myself, this situation is going to be over long before I ever sink inside of her.

I grip her around the waist and walk backward with her in my arms until the edge of our bed hits the back of my thighs. I lie back in the center of the bed and position my thick erection at her entrance. She places her hands on my chest and slowly begins to sink down my length.

"Oh!" She pants just as "Fuck," slips past my lips.

I'm not afraid to admit that of all the women I've been with Lorali has the tightest, sweetest cunt I've ever had the pleasure of well, pleasing. The feel of it with the plug? Out-of-this-world amazing.

Two trips up and down and I'm blowing my load like a sixteen-year-old virgin in a tube sock. Feeling the pulses of my orgasm, Lorali stills and glares down at me, obviously unimpressed with my impromptu climax.

"Seriously?" She chastises and playfully slaps my chest.

I shrug and grin at her. "What do you expect? You tease me all night, show me that damned photo album, and then gift me with the promise of taking your ass. You're lucky I made it inside of you before I came!"

"Lucky me," she says rolling her eyes, but she squeals loudly as I flip her over on her back.

"Has there ever been a time I didn't take care of you?" I kiss her lips before she can answer because honestly not too long ago I got too drunk and passed out before taking her.

I shift my hips and slide easily, if not tightly, through her swollen sex. She moans; I smile. "That's what I thought."

I spread her legs wide and sit back on my knees, making sure to hit the plug with every heavy slap of my balls against her body.

"Ian!" She chants and when I can tell she's right on the edge I reach down, pinch her clit between my fingers, and pull the plug from her body with my other hand. Her body immediately clamps down on me and begins to pulse erratically; the tiny muscles of her core rippling down my shaft. I groan and slowly pump in and out of her milking every last tremble of her orgasm from her body.

"Lorali," I whisper and pull free of her body.

I watch her sated face with half lidded eyes of my own as I use the head of my engorged cock to sweep the remnants of both our orgasms over the puckered entrance she promised to me. She arches her back at the sensation and I take this as the go-ahead I was desperately hoping to find.

I'd be lying if I said this was something I'd never done before. Some women in my past were down with just about anything and I'm sure some of them used anal sex as a way to try to get me to stick around longer. It was great while it happened but was never anything to make me want to go back from more from that particular woman.

Never doing this with Lorali was never going to be a problem for me. If she didn't want to, then I was fine with that. It's not like it's something I spend any amount of time feeling deprived of the last ten months. Now that she's given me the go-ahead? I have to restrain myself and remind my brain that this is something she's never done, ever. I smile knowing I will be the only man to ever have the privilege of entering her here.

"Relax," I coo at her as I press against her and I nearly faint at the sensation when the head slips past her tight ring of muscles. I thumb over her swollen clit as I incrementally push further inside of her.

She whimpers and I slowly begin to retreat. "Lorali, if you don't…" She grabs my neck and pulls me down so her mouth is on mine.

I'm delirious with passion as she hungrily attacks my lips. I almost bite her tongue when I clamp my teeth together as she shifts her hips upward and takes more of me inside of her.

I take this as my cue and begin moving my hips, never breaking our kiss. After what seems like the shortest, most magnificent minute of my life she pulls her mouth from mine and stares into my eyes briefly before they flutter closed.

"I don't… how is this even?" I feel the pulsing clenches of her orgasms through the thin wall separating me from her pussy.

"Fuck, baby," I groan and begin to come unceremoniously, my body jerking and shuddering irregularly.

I rest my forehead against hers as we pant against each other, our breaths combining at our lips.

I hear her whimper and I know, now that her orgasm is tapering away, she's growing uncomfortable with me inside her still. I lean back slightly and swipe my fingers over her sensitive clit, simultaneously pulling out of her.

"Jesus," she says still trying to catch her breath. "If I'd known this is how married sex was, I would've gotten married a long time ago.

I grin at her sentiment even though she pretty much just said she'd have gotten married before meeting me. I turn my body toward her. "It's only like this with me, Baby," I swear to her before kissing her lips delicately.

I pull her against my chest and kiss the top of her head. "Thank you for making me the happiest man in the world, Lorali."

Epilogue
Kaleb

"How's my boy doing?" I ask as I position myself on the couch beside Josie.

She grumbles something under her breath about injured ribs and back pain. I kiss her round belly and then lean over and kiss her lips. She's less than two weeks away from her due date and ever since the doctor mentioned at her last appointment that any time from then on out was safe to deliver the baby as he is full term, she's been doing everything in her power to make that happen. Needless to say, there has been a lot of walking and spicy foods going on.

Mia has loved it. She gets walked around the neighborhood several times a day when she's not at the precinct with me working. I'm tasked with grabbing spicy food each evening before I head home from work.

We've tried more traditional ways to induce labor as well. Nipple stimulation and lots of sex have become my favorite way to try to nudge her body into labor. It hasn't worked and I'm not really complaining. I'm ecstatic about the imminent birth of my son, but I also love spending alone time with my wife. I know that makes me sound like an asshole, but it's honest. He will be here before we know it and we will then always be a family of three.

I'm having a good time saving up the intimate touches and the kissing and the free of worry caressing that eventually will have to be monitored once he's old enough to pay attention. No doubt he'll grow up in a home that's full of love, knowing he has parents who not only love but are totally dedicated to one another, but some things aren't appropriate for children to see. Some of those things I'm hoping Josie's is going to be in the mood for this evening.

"It won't be much longer, Mariposa," I promise and slide my hand down her back, kneading it with the palm of my hand where she typically has pain.

"Mia is getting super clingy," she says looking down at the K9 asleep on the floor. "She's under my feet constantly. I almost tripped over her today," she admits with a small giggle.

I frown down at the SWAT trained, Denver PD badge wearing animal. Not news I wanted to hear. I don't even want to think of the damage a fall would mean right now for Josie and the baby. I twist and pop my neck, trying to push down the urge to put the dog outside.

Josie groans and I turn my attention back to the knot I'm working out in her lower back. "That feels so good," she groans quietly.

I nip her ear and gently roll her nipple through the fabric of her tank top.

"Ready for your medicine?" I whisper seductively in her ear. We've been calling it that since she read in one of her pregnancy books that scientists believe semen can actually promote cervical softening and her own orgasms can cause contractions. Needless to say, there's been a ton of orgasms all around.

She smiles but her head lolls on her shoulders and she doesn't give a definitive answer with her mouth, but I'm thinking that the hand gripping my cock right now is as good a sign as any that she's leaning toward the affirmative. I scoop her up in my arms and carry her to our room like a bride.

I walk her toward the bed and release her lower half so she can stand. I pull her shirt over her beautifully swollen belly and tug it over her head. Her incredibly short shorts are next and I discard them quickly.

I narrow my eyes. "Did you walk the neighborhood in these shorts today, Mariposa?" I've seen her in them before; the bottom curve of her luscious ass is visible.

She bites her lip and gives me a faint nod as she bites her bottom lip. She loops her hands around my neck in an attempt to abate my frustrations; it almost works.

"I bet Mr. Childress was out in his front yard watering his dead grass again also, right?" I pull my hand back and give her a sharp slap on her ass.

She hisses and groans at the same time and it is the most erotic thing I've ever heard. My cock stands at attention.

"I wore sweats over them," she confesses. "It was too cold out to only wear the shorts."

I laugh and scoop her up to place her on the edge of the bed spreading her legs wide so I can stand in between them.

"I think you like it when I get jealous, don't you?" I nip at her neck and revel in the moan from her lips.

I slide my fingers over her already swollen clit and through the evidence of her arousal. I don't waste any time gliding two fingers into her hot, wet heat; expertly stroking her front wall with the curve of my fingers.

I kiss her deeply, probing her mouth; my tongue tangling with hers. She has managed to get her hand down my pants and under the elastic of my boxers. I can never get enough of the feel of her tiny hand wrapped around my raging cock. I moan into her mouth.

"Kaleb!" She wails as her orgasm takes both of us by surprise. I suckle her lips as she convulses on my hand.

"Fuck Mariposa, you're so wet for me." I look down at the burgundy duvet and notice it is practically black under her thighs, and spreading.

"Ah!" She screams and clutches at her stomach.

"Josie, what's wrong?" My vision is tunneled and I can only see my wife, nothing else even registers in my brain.

She winces again. "I think my water broke," she admits.

I look down and can't help but agree with her. I mean she's come a lot in the past, but the level of wetness on the blanket is ten times what she's done before.

"I think you may be right." I grin at her. "Let's go have a baby."

She smiles at me and I can see the excitement and the terror in her eyes.

***

"Would you like to cut the cord?" The doctor asks as he holds up the most incredible thing I've ever been involved in making. Six hours of labor and forty-five minutes of pushing later my son has entered the world.

I wipe the tears from my eyes and close the distance from near Josie's shoulder to the precious baby he holds in his hand.

Afraid I'm going to hurt him, he has mercy on me and tells me exactly where to snip the umbilical cord. I'm a blubbering idiot as he places Gustavo "Gus" Angel Perez on my wife's breasts. She coos at him and talks to him. Letting him know how happy we are to meet him and how perfect he is. I have to agree, my son is gorgeous.

We don't get much alone time with him before the nurse sweeps him away to clean him, weigh him, and do some type of baby wellness test. I caress Josie's cheek and tell her how much I love her and how she's made me the happiest man in the world for the second time; the first of course was the day she married me. I whisper in her ear words so precious they can only be spoken in Spanish as the doctor does whatever it is he has to do below since her delivery.

We cry even more when the nurse brings him and places our tightly bundled son back into Josie's arms. Before long the hospital staff clears out and the family starts to filter in.

At some point during the evening, everyone that we hold near and dear makes it by to visit. Alexa, Garrett, Lorali, and Ian are the constants, refusing to leave even when the room gets overcrowded. Gus makes his way around the room to be snuggled and loved more than once.

I can tell Josie is growing weary and Gus is getting cranky, a sure fire way to tell he's tired and hungry. I love all of these guys, no doubt, but I'm not okay with my wife pulling out her breast to feed the baby in front of the men.

I clear my throat as I take Gus from Ian's arms. "I hate to run you off, but I think we need some rest."

"Of course," Garrett says and reaches a hand down to help pull Alexa from her chair.

"Oh, I almost forgot," Lorali says standing and holding a tiny blue bag with white tissue paper flowing out of the top. "A little gift for Gus."

She hands the bag to Josie, who promptly pulls the tissue paper out and hands it to Alexa. Reaching into the bag, she pulls out a little onesie and lays it on her legs so she can get a better look.

Out loud she reads, "Coolest. Cousin. Ever."

She tilts her head for a second. "No way!" She shrieks finally catching on. "You're pregnant?"

Ian beams and Lorali shakes her head up and down with a smile on her face from ear to ear. Hugs all around and black slapping commences.

Once everything settles a bit. "How far along are you?" Josie asks her sister.

"Almost three months," Ian responds proudly.

"Perfect," Josie says. "So that only leaves…" She looks pointedly at Alexa.

"Not a fucking chance!" Alexa says holding her hands up as if she's trying to ward off the baby juju. I don't miss the glint in Garrett's eye.

Acknowledgements

What can I say?

With the end of this series, also comes the end of a year of pain, suffering, and eventually a level of healing. Writing, although something I always wanted to, never came to fruition until I had no other place to focus after a devastating miscarriage.

I mentioned M. Never in my book because the quote *"A certain kind of darkness is needed to see the stars"* rings true with my struggle. She deserves the recognition. Reading that in *Owned* gave me not only the ability but the permission to grieve as well as grow simultaneously, and for that I'm forever grateful to her.

My husband has been my rock and biggest supporter as I've journeyed through the chaos that is Indie writing. He reads and rereads (even though he complains about the sex: which he never turns down but some reason grows weary of reading, men who can understand them). He makes suggestions and shows me the error of my ways. Without him, as an author I'd be in trouble. Without him, as a woman I'd be lost.

Jody, my bestie, is also showcased in the books, takes the time out of her busy life to help me plot out the Hale Series and I'm forever grateful for her time and dedication to my stories.

My beta team! What can I say....you gals are the best!! Brenda, Brittney, Diane, Jessica, and Tammy (Alphabetical order because they are ALL number!!!) I couldn't do this without you! When I started this journey and I thought I could do it alone, I was correctly very quickly. Each and every one of you has helped tremendously!

The people in the background are ALWAYS the ones who do the most work. A big THANK YOU to Wendy and Claire of Bare Naked Words, who bust their asses promoting for me. I could NEVER do this without you ladies!

Amanda and Ena, from Enticing Journey Book Promotions, have put up with my kind of crazy since the beginning. Thank you for all you do!

Kylie of Give me Books has joined my team of promoters and has done so with a bang! Love you lady and thanks for everything you do!!

Kari Ayasha did another bang up job on the book cover! She's the best...check her out at Cover to Cover Designs...you won't be disappointed.

My supports at One-Click Addicts Support group and my Fictional Ho's have been instrumental in spreading the word about my books and I'm forever grateful.

Now....my dear Smuffins. Your posts and pictures have not only assisted me personally but have also gotten the creative juices flowing where my writing is concerned. Keep up the good work bitches; I need you in my life!

My fans.....man I'm blessed. The ladies and gents who read my books, share without asking and send me messages. I love you people! You are the backbone of the Indie writing world. Without out you, there would be no us!!

If you loved my books make sure to head over to Amazon or GoodReads and leave a review! 20 words are used up in a flash.

If you want a signed paperback don't hesitate to send me a PM on Facebook and I'll get one to you!

I appreciate each and every one of you!!!

It's been One Hale of a Ride.

~Marie James